MATTERS OF STATE

A Corps Justice Novel

C. G. COOPER

"MATTERS OF STATE"

A Corps Justice Novel

Author: C. G. Cooper

Warning: This story is intended for mature audiences and contains profanity and violence.

A portion of all profits from the sale of my novels goes to fund OPERATION C4, our nonprofit initiative serving junior military officers. For more information visit OperationC4.com.

Want to stay in the loop?

Sign Up to be the FIRST to learn about new releases.

Plus get newsletter only bonus content for FREE.

Visit cg-cooper.com.

PROLOGUE

TIPTON - PARIS, FRANCE

How was he to know that the next five minutes would spark fear in the highest echelons of state? There was no fear in this place. He had marched down this particular path hundreds, possibly thousands of times. He might not have called it part of his routine, for routine means death to a spy. But there wasn't a week that passed that he didn't mark a steady cadence down this silver slice of heaven with his newly resoled boots.

Bo Tipton stopped to inhale the sweet tidings of spring. If he had to choose, he'd say it was his favorite time of year. Death had marked him on too many occasions to count, so he preferred not counting favorites. Thugs. Spies. Cancer. They had all tried, and Tipton beat them all. He hadn't made it this far in life by being careless. At any given time, there were four weapons on his person. He might be 72-years-old, but he could still wield a stiletto or conk a would-be mugger with a truncheon. And he never crossed a path without checking it three times, especially when it came to business.

But business was slowing. His former employer talked a good game about deploying human assets to the field. But intent and action are two vastly different things. It was easy to rely on cameras and gizmos when you were halfway across the globe. Much harder to manage a spy who might have all manner of proclivities. A man didn't become a spy because he acted like Ward Cleaver. Not in private anyway.

Maybe it was time to retire. The taskings from Langley came sporadically now. It wasn't that Tipton didn't like the excitement. In fact, he adored excitement. But there wasn't much excitement anymore and that's why he'd done it. That's why he'd married and divorced three women. No, four—there was that fling in Marseilles that ended in Bordeaux-soaked nuptials and was dissolved five minutes after the case of magnums ran out. But now his hands ached on cold days, and the snide children who occasionally came along to "supervise" him got on his nerves more than he cared to admit.

A pair of sparrows streaked by close enough to touch. Tipton watched them for a moment, then squatted to pat a patch of new grass. Yes, this was how he'd like to spend his final years. Tending to life rather than chasing the next target.

Suddenly he felt tired. Like he might lie down right there and take a much-deserved nap.

No. He had work to do. One last job.

His bones cracked when he rose, but he still smiled. This was life. The passing of time ticked off by tiny pops in his knees.

His smile faded when he saw the woman.

He knew her. Not personally, but by reputation. It was impossible to work in Paris for close to forty years and not know who she was.

Tipton forced the smile back to his lips as the sweat beaded up on his back.

"Bonjour," he said.

"Bonjour," she replied.

That voice. Still as beautiful as always.

That was how they'd first found her. She'd been a voice in the dark, untraceable.

"It's a wonderful day."

Tipton's French was native. At one point he'd even thought about changing his name. In the end, he remained an American, though his politics had shifted through the years.

The regal figure didn't answer. She kept her hands in her overcoat pocket and walked his way. In America, he might've been armed with a pistol. But this was Paris, and it was peaceful on the surface.

"I really must be going," Tipton said, unafraid. He could take care of himself.

He made to leave, taking a step back the way he'd come.

"Look at me," she said.

He couldn't help but look. She had to be in her fifties now. But she was timeless.

And that was when he realized his mistake. The *look*.

He raised his hands when her pistol came out. It was as beautiful as she was, slender and shining. It had to be. She had a reputation to uphold.

"Just tell me why," Tipton said.

It had been a good life. So many adventures. No two days the same. He held no regrets. But he wanted an answer, nonetheless. That's what led him to become a spy. He liked answers. He loved puzzles of every kind. And this was the ultimate puzzle—life on life's terms.

Bo Tipton frowned at the first shot. He died on the second. And he went to his grave wondering why the Duchess had resurfaced.

CHAPTER ONE

STOKES - PARIS

The JURA coffee maker whirred to life, grinding the coffee beans, then setting the grounds to water, a hair off the boil. The lifeblood sputtered once, then flowed into the espresso cup below. Less than thirty seconds and it was done.

Cal Stokes picked up the cup and deeply inhaled. The perfume of Elysium. Better than any of the coffee back home.

"Down the hatch," he said, raising the cup to the Louvre across the River Seine.

One ristretto down, Cal filled another. He found that he preferred the smaller size—more of a shot, really, at an ounce and a half. His second splash of caffeine down, he waved to the first tour boat of the morning. The larger vessel sent a wake his way and rocked the houseboat that he currently called home.

Two weeks in Paris. Who would have thought?

"Ready to go?" came the voice from below.

Uncle Adam trudged up the ladder to the kitchen and

eating area. This was his home. Three bedrooms of river living. Priceless real estate.

Until recently, Cal hadn't known his uncle existed. He was still getting used to the fact that he had even a single surviving family member. What was even creepier was his uncle's resemblance to his father, the now-deceased Colonel Calvin Stokes, USMC.

"Let me get my boots on and I'll be ready," Cal said.

This was their routine. First, coffee on the boat. Then, a leisurely stroll up the way to Uncle Adam's favorite boulangerie.

It hadn't taken much to convince Cal to come to Paris. After losing another love of his life, Diane Mayer, the sudden appearance of an unknown uncle came at an opportune time. When confronted about their divergent past, Uncle Adam explained that he had been disowned by Cal's father long before Cal was born.

"I was an ass of monumental proportions," he explained. "But once I got clean, I stopped blaming him. Addiction does that to a man, you know. Makes him blame everything and everyone for his own problems. But your father was my hero. I didn't realize it until I was too old to do anything about it."

"Did you ever tell him as much?"

His uncle smiled and said nothing. And that was all Cal got from the man.

He knew from his own digging that Uncle Adam moved to Paris in the mid-nineties. He'd spent time with a handful of larger consultancies, having hung up his retirement shingle a decade before. He had no debt, just enough cash in investments to live out his days in relative comfort, and no federal or international criminal records.

"You going with chocolate or raisin today?" Uncle Adam

asked, knotting his tie after selecting 'espresso' on the coffee machine.

"What was that ham and cheese thing you got yesterday?"

"*Croque madame*."

"Yeah, a croak madam," Cal said, putting emphasis on the mispronunciation. "I'll have one of those."

Uncle Adam smiled. "Paris is finally soaking into my nephew."

The full suit Uncle Adam wore—blue, double-breasted—showed the extent to which his own persona had overlapped with his home city. There wasn't a day that he wasn't dressed to the nines, another well-to-do Parisian, something Cal Stokes could and would never be.

He couldn't really be sure his uncle wasn't phoning it in himself.

CHAPTER TWO

STOKES - THE SMITHS BAKERY, PARIS

"Merci," Cal said, grabbing the proffered pastry and trying not to salivate on his way to the door. He had learned to wait until he was at the table before chowing down. The first morning he had failed to do so and received a look from the owner of the shop that could freeze gin. He would've taken it as a compliment if he were in her shoes, but, when in Paris...

Uncle Adam had finished his breakfast and was sipping thoughtfully on his coffee, watching life pass by on the Rue de Buci.

"I stay here much longer and I'm sure to put on fifty pounds," Cal said, taking a seat also facing the one-way street, his back against the brick wall.

"Stay as long as you want, nephew. I hope you've felt welcome."

Cal laughed as he fished the first of two pastries from the brown wrapping. "I have. I think I was in dire need of a vacation."

"From what you've been through, I believe it."

He'd lost her twice, his love. Diane. He'd thrown her away once. Miraculously, she'd returned. And he knew he had nothing to do with that. She was smarter than he was. She'd probably known all along that they belonged together. She challenged him in all the right ways. She knew what he did in the shadows and didn't care—and it had cost her nothing less than her life. The loss had hollowed him out. There were nights when he lay in bed unable to breathe at the mere thought of what was missing.

"What do you think Dad would say if he saw us now?" Cal asked, not yet ready to dive into the Diane conversation.

Uncle Adam looked up at the sky and pointed. "I'll bet he's looking down at us right this second, wagging his finger and saying, '*I told you so*'."

"Told me or you?"

Uncle Adam frowned. "The first chance I got I ran from my family. Broke my mother's heart. What can I say? I was young and stupid. I didn't know what I wanted. I thought I did. I thought I was hot shit, out to change the world." He looked up at the sky again and nodded. "You were right, big brother. Family."

They sat and enjoyed each other's company, Cal diving into the second pastry with sheer, unadulterated delight. When he was done, he took it all in—the bustling street, Parisians going about their morning, some chatting, others walking along with cigarettes bobbing at their lips. He'd never thought of himself as a city guy. The wilds of Tennessee were more his speed. But there was something to be said for being in the middle of civilization, one that had been around since before the Declaration of Independence was even a thought. Paris, with its sprawling boulevards and tiny alley conclaves, was living history. It positively pulsed with life in a way that pulled at Cal like no other city had.

"A guy could certainly find himself enchanted by this place. You ever miss the States?" Cal asked.

"I miss a good cheeseburger and a slice of cherry pie from the diner. But you have to understand, Cal, most days I'm simply happy to be alive. I'm sure you understand that."

Call nodded. "Ever think about going back?"

"Not anymore. This is home. I'm not sure I'd be much good back there anyway. Too many bad memories make a man useless. I have better memories here."

Uncle Adam had the look of a traveler who'd seen the world and all its ills. There was a weariness in his eyes that only came out after enough wine or an instance of surprise nostalgia, like the time Cal had shown his uncle the pictures on his phone from his parents' last visit to Charlottesville.

They'd kept their conversation light, like train companions. Cal didn't think there was a fight to be had here, but there had to be stories—and he wanted to hear each and every one.

CHAPTER THREE

ZIMMER - WASHINGTON, D.C.

"Edmond, I wanted to take a minute to thank you personally for all you've done in your short time in office." President Brandon Zimmer reached across the table and shook the director of the CIA's hand.

"Thank you, Mr. President."

"I have a good feeling about our working relationship going forward."

"As do I, Mr. President. And if I may, it's a breath of fresh air when a career politician opens his door to an old spy like myself. You'd be surprised at the looks we used to get, like we were lepers fresh off the boat from the copper mines."

They both laughed at the smaller man's joke. Zimmer was pleased. Edmond Flap didn't look like much. His head was a bit too big. His eyes a bit too small. He wasn't going to win any beauty contests. Maybe that's what made him a good master of espionage, though these days a CIA director seemed to need more political blood than anything else.

"Are they giving you any trouble? The old guard, I mean."

Flap shrugged. "There's bound to be turnover when there's a change at the top. Nothing I can't handle, Mr. President." Flap looked like he was going to continue but didn't.

"There something else?"

"I don't want to bother you, Mr. President."

The last thing Zimmer wanted was for his new director to think that he couldn't bring an issue to his boss. While the president was far from a micromanager, he'd made it known that his door was always open, as long as problems were presented with possible solutions rather than simply dumped in his lap.

"That's my job, Edmond. I'm here to help if I can. And if I can't, I'll tell you."

Flap nodded. "You'll have to excuse me. It takes some getting used to. Years spent cleaning up messes before they hit the headlines... well, that's all in the past." Flap pursed his lips and took a short breath. "We may have a problem, Mr. President. In the past week, four operatives have gone missing."

"Does missing mean dead? I know the CIA has a penchant for ambiguity."

"In this case, missing means missing, Mr. President."

"What's the story?"

"Well, each operative was a veteran of the agency. One had close to forty years of service under his belt."

"Were they working together?"

"No, sir. One in Paris. Two in China. One in Japan."

"And there's no link?"

"Not that we can see."

Zimmer nodded slowly. "You've obviously brought this up for a reason."

Flap rubbed his hands as if they were suddenly clammy. "Mr. President, as I told you before you so graciously offered me the director's chair, I want to be as transparent as I can. I will bring issues to your attention. This is a potential issue. In the past, we've had agents defect. Sometimes it coincides with a transfer of power. Sometimes it's a random event. A spy gets into debt or falls in love with the wrong woman. They get turned and we have to figure out why and what we should do."

"Something in your tone tells me these disappearances have nothing to do with debt," Zimmer said.

"I don't like to speculate, sir, I like facts. But this is a murky business, and I can't help but think that our recent run-ins with the Russians might have something to do with our missing spies."

Zimmer wondered how much Flap knew. It wasn't but a few weeks earlier that President Yegorovich had been kidnapped by an assassin who just happened to be under the watchful eye of Zimmer's good friend Cal Stokes. All had parted as friends, or at least that had been the intent. Zimmer knew he'd have to offer amends one day, maybe in the form of a treaty that tilted Russia's way, but he could work with that.

"Why the Russians? What would this accomplish?"

"We've seen them flexing their muscles. Two of our people were roughed up in Moscow last week. The wife of an embassy official was followed by supposed Spetsnaz soldiers in South Korea. Little things that might appear to be isolated incidents when individually scrutinized. Some might say it's the price of playing the game."

"So, you're telling me the Russians kidnapped or killed four of our veteran spies for what? To show us that they're back in the game?"

Flap shrugged. "We don't know yet, Mr. President. And right now, it's no more than a hunch. I've got my people working on it, but I wanted to bring it to your attention before we dive deeper."

Zimmer thought on that for a moment. If he brought Flap into his confidence and told him about the latest run-in with the Russians, what would unfold? A mess potentially, and there were plenty of those to go around. No, better to let Flap run this without his input. That way the president could better gauge how the man worked.

"I trust you, Edmond. Do what you think is right. And if you need me to make some calls—"

"I hope I never have to ask you to do that, Mr. President. If I do, I'll hand in my resignation that very day."

Zimmer smiled. "Edmond, I think you and I are going to get along just fine."

CHAPTER FOUR

FLAP - FALLS CHURCH, VIRGINIA

There are men with secrets and there is Edmond Flap. He liked to think that through the decades he'd logged enough secrets to fill up his own bible. That would be an apt term for it too, for Flap believed the Holy Bible was the greatest propaganda tool of all time. It wasn't that he didn't believe there might be a God out there, somewhere. It wasn't even that he didn't believe in good people. He merely refused to rely on the possibility of that speculation being true. What he did believe was that the Bible, whether spiritually inspired or not, had served to foment just as much evil as good—maybe more. The same could be said for Islamic texts or even some of the misinterpreted texts of the Buddha. But Flap really admired the Bible, and the way some folks latched onto it and used it as their rallying cry.

In Edmond Flap's mind, they were weak.

He, on the other hand, was very aware of who he was and why he'd become his present manifestation. Psychology showed him that he had mommy and daddy issues. Elementary school showed him that he didn't have the knack for getting along with his peers. College showed him that the rich kids always got their way. And finally, the CIA taught him that there was no such thing as loyalty. Not in the spy game. It was fight for every inch or you get left behind.

None of these thoughts ever tainted his actions. He learned to keep his own counsel, and never showed more than the first two cards of his hand.

As he walked through the Walmart parking lot, the lunch crowd bustling, he thought about the amount of effort it had taken to get him to where he could now sit in the Oval Office with the president, batting niceties back and forth like he'd been born to the upper crust of society. Was it easy? Not a bit. Had he suffered? Immensely. Any other man—or woman these days—put in the same position would've folded years ago.

The greatest example could have been his greatest failure: Berlin. A plum assignment. The height of the Cold War. Edmond Flap was a young and ambitious station chief of that vaunted outpost. He'd made the mistake of thinking every i was dotted and every t crossed. He'd gotten complacent. He'd forgotten that good men, seemingly infallible men, would go to the lowest depths to maintain their sterling reputations.

The result was that he wound up framing an innocent man, fully expecting that man, that Marine, to take his medicine and get shipped home. Then again, Major Calvin Stokes was anything but ordinary. He'd made a deal with a spy from the other side. Flap didn't know the particulars, just that he, Edmond Flap, was the target, and the end result was being fed to shitbricks at Langley. A dark hole to get tossed into. It was only by the skin of his pinky toes that he survived. And it was only because he knew too much and had too much experience for the agency to just throw him away.

He'd started at the bottom. They threw him into every rat-infested, shit-stained city they could find. Flap took the drumming with relish. He kept his outward appearance stoic, careful not to reveal the physical effects of an eagerly relished challenge. There was still a chance. And if there was one thing Edmond Flap was good at, it was taking a sliver of hope and turning into a heaping pile of opportunity.

Perseverance won out. The CIA was no different than any other government agency. The cream of the crop left for high-paying jobs on the outside. The rock stars who stayed pushed their way to the top and eventually retired. Sure, there were a couple of dinosaurs still kicking around in the espionage ring, but they were rare.

As administrations came and went, the CIA's memory faded like so much old ink. So when the opportunity presented itself, Edmond Flap's personnel file was as clean as a spy's should be. Just enough grit to impress.

Flap pushed an errant shopping cart back into place and continued on his way. He'd missed the chance before—9/11 had seen to that. Calvin Stokes, Sr. was dead. What a waste. Flap's dossier on the man had only grown throughout the years. It helped that he had his own friends in high places.

One friend was his favorite. Flap's cherry on top. While this friend rose like a Phoenix, Flap languished like a prisoner being given only enough to survive.

When the call came from Flap's old friend to tell him about the son of Stokes, Sr., that familiar anticipation tingled in his skull. His friend: President Konstantin Yegorovich. The man who'd helped Stokes in Berlin, and then saved Flap from ultimate doom, told him that Cal Stokes, Jr. turned out to be a chip off the old block. When word came that Cal Stokes had his own high-placed friend, one who happened to live at the White House, Edmond Flap's career aspirations went into overdrive. He rallied every favor he was owed and snatched the opportunity.

Calvin Stokes, Sr. was dead and gone. Cal Stokes was his only surviving heir. The debt passed to the son. That debt was not death. Death was too easy. Too clean. Too simple.

No. Edmond Flap would exact his pound of flesh the old-fashioned way—slowly and deliberately. And when he was done, the Stokes name and legacy would rank down there with pig shit in backwater Thailand.

"You wanted to see me?" the man shuffling through Valentine's Day cards said without looking up.

"I have something for you."

"Not here. The cameras."

Flap chuckled. "They're down for servicing. We have five minutes."

Now the man turned. Dirk Springer had the mustache of a swashbuckler. It actually twitched when he smiled.

"I hope this is good. My editor's been on my ass. I'd love to have something that I can shove right up his."

"No need to be vulgar, Springer." Flap pulled an envelope from his coat. "This is the first. If it plays well, there's more."

"How do I know if it's legit?"

Flap gave him a sorrowful head shake. "Have I ever given you a bad scoop?"

"No. But I get paid by the word, you know? And the *Post* ain't paying what it used to..."

It was the same old spiel. If Springer wasn't complaining about money, he was complaining about money.

"You'll like it. I promise."

Springer's mustache twitched. "Okay. Then thanks. And my girlfriend thanks you, too."

CHAPTER FIVE

SPRINGER - GEORGETOWN, WASHINGTON, D.C.

Dirk Springer stumbled into his penthouse suite, almost toppling a pile of packages that the doorman had left inside. He stood up straight, covered one eye.

"That's better," he said, staring at the pile. "Now, down you go."

He took a swinging kick at the pile and somehow managed to hit the middle. Half of the pile flew across the room. The other three packages stayed put.

"Still got it," Springer said, nearly falling again. He'd been a soccer player at Georgetown University. He loved the game. And why not? It had gotten him plenty of tail. He missed the sport, and if he ever took a minute to analyze what he'd become, he would've realized that everything he had done since was an attempt to regain the easy days of playing soccer, skipping class, and getting laid whenever he wanted.

He slipped out of his boots and left them at the door. The place was a mess. He was about to quick dial his maid when he remembered that he'd fired her the week before. The bitch had the audacity to say that he hadn't paid her. Whatever. He would find another maid. A prettier one. One who liked to shake her ass as she worked and maybe play housekeeper. Springer laughed at the empty apartment and shuffled to his bedroom that doubled as his office. He often slept on his couch. It was closer to the kitchen and he liked to save the bed for his fans. He still had a few. The Pulitzer helped, especially when he visited his alma mater and gave a talk on the current state of journalism, lamenting the extinction of the serious journalist.

Because that's what he'd been in the beginning—a serious journalist. His skill level wasn't high, but he'd worked and he'd learned. He took the crap assignments that nobody else wanted and made them shine like diamonds. That's how he'd won the Pulitzer. A story about a little girl who lost her parents to fire from faulty wiring. Trips through foster homes. Abuse. Rape. Drug dependency. The little girl with so much potential died at the age of seventeen, and Dirk Springer had turned her wasted life into a Pulitzer. Not bad.

He took off his coat and threw it on the bed. Then he remembered the envelope. He'd forgotten about it. Hard not to when you get an invite from a rich alumnus who wants to take you out to dinner. Didn't hurt that he had a hot daughter who wanted to be a journalist. Who was Dirk Springer to say no?

He flopped back on the bed and looked at the envelope. It was identical to the many he'd gotten from Edmond Flap in the past. In the beginning, he'd cherished these moments, opening the envelope like a Christmas present when he was six. But that was then. He was too tired, too broke, and too jaded to be impressed now.

He slid a dirty nail under the lip of the envelope and tore it open. A single black and white picture fell out and landed on his face. He picked it up. It was a Marine. Springer hated Marines. Them with their shiny medals and spic-n-span uniforms. Haughty bastards. Not to mention the fact that the smallest service in the U.S. Armed Forces never granted his requests for interviews. Bastards.

The kid in the picture had light hair. Probably blonde, though the black and white image didn't give that detail with a 100 percent accuracy. The guy wasn't smiling, like the Corps issued the guy a rusty spoon to keep up his ass. That made Springer laugh.

He flipped the picture over. A simple description in untraceable type. A name, social security number and date of birth. Springer had done a lot with a lot less. Then, as was customary with the new director of the CIA, came the tip. Never a list of instructions, just a tip to send him out sniffing for more. Springer had always appreciated that. It made him feel like Flap was on his side, that he wasn't trying to manipulate their relationship. It was a win-win, baby.

The note read, *"Check out his citations in relation to his time after service."*

He placed the photo on the bed and sat up. He felt energized, like the words were an edict from God Himself. The possibilities rolled around in his head. He'd need the right hook. Luckily, his editor had a hard-on for the service, though they were getting way too much of the Federal budget. Springer didn't give a damn about budget. His budget ran consistently in the red. But with this story, this could be his rebirth. There wasn't money in writing about heroes or victims. Readers wanted to read about villains. The Bernie Madoffs of the world was what sold books, magazines, and movie tickets. Springer saw it all. He knew this was why he'd been chosen. If Edmond Flap was a drinker, Springer would've sent him a bottle of tequila. Hell, if Flap swung for the other side Springer might have... nah, forget it. No story was that good.

He fished around in his pocket and pulled out the vial of coke he'd filched from the frat boy who'd left it on the counter in the bar bathroom. Meathead.

He tapped out enough to form two lines, was careful to etch the lines with a business card, then snorted one line through each nostril, reveling in the jolt of a thousand needles that filled his skull with pure elation and life.

Sucking the remnants of the cocaine from his mustache, Springer flipped open his laptop and got to work. There was so much to do. Start with research then expand from there.

He opened Google Chrome and typed in his first search of the night: *Daniel Briggs, USMC.*

CHAPTER SIX

STOKES - PARIS

Cal couldn't help but smile when he heard the impromptu quartet singing at the top of their drunken lungs. The tour boat skimmed by to a bawdy ballad that was probably a tad too Scottish for this neck of Paris. But no one cared. As long as you weren't stabbing or shooting, Parisians pretty much let you have your fun.

The quartet went on singing until they were under the bridge and looping their way toward Notre Dame, or what was left of it. The national treasure still lay in ruins after the devastating fire ripped through its ancient boughs. Cal hadn't been to the site yet. Uncle Adam mentioned something about having a friend who could get them in for a look. Maybe they'd go, although Cal was more than content lounging on deck, sipping his wine, and watching the world go by.

Tonight, he was flying solo. Uncle Adam was off to see an old friend. Something about a "monthly gathering of geezers." Cal never once thought of the older man as a geezer. He could probably give men half his age a run for their money, though he had never seen his uncle lace up a running sneaker or do a single push-up. He was one of the old breed who would look impressive until the day he died.

One bottle of wine gone, Cal thought about getting to bed early. Sleep hadn't been easy to come by. The wine helped some nights and not so much others. Diane kept coming to mind. Her memory lingered in the periphery like a wraith, a shadow he couldn't quite define.

He reached over the side cabinet and pulled out another bottle. French wine was supposed to be good for you. Might as well avail himself of the fountain of youth while he had the chance.

The tour boats were done for the night and so was Cal. There was still plenty of wine left in the second bottle when he decided to pack it in. Maybe it would be a good night for sleep. The demons seemed to be at bay tonight.

He corked the bottle and was just setting it on the counter when he heard the electric motor that powered the gangplank. Uncle Adam was home.

He grabbed the wine bottle and snagged two fresh glasses. Sleep could wait.

He settled back in his chair as Uncle Adam appeared from the dark, pulling the heavy glass door open with an inhale of air.

"Can I pour you a glass?" Cal asked, already pouring himself one.

Uncle Adam didn't answer. Instead, he moved across the room and started rummaging through drawers, his face a mask of concentration.

"Everything okay?"

"I'm not sure," came the eventual reply.

"Anything I can help with? I'm pretty handy with a screw-driver if you give me good direction." Cal hadn't heard the gang plank go back up, so he assumed this had something to do with that.

"Dammit," Uncle Adam said under his breath, slamming the last drawer shut. "My brain must not be working."

"How was your friend? Good meetup? The bards were loud and proud around here tonight."

Uncle Adam began scrolling through his phone. "He didn't show. He's never not shown."

Cal watched him dial one number and heard the voicemail greeting on the other end in French. Uncle Adam tried another number. This call went through, though Cal couldn't understand the conversation apart from the yeses and nos. Uncle Adam became more and more animated as the words kept coming. Finally, with a grunt of frustration, he ended the call and rested his hands on the counter.

Cal stood on the opposite side of the counter.

"You must think I'm crazy," Uncle Adam said, not looking up.

"I never said that."

"Well, I feel crazy." He ran a hand through his gray hair. "For close to twenty years we've had these plans. Every month, no matter what's happening in our lives. Once I had gone with the flu. And he went right after he found out he had cancer." Deep worry lined his face. He shook his head. "This can't be happening."

"If you tell me who it is, maybe I can make some calls." They hadn't talked about what Cal did for a living. No need to bring that up with a civilian. Too many complications. And besides, Cal had no desire to burden his newfound uncle with his own baggage.

"I'm pretty sure that's not possible."

"And I'm pretty sure I'll surprise you with the resources I can bring to bear."

Now Uncle Adam looked up. But it wasn't hope or even apprehension that showed. It was anger. Pure, thin-lined anger, directed right at Cal. "You wanna know the reason I can't ask you for help?"

The level of animosity surprised Cal enough to make him feel the outer edges of defensiveness.

"Of course I want to know."

His uncle's hands balled into fists. "Ok, smart guy. It's because of your friend Zimmer. If it weren't for his meddling, my friend would still be alive."

CHAPTER SEVEN

ADAM STOKES - NASHVILLE - 1973

KC and the Sunshine Band's *Blow Your Whistle* piped from the radio, the tinny pop tune bopping perfectly to the rhythm of the marijuana smoke puffing from Adam Stokes's lips.

"Sock it to your biscuit, baby," he murmured to himself, stifling a cough from the sting of the ganja. He tipped to the side and tapped some ash onto the floor. Littered with beer bottles and throwaway clothes, nobody was going to see it anyway.

Bang, bang, bang, came the interruption from the apartment door.

"Go away!" Adam yelled, though there wasn't a smidge of malice in his voice. No, that anger was gone, lost in the haze of pot smoke.

Bang, Bang, Bang, came the sound again.

More annoyed than upset, Adam sat up and steadied his gaze on the door. All he wanted to do was sit here, smoke his brains to oblivion, and listen to some tunes. Just on cue, Glen

Campbell's *Bring Back My Yesterday* faded in. Adam had met Campbell once. He lived not far from where the young Stokes now sat stoned out of his gourd.

Bang, Bang, Bang...

"Keep your shirt on," Adam said, slipping into a pair of swim trunks he'd worn the week before. He wasn't expecting visitors. He never was.

He opened the door, frowned at the sunshine that assaulted his eyes, and then frowned deeper when he saw who had come to call.

"What the hell do you want?"

His older brother, Calvin, stood like a Marine Corps poster, resplendent in his dress blues. "Aren't you gonna ask me in?"

"Dressed like that?" Adam snorted. "Why are you all gussied up anyway? Been to a funeral?"

It was Calvin's turn to frown, a not uncommon practice when the two brothers were together.

"I was around the corner informing a mother that her son died serving his country, as a matter of pure fact. Now get out of the way."

Calvin pushed past his little brother. Adam had no choice other than to follow. He flicked his spent joint out the door of his sun-free cocoon.

"You used to be the neat one," Calvin said, trying to find a place to stand on a floor littered with a grown man's belongings.

"Yeah, well, things change, you know?" Adam heaved his heavy feet back to the couch and managed to find an acceptable perch. It was a good, clean high, one that couldn't be pilfered by his overbearing brother. "How's the Corps anyway? They got you cleaning latrines and burning shit in the desert?"

Adam laughed at his own words and melted back into the couch. His brother remained stoic, standing and staring down at his only sibling.

"You could be on your way to wearing this uniform, you know. Just give me the word and I'll make some calls."

Adam sputtered out a laugh. "First of all, what makes you think I want to turn into some jarhead Frankenstein who hops when some other Frankenstein commands him to? Second, who the hell are you, Mr. High and Mighty? What, do they give butter bar lieutenants a direct line to the president? I'll bet Señor Nixon would kick your ass all the way to China."

Calvin didn't take the bait, though even through his haze Adam wished he would. He wanted a fight and his brother was the only target available. A good, high fight was just what the medicine man ordered.

"What I mean is, I know the guy who's recruiting officers. You could try for a slot. You've got the grades, and with a little work, you could get back in shape."

"*Pfft*. I could still whoop your ass and I'm high as Mount Everest."

Calvin still didn't budge. Oh, how Adam wished he would. He really hated that turn the other cheek routine. Lieutenant Stokes had perfected it.

"You know what I mean, Adam."

Adam selected the next joint from the only clean spot in the place. Three left and he meant to smoke every damn one. "Don't you worry your prissy little self about me, dear brother. I'm good. A-okay. Peaches and cream. You can keep your precious Marine Corps. It's not for me."

"That's not what you were saying last month."

"Yeah, well, things change, you know?"

The only sound for the next minute was Adam lighting his joint and taking a piping hot inhale.

There. That was better. The stress melted away along with every problem he'd ever had. Maybe those old hippies had it right. Stay high and stay happy. That sounded like a helluva plan to Adam Stokes.

"Mom says you haven't been around for Sunday dinners."

"I haven't been hungry."

"She's worried about you."

"She'll be fine. She's got you to make her proud. No need to be looking to me anymore. I'm not the star of the football team. No, sir. I'm a stoner and a loner. Sound about right?"

Calvin shook his head. "Sounds like you're giving up. Come on. Let me help you. I've got a little leave saved up. Why don't we work on this together?"

Adam looked up through the cloud. "Together? You mean like in the old days? The old Stokes boys back together in the O.K. Corral?"

"I should come back. You're in no condition to talk."

Big brother took a step for the door and even the sweet high couldn't temper Adam now. Some corks are made to be popped.

He rose and balanced himself on knocking knees. "You know what? You're right. But with one amendment. Don't ever come back. And you can tell mom and dad to forget about me, okay? I'm no good to them anyway."

His brother turned. "Is this you or the drugs talking?"

Adam's grin felt like it touched his ears. "It's all me, big brother."

"What happened to you? You had everything. You were on your way."

Adam steadied his knees and looked right into his brother's eyes. "You wanna know what happened to me? The goddamned United States of America is going to hell. You're right, dear brother. I *was* on my way. I volunteered for Viet-freakin-nam like any good little apple pie-munching American boy should. And what do they do in return? They tell us we're not going, that the war is over. Well, I'm not about to be part of a country that can't keep its word. I'm out of here, big brother. Keep your country. Keep your Corps. Screw the rest."

CHAPTER EIGHT

STOKES - PARIS

Uncle Adam had mentioned a friend. That friend was now potentially dead. What did said friend have to do with President Brandon Zimmer, and why did Uncle Adam blame the president for his friend's death? And now, Uncle Adam had disappeared for three days. Three days that left Cal to consider his options.

So—options.

Option 1: Go look for Uncle Adam. On his own this was nearly impossible. Was he, Cal, an elite operator? Yes. Did he have corresponding elite assets at his disposal? Yes. But until he figured out what Uncle Adam meant he had no real reason to call on said assets.

Option 2: Go home. One day alone pushed his patience. Two days alone made him pace back and forth on the houseboat. He probably looked like a crazy person to any tourists who happened to watch the portholes. No, going home wasn't an option. Zimmer aside, there was so much he wanted to know. He'd barely dipped his toe in the pond of his uncle's life. Cal wanted to hear the stories, wanted to get to know his one-and-only living blood relation. So, no, going home was definitely not an option.

Option 3: The one Cal wasn't very good at: wait.

That's what he did. Wait. When he wasn't pacing, he went topside and scanned every street and corner he could see. The lady on the bridge making crepes from morning until night. The tourists leaning a bit too far over every conceivable ledge they could find. Selfie heaven, apparently.

Thank modern technology for food delivery because leaving wasn't an option. Paris had every conceivable meal ticket in the world. He'd just cracked into the menu of a local ramen shop when the electric buzz of the gangplank sounded overhead. Cal climbed upstairs and was ready and waiting when Uncle Adam opened the glass door.

His uncle paused, then threw his keys on the table and kicked off his shoes into the corner. "I was expecting you to be gone."

"Why would I leave?"

Uncle Adam sighed and grabbed a bottle of wine. "I don't know. Maybe because I left. Maybe because of what I said."

"I'm working on my patience," Cal said honestly.

"You sound like your father."

"He was one of the most patient men I've ever met. Though my buddy Daniel would give him a run for his money."

Daniel Briggs, sniper extreme, was like a warrior monk, fully attuned to the world around him and virtually unflappable.

Uncle Adam poured himself a full glass and tipped the bottle Cal's way. Cal motioned with his fingers that he only wanted a bit. He got a full glass anyway.

"You know, I think I'm the only man in the world who had the ability to test your father's patience."

Cal nodded his appreciation at the wine. The French really did know their grapes. "Sounds like I take more after you than him. Tell me about my father. What do you remember?"

A long swig went by before Uncle Adam replied. Cal didn't know if it was the ride down memory lane or the current predicament with his missing friend that had his uncle distracted.

A long exhale started the tale. "He was a good man. A great big brother. I've always regretted how things turned out."

"What happened?"

"I'd rather not talk about that. Not yet. I will in time, but it's my boulder to bear. I'll tell you about the time before I fucked it all up. How about that?"

"Sure. I'd like that."

Uncle Adam downed the rest of his wine and poured a refill. "First of all, it was my fault. I want to say that upfront. I'll put that in writing if I have to."

Cal realized that the downed glass of wine probably wasn't Uncle Adam's first. "I understand. Tell me about the time before then."

Uncle Adam swirled his wine and looked deep inside the rich purple. "Your dad was the perfect older brother. Good student. Good son. Pretty good at everything. Never got in trouble. But me, I was the favorite. Things came to me, you understand? Sports. Grades. Girls. I never had to try. Not once. In most families, a brother might resent you for that. Not your dad. No way, no how. You know why? Because I was his favorite, too. He looked out for me when I was too big of an idiot to make the smart move. I had a hot head, always reaching for things that weren't mine. I even stole one of his girlfriends once. I did it fully expecting a knock-down, drag-out fight. You know what your dad said when whatever her name was broke up with him?"

"Probably something levelheaded."

Uncle Adam snorted. "Yeah. Something like that. He said, 'She's better for you anyway.' That was it. No punches. No screams. Nothing." A deep drink and Uncle Adam gazed off into the past. "I miss him."

"So do I."

Uncle Adam returned to the present and grabbed Cal's hand. "I'm so sorry, Cal. I really am. I can't imagine what you went through losing your parents. Not like that. I should've been there for you."

The wound was still there. Cal felt it every single day. His parents had been everything to him.

Cal squeezed his uncle's hand and raised his wine glass. "To new beginnings."

"New beginnings."

CHAPTER NINE

BRIGGS - ROSEMARY BEACH, FLORIDA

The beer-gutted tag team guffawed drunkenly. “Look at blondie over here. I’ll bet he’s one of them, what with his pretty blonde ponytail.”

“Sir, could you and your friend keep it down please?” the bartender whispered.

“Isn’t this a bar?” the louder of the two asked, a spittle of beer trickling out of his mouth. He slurped it back with a suck.

“Yes, sir, but we like all our patrons, bar and restaurant, to enjoy their time in this establishment.”

The bartender was waved over by a woman toting a suntanned husband and the surly duo were left to grumble.

“I’ll bet I could take him out with one punch,” Beer Belly Number One said.

“I’ll bet I could blow him a kiss and he’d flutter his pretty little butt on down to the ground.”

Number One punched Number Two in the meaty flesh of the arm. “You do that, I’m Peter Pan.” They rocked back in laughter, the restaurant customers turning from their meals, obviously unaccustomed to raucous anything in the quiet hamlet that was the beach town of Rosemary Beach. The streets were paved with wood and brick and you could smell the money in every shop you perused. You might forget that Panama City Beach was a few miles down the way, though that once-capital of the Spring Break college crowd was cleaning up its own act to attract families instead of oversexed and overindulged coeds.

"This place makes me want to puke," Number Two said, spitting on the floor. "Look at all these rich bastards and their babies. Bet they wouldn't offer me one of these fancy napkins if I got a paper cut." The second spit on the floor elicited a shocked gasp from a rail thin mother bedecked in Lilly Pulitzer frill. She forcibly turned her toddler's head away from the scene.

The manager of the place, a man with a calm demeanor and soothing voice marched up to the bar and said quietly, "Gentlemen, can I get your check?"

"What, are you kicking us out?" Number One said, puffing his chest and bumping his belly into the owner.

The owner stepped back from the offending stomach. "I'm happy to have the chef make you his signature dessert. You can take it to go."

His tone marked finality. He might be calm, but this was his house, not theirs.

"I think he's kicking us out," Number Two said, not just to his buddy, but to the entire room. He looked at Mrs. Lilly Pulitzer. "What do you think, pretty britches? You think we're misbehavin'? Maybe you could give me a spanking!"

He really laughed at that, but it stopped when the owner placed a hand on Number Two's hairy forearm.

"I think it's time for you to leave."

Number One's eyes went wide like he was ready for the show. Number Two looked down at his arm then into the eyes of the owner who wasn't backing down.

"Why you son of a—"

Everyone in the place saw the cocking arm and the punch that was meant for the owner's face. Even the toddler knew the old man's face was going to get squashed. But it didn't. Not even close. Halfway to its target, the arm stopped, straining, withheld from glory by another arm braced squarely across Number Two's bicep.

"He said it was time for you to leave," Daniel Briggs said as calm as snow.

Number Two pulled his arm back. "You fucking fa—"

Daniel put a finger to his lips. Number Two stared at him in disbelief. It was Number One who made the move, an identical fist that came at Daniel's face. The Marine sniper sidestepped, grabbed the extended arm, and wrenched it in an unnatural direction. Number One bellowed and fell to his knees. Number Two tried to slip off the bar stool, but Daniel wagged a finger back and forth. Number Two got the picture.

"It's time for you to leave," Daniel said, the whole room watching. When neither offender spoke, Daniel wrenched Number One's arm just enough.

"Okay, okay, we'll leave."

Number Two slid off the stool and gave Daniel a wide berth. Once he was headed for the door, Daniel let go of Number One and let him get up. He seemed sober now and avoided every gaze as he followed his friend out the door.

"Thanks for the help," the owner said. "Let me take care of your dinner. It's the least I can do."

"No need," Daniel said, pulling a hundred-dollar bill from his pocket and setting it on the bar. "This should cover mine and theirs, right? Thanks for the hospitality. I'll make sure those two are on their way home. By the way, the ceviche was fantastic. Something about the sauce. Just enough heat. And the potatoes, some of the best I've ever had. Soft on the inside and crispy on the out. Please give the chef my compliments."

The owner, who had the God-given gift to talk to anyone with a pulse, was suddenly struck mute, and could only nod quietly as the Lone Ranger left his small eatery.

After making sure the two instigators were gone for good, Daniel took a leisurely stroll toward the beach. The place had an air of creepiness to it, the fog taking visibility down to fifty yards, max. It felt like he was walking through a literal ghost town, figures coming out of the night like they materialized from the mist.

Sometimes he wished he could see real spirits. Maybe one of his old friends would come to call. But that was God's domain, and as he walked and thought about his friends who were living, he couldn't help but settle and pray on the well-being of his best friend, Cal Stokes.

CHAPTER TEN

SPRINGER - ST. LOUIS, MISSOURI

It's amazing what a couple hundred bucks could buy. Sure, Springer could have gone the long route and requested records through ordinary channels. Sure, he could have let the system work for him while he made the next leap for his story. But there was something about this story regarding the Marine sniper. It was that Pulitzer feel all over again. Springer could almost taste the congratulatory champagne.

"Let me know if you need anything else," the sergeant said.

He was an eager one, chosen perfectly. Springer knew all about the sergeant's late-night trysts and video gaming marathons. An addict like that needed dough, and dough wasn't something an Army sergeant had.

"Yeah sure," Springer replied. "Probably something else next week."

The sergeant didn't need to know that Springer wouldn't be back, at least not for this story. Springer was many things —a liar, a cheat, and gambler—but where he drew the line was the story. He never embellished and he never lied on paper. He saved that for his ex-girlfriends and his parents. No, this was a fact-finding mission of the tallest order. A serious story that would find the front page. He knew it.

The sergeant drove away $400 richer merely for expediting. Nothing illegal about it. Springer just got to the front of the line at the military record weigh station. Better than being one of the many cattle mooing for their turn.

Springer drove to a secluded spot in a motel parking lot and cracked open the file. The sergeant had done the extra work of tabbing each section by year. The front of the file consisted of medical records. All clean. There was some dental work and mandatory checkups. Nothing else. Springer had been hoping for a psych checkup or maybe a rehab stint. Nothing. Marines rarely sought help unless forced.

Reading the report, Springer realized he would have to school himself up on military lingo. They had more acronyms than Scientology. Then again, that's what researchers were for, and there were plenty of researchers who wanted to work with a Pulitzer winner. It was one of the perks that Springer loved.

He flipped page to page, year to year, following the progression from recruitment, to boot camp, to what the Marines called School of Infantry. Then it was Camp Lejeune and the 1st Marine Division, who recommended the young PFC for sniper training.

The sniper instructors were to the point, no fluff. But Springer read between the lines. They obviously thought highly of the guy.

Springer wondered if it was something like he read about pilots, how some just had the knack. They took to the sky like eagles tossed from a cliff. Was it the same for snipers? Another thing to find out. Anything to build the case and make this Marine extraordinary would only help to make the copy stand out. Yes, it was coming together, the story slipping into his head, line by line.

He devoured the rest of the documents, including the citation for the Medal of Honor. Springer wasn't familiar with the process of awarding the nation's highest medal for gallantry, but he found it odd that there were no notes mentioning why the medal was never given to a Marine who, in Springer's humble opinion, very much deserved it. It wasn't every day you ran across a story about a Marine who killed what might have been more than one hundred enemy combatants in the course of a battle.

So yeah, this guy deserved the award alright, so why didn't he get it? And more importantly, what had led this otherwise exemplary Marine to commit the acts Springer had so recently uncovered.

Springer tossed the file on the passenger seat and pulled a vial from his coat pocket. He spooned out a small mound of the white stuff, snorted it, then repeated it on the other side.

Springer felt the familiar pull of the story just as the drug kicked in. Yes. This wasn't work. It would never be work. He would do it for free if they paid for his food, lodging, and an occasional babe to sleep with. A purist at heart, Springer's need for the truth was as strong as his need for adulation and a good bump every now and again. The good news was the truth paid well when it was presented with skill and perfect timing. Springer had the skill, and with a little luck, he would also have the timing.

CHAPTER ELEVEN

ADAM STOKES - PARIS - 1974

Adam Stokes felt like he'd been bred to live in Paris. The cafes. The laid-back lifestyle. The loose rules on sex. He could get used to this. Maybe he'd become an artist. Bohemian like the ones he saw lining the River Seine trying to catch that perfect millisecond glimpse in time. Or maybe he'd do odd jobs until something real struck his fancy. Adam didn't mind manual labor. He'd been raised on a farm. Getting up early and earning a fair keep was tangled up in his DNA.

He had a little cash, what was left of the high school graduation gifts from his family. So what if he had to sleep on a floor? No problem. And so what if he could only afford coffee and pastries? Definitely no problem there. It was a perfect set up. No attachments. No responsibilities. No nagging family. That last one might be the best of the three.

Adam stretched an arm around the pretty Brit he'd picked up at the anti-war rally. She was vivacious, full of alcohol, and possessed a willingness to shag until the next millennium.

"Want another glass of wine?" she asked. He loved how

her eyelashes drooped down when she drank, like she was already halfway to bedtime.

"Sure. Why not? I don't have anywhere to be," Adam said. She gave his crotch a light squeeze. "Whoa, careful there, honey. Don't want to damage the merchandise."

She all but purred, planting a sweet kiss on his mouth.

HIS SHIRT WENT FIRST, then his pants—both flew over his head and nearly out the window.

"Don't even think of coming back. I ought to call the police right now!" the proper-looking English gentleman bellowed, looking properly puffed and bedraggled. He probably would have rattled a saber at Adam if he had one. The man's daughter stood behind him. One arm draped across her bare breasts. Her pink underwear was the only other cover she had. She winked and blew him a kiss.

Adam scooped up his clothes and blew her a kiss back. The door slammed shut just in time for him to hear the father say, "Now get some bloody clothes on, girl!"

Adam chuckled drunkenly, staggering as he put on his clothes, trying to figure out where he was going to sleep. It was about three in the morning. He turned around and blew another kiss.

"I'll be seeing you, darlin'!" he yelled from the cobblestone pavement below. An old woman stuck her head out of a window and grumbled in French. "I'm very sorry, madam, I've been kicked out of my sweetheart's flat."

"Stick it up your bum, Yank," the woman grumbled, and slammed the window shut.

Well, it wasn't how he had planned the night to go, but all in all it was quite the day. Quite the day indeed.

He spent some time roaming, looking for a place to sit, but he was in a part of town he didn't know. A park bench would be fine. He'd sleep in a corner if he hadn't seen so many Parisians take a leisurely piss in them.

On he walked, whistling at times and listening to the dark. The place didn't sound like home, and in that moment he wished he could hear the crickets in the fields and a lonely owl's call. He wished for the smell of fresh hay and dirt recently turned for seed. Maybe he should go home. His parents might be upset over his leaving, but they'd take him back. He was their baby boy. Their favorite.

He was just making his mind up to place a call, maybe ask for a plane ticket home, when three men stepped out of an alleyway. Like all good Parisians, they were smoking. They talked animatedly and Adam pegged them in their early twenties. There was nothing special about them. Just a group of guys up late, probably heading home from a house party.

Then he saw the flash of jewelry. A handful of it. One of them laughed and the jewelry disappeared in a pocket.

Shit, Adam thought to himself. What a way to end the night. Get kicked out of a beautiful girl's pad, or her father's, and stumble upon the aftermath of a robbery. Adam didn't want any part of it. Maybe if he was home he would have done something about it, but this was Paris, a strange city that suddenly felt a bit more sinister. Time to hide.

One of the trio barked something in French. Adam ignored them and kept walking. He should've paid more attention to learning the language instead of the local menus. Up ahead he saw a park. He could lose them. He was lightning fast, but maybe they'd leave him alone. He hunched a little further. Maybe they'd think he was a mute or a cripple.

"Hey, American!"

That's when Adam realized two things: 1) that he had just

passed under a streetlight, and 2) that he was wearing the same clothes his British lover had told him to get rid of.

"You stick out like a boorish American," she said. "You need to learn to fit in, dress like you're a Parisian."

But he hadn't cared enough or had enough money to even think about a new wardrobe.

He ran.

Adam heard the footfalls behind him. He was fast. Fastest at his high school.

But it was nighttime in a strange city, and he was still partially drunk, and he hadn't run in weeks. And they were gaining.

He broke through the first line of trees and off to the right saw the lights lining the river. Maybe he could leap in.

He went right, noting how close the three robbers were behind him. No time to think, Adam. Just run.

And he got close. Not ten feet to the edge where a long jump would've sent him splashing.

Someone tackled him from behind, and suddenly there were bodies all around, kicks all over and punches raining down. All he could do was bunch up as best he could and take the beating. When he covered his head, they kicked all the harder. He lost all sense of time.

WHEN IT WAS FINALLY OVER, Adam Stokes was covered in spit, blood, and dirt. He knew there were multiple broken bones in his hands, possibly a cracked skull and bruised ribs. But that wasn't even the worst of it. They sealed the deal by taking all the money he had left and every form of ID he owned.

He lay back as the sun peaked over the horizon, the birds swooping down to the river to find their morning meal.

How a single day could change.

He had one thought as he struggled to his feet: "Now what?"

CHAPTER TWELVE

FLAP - WASHINGTON, D.C.

The Republican senator stroked the leg of the leather-clad mistress as he spoke. "You're telling me you're sure. Because I can't have any opposition on this, Flap."

"I've confirmed the information myself, senator. No fewer than five corroborative sources."

There was a muted grunt from the senator as the masked mistress nibbled on his ear.

"Good enough," he said. "Now, if you'll excuse me, I've got business." He grabbed the chain looped around the woman's neck and pulled her up to a standing position. "I'm in charge tonight."

"Anything you say, senator."

The woman's voice was equal parts the finest wine in Paris and the smoothest silk in Persia. She had curves in all the right places and Flap approved of her alluring scent. It was an intriguing thing. He'd essentially been celibate for his entire adult life.

He waited for the pair to leave and then knocked on the wall behind him. A bodyguard appeared.

"Tell them to take my twin across town," Flap ordered. "We've got one more stop to make."

Flap had a handful of body doubles that could pass all but the most intrusive scans. They were more than useful in his line of work. They were necessary. Much like this sex club. You could buy off a bartender or a flight attendant, but Flap had learned from a long-dead spy that a plyer of the sex trade wrapped themselves in anonymity like a bat in its wings. It didn't hurt that there were plenty of clubs scattered around town. They were favorite haunts of bachelors and married power icons alike.

The beat-up old Chevy swerved to the curb and Flap waited for his bodyguard to do his diligence in the brownstone apartment. The place had seen better days, much like this vehicle. But that didn't mean it wasn't secure. The car was armor-plated and could take up to a .50 caliber round. The window was shatterproof and thick as a wrist. Flap never understood riding around in a souped-up Suburban like you were some Hollywood wannabe. He'd leave that to the amateurs.

The bodyguard nodded from the front stoop and Flap wasted no time. He was up the stairs and inside in seconds, a man surprisingly spry for his age and awkward build.

"Dinner is almost ready," came the voice from the kitchen.

Flap was starving. It was one of the few vices he allowed. No booze. No women. But good food was a must.

Konstantin Yegorovich stood at the massive stove, dancing to the strains of Prokofiev's *Alexander Nevsky* score as he swapped one hot pan for another and flipped with expert ease.

"Are you hungry?" he asked.

"Very."

"Good. I've made you something special."

Flap drank two full glasses of water before dinner was finally served.

"Et voilà," said the Russian president, setting six dishes on the kitchen island. "I would ask you if you'd like to join me in a celebratory vodka toast, but I know that's beyond my powers of persuasion."

"Your American English is getting better," Flap said, stabbing a pork loin and moving it to his plate.

"I'm glad you noticed. It's the slang that gets me." The Russian waited for Flap to take his first bite and then asked, "Do you like it?"

"You know I do."

The president clapped his hands together and set upon the food. Whenever they could arrange it, this was their routine. Flap knew there were Russian guards stationed throughout the house, but he'd long since stop caring. These two were in it together. They'd forged their parallel paths with great care.

Flap was well into his second helping when the real discussion began.

"How are you liking your new job?" The Russian said with a distinct Midwestern drawl, making *job* sound like *jab*.

"It takes some getting used to..."

"Do you miss the field?"

"Always."

"But you're closer to your goal."

"And what goal would that be? I thought I'd already gotten everything I wanted."

They both smiled at the quip. The CIA directorship had been a lofty pipe dream twenty years before, when Flap was slugging it out with ruffians in Kazakhstan. But the Russian knew Flap's real objective. They'd talked about it many times before.

"So, how is Calvin's son? I hear he's in Paris."

Even without Flap's considerable input, the Russian's resources were impressive.

"He's stepping closer and closer to my noose. Would you like to know the details?"

The Russian dramatically waved his hands in the air. "Absolutely not. I'd rather watch as it unfolds. His father was a good friend, after all."

Again they both laughed, and then began a process of immersion into their shared stratagem.

CHAPTER THIRTEEN

STOKES - PARIS

The Louvre entryway cast down light that seemed both natural and manufactured. White on white on white in every direction. Tour groups milled, waiting for guides. Mothers tried their best to bribe children before stepping off into the passageways of history.

Cal sipped a bottle of water and waited for his uncle. Adam returned with a pair of maps.

"I don't care how many times you've been here, if anyone says they know their way around, they're lying." He handed a map to Cal and off they went.

Uncle Adam was the perfect guide. He didn't know everything, but he knew enough to keep his nephew's interest. It was tidbits about a certain painter, how a reckless string of debauched marriages had almost derailed a career, or the rich patrons who had been the only reason such-and-such artist ever had a chance of standing out.

There was the political history, too, rich and vibrant in

paints as real as the present. Figures cut from stone by expert hands and lovingly given to the world.

"We wouldn't have any of this if it weren't for money," said Uncle Adam. "Money rules the world and makes things *happen*. I didn't believe it when I was your age, but I'm pretty damn sure about it now."

Adam kept philosophy in his deep bag of secrets, but as they walked further into the honeycomb that once housed French kings, he seemed to come alive, to channel whatever power the place held. They passed a giant sarcophagus of ornamented marble, its very presence a testament to the continuation of life in sculpture.

"When did you first come to Paris?" Cal asked.

"I was eighteen. Young. Stupid. Lost. I thought I knew what I wanted."

"Sounds about right for that age. I was in my early twenties when I decided to run off to war." Cal stifled himself again. It was a time in his life that he never talked about and rarely wanted to even think about.

His uncle pressed him. "Tell me about it, about that time."

"You don't want to hear about my garbage years."

Uncle Adam stopped walking. "I want to hear about all the years. In fact, I realized as we've been walking that I've been a poor host. We've had a couple laughs and we've gotten to know each other on the surface, but I suppose I was afraid to know more. I can admit that to you now."

"Afraid of what?"

"I've made more than a few mistakes in my life, Cal. The biggest, by far, was walking out on your dad. Even bigger than leaving my parents if I'm being honest." He led Cal into a quiet alcove and his voice lowered. "I guess I've been scared of hearing everything I missed because of my decision to leave. You have no idea what it means to me that you trusted me enough to come stay, but it opened a wound that might consume me. Every time I see your face, I miss your father and want him here with us. He really was the best of us, Cal. I want you to know that. And I want to know everything. I really do, but don't be surprised if your old uncle sniffles a little every once in a while."

Uncle Adam's words cut clean into Cal, welling up all the memories of not only his mom and dad, but of his friends, of Diane...

"Okay," Cal said after a moment, "so, 9/11 happened. I was in school at the time."

"University of Virginia, right?"

"Right. It was horrible. I remember it like it was yesterday."

Cal told his uncle how he'd missed the call from his dad, who was aboard the plane that crashed into the Pentagon. "I kept the message."

"I'd like to hear that, if you'll let me."

Cal nodded, his mind still back all those years ago. "I lost it. I demanded from everyone who would listen that they send me to kill the sons of bitches who killed my parents. Long story short, I went to boot camp, thought I was God's gift to the Marine Corps, got humbled, made some great friends, and eventually went off to war."

"Did you deal with it or did you bury it away? The pain, I mean."

Cal smiled wryly. "What do you think? I buried it. I was gonna ask you if that was a family trait."

Uncle Adam laughed. "Passed down through generations of Stokes men."

"That's what I thought." It felt good to talk to someone of his own flesh and blood who knew. Friends were life, but family was family. He'd forgotten that simple fact. "So, I come home, fresh out to the Corps, engaged to a beautiful girl—"

"Jessica, right?"

"That's right. She was the vanilla ice cream to my stale apple crumb cake. Where I had rough edges, she had beautiful lines and perfect emotions."

"She sounds like a special girl."

"She was. I lost her and then things really hit the fan. But what do they say, something about in the midst of horror one either finds themselves or succumbs? Well that was me. I was on the razor's edge. And it wasn't the last time. I was lucky enough to have friends who dragged me kicking and screaming into the light." Cal thought of Brian Ramirez and his cousin Travis Haden. Both dead. Both heroes. "I wouldn't be here without them. I know that and I try to live by their example."

"You've been lucky."

"I'm not sure I'd call it lucky, but yeah, I've come out okay."

They kept walking, past the gold and jewels left by ancient pharaohs, through a pod of art students sprawled around the next chamber, each engaged in their own private Picasso moment.

"Can I give you a little advice," Uncle Adam said, "Stokes man to Stokes man?"

"Sure."

"It's born out of experience. I say that so you don't think I'm climbing up to my pulpit." They scooted past a child who was stomping on stack of crayons, his father oblivious two feet away. "I know you've been through a lot. You've probably seen more than any mortal man should ever witness. But I've found, through my own dark times, that if I stick with the ones who really matter, the ones who've been with me through the good times and bad, that I'll come out the end of the shit-stinking tunnel in one piece. And I want you to know that I'm here with you now. I want to be part of your family, Cal, I really do. Will you let me do that?"

Cal felt something well up inside, the pressure building so much that all he could do was nod and take his uncle's offered hand.

CHAPTER FOURTEEN

BRIGGS - ROSEMARY BEACH, FLORIDA

Liberty disappeared into the fog, the German Shorthaired Pointer sprinting after the tennis ball like it was a leg of lamb. Daniel estimated visibility at fifty yards. It deadened the sounds of the crashing waves and made him feel like he was the only human being in a mile's radius.

Liberty bounded back toward him, the tennis ball found, the tongue lolling out one side of her mouth.

"Good girl," Daniel said when she was close enough to drop the ball and roll it toward him with her nose. She got a coating of Florida Panhandle white sand for her efforts.

The ball sailed through the air again and off she ran, her enthusiasm for such a task contagious. Daniel had come to understand the importance of these downtimes, these moments between moments. Others might call it boring, the calm before the proverbial storm, but this was the time Daniel used to recharge, reengage, find his spiritual center. And he needed it. Especially today.

A muffled bark sounded from where Liberty had gone,

and a figure appeared, trailed by the wagging tail that moved so hard it shook the dog's rear half from side to side like a metronome. Daniel raised a hand in greeting and the woman, sandals in hand, waved back. She could be a 110-years-old and Daniel would still find her beautiful.

"Anna," he said, when she came in for a hug.

"I've missed you," Anna Varushkin said, giving him a good squeeze. "Now, let me look at you." She held him at arm's length. "Hair still ponytailed and scruffy. Face in dire need of a shave. But it looks like they've been feeding you well. As well as when we first met?"

"Not quite. You'll have to challenge Top to a duel. I'd love to see you two duke it out in the kitchen."

Top was Master Sergeant Willy Trent, USMC, Retired. At close to seven feet tall and as chiseled as Zeus, the Marine was a classically trained chef, and The Jefferson Group's reigning stand-up comedian.

Anna hugged him again. "I really have missed you, you know. I'm so glad you called."

They spent the first hour of their walk talking about mundane nuggets of life, though both lives had been far from mundane. Daniel was a covert operator who spent his time finding bad guys and either putting them in the dirt or in a cell. Anna led the Fund, a powerful conglomerate founded by Soviet and Russian expatriates. Daniel didn't know how many billions the Fund had in its coffers, but he did know that since Anna took the reins following her grandfather's death, returns kept growing with the influx of capital and partnerships.

"I was so sorry to hear about Diane. My time with her is something I'll always cherish."

"She was one of the good ones," Daniel said, picking up the tennis ball and throwing it into the fog.

"And how is Cal? I can't imagine what he's going through. This is the second time, am I right?"

Daniel nodded. "First he loses Jessica and now Diane."

Anna squeezed his hand. "There's something you're not telling me. I can tell, remember?"

Yes, she could. She might be the only person in the world who could read the unreadable Daniel Briggs. There was no sense hiding it.

"It was my fault. I should've protected them. I don't know how to tell him I'm sorry."

He had already said it to God. Now he was saying it to the woman he most respected in the world. She had all the power of a world leader, and yet, she chose to stay humble and loving.

"Tell me what happened."

Daniel explained, going into just enough detail about the operation in Canada months before. He left out the major players, at least for now. He described how the rogue sniper lured Diane out in the open, then shot her probably thinking it was Cal.

"That's a tough one. I'm sorry," Anna said, not letting go of his hand. He needed that hand, that human touch.

"I should've done more," he said. "I should've secured the area, had more men, something."

"This doesn't sound like you, Daniel. I know you're hurting for your friends, but you know as I do what happens in the head of a madman when he gets the scent of blood and revenge. There's no stopping that unless it's a bullet."

And she knew from experience. They both did. That was the bond that first brought them together. Anna's father, a wolf in sheep's clothing. Actually, a preacher's clothing.

And then she went into CEO mode, the calculations

kicking into gear. "Tell me what you learned. What's the silver lining?"

At that Daniel smiled. "I didn't tell you about Lena."

Anna's eyebrow arched. "And who, pray tell, is Lena?"

"Lena is a 19-year-old woman with quite possibly the best natural instincts of any sniper I've ever met."

"High praise coming from nature's gift to Marine Corps sharpshooting. I want to hear more."

"You will. In fact, I was hoping you would meet her in person. Up for a road trip?"

"I'll be your beck-and-call girl," Anna said with a happy twinkle in her eyes.

"Good. Because there's more we need to discuss."

"Oh? I was hoping this would be a vacation." She sank into the seriousness of the situation. "But I should know better than that when I'm with you." She wrapped her arms around his midsection. "So, what is it?"

There was no other choice. He had to call on her. She would know or she would be the person with the best resources to find out.

"I need you to tell me about the Russian president."

CHAPTER FIFTEEN

LENA - CAMP SPARTAN, ARRINGTON, TENNESSEE

Jab. Jab. Jab.

Hook.

Miss. Miss. Miss.

Whiff. Lena blew a stray hair out of her eyes and squinted through the sweat.

"You're trying too hard," Top said.

She didn't know how such a big target could be so hard to hit.

Jab. Jab. Jab.

He grabbed her wrist and applied just enough pressure. Before she could comprehend what had happened, she was on her back, looking up at the grinning Marine. He offered her a hand. She took it.

"What am I doing wrong?" she said, going for a quick sip of water.

"You're not doing anything wrong."

"You said I was trying too hard."

"You are. But you're learning. For example, you took my

hand when I offered you a help up. That's called being smart. You always take a friend's hand when he offers it."

It was one of many lessons the huge man liked to sprinkle into their training. She'd tried to ignore them at first, but it was hard not to like Top. He was too fair, too nice, and holy moly could he cook.

"Okay, so I'm not doing anything wrong. You're saying that I'm getting better?"

Top nodded. "That's right. You're gettin' it. But let's talk turkey. You're what, 115 pounds soaking wet with a pack on? Now, look at me. Aside from all the pretty in my face, do you think this is something you'd take on hand to hand in real life?"

"Not unless I was crazy."

"Right. So why are we doing this? What am I trying to get you to learn?"

Lena thought about that. So many lessons. What was the common theme? Or was there one?

"That I can push through the pain?"

Top smiled. "I had a pretty good feeling that you already knew that before you stepped in the ring with me. Tell you what. I won't make you guess, cuz it's not something on the surface." He threw her a towel and she mopped herself off. "You have any friends?"

It should've been an easy question. Every 19-year-old female had friends. "I used to."

"And what happened to them?"

"They're dead or gone."

Top's eyes softened now. He saw her pain even when she tried to hide it.

"I want to be your friend, Lena. *We* want to be your friends. That's the lesson. The rest of this training, your sessions with Doc Higgins, shooting with Daniel or busting through doors with Gaucho, it's all icing on the cake, honey. We see you. Do you understand that? You're one of us."

She'd lost so much. Her traitorous father. Her old friends. Any semblance of a life. Then again, had she ever really had a life? No. She couldn't accept his words that easily.

"So, am I free to go, or am I still under house arrest?" Lena asked.

"You know why you're here, Lena. People much more important than me have to decide what to do."

"And when they do, if they say I can go, will you let me go?"

"Of course. But we hope you'll stay. Not because you have to stay, but because you want to stay."

Lena took another sip of water and dropped the bottle on the ground.

"Ima pummel your ass now, punk," she said, holding up her fists.

Top grinned and waded in for the thrashing.

CHAPTER SIXTEEN

SPRINGER - JACKSONVILLE, NORTH CAROLINA

"Tight-lipped simpletons," Springer said, putting his car in drive and watching the rearview mirror at the three jarheads staring him down. He hated this town. It only existed because of Camp Lejeune, the largest Marine Corps base on the East Coast. Springer wondered what would happen when the uppity bastards read his story, right there, smack dab on top of the headlines. "Probably can't even read," he muttered, steering his way past strip malls and traffic waiting to enter the base.

Springer liked to follow a trail like a hound on scent. He'd started at the beginning of Briggs's career. The training didn't count. He knew there were a host of veterans who stuck close to their former calling after they left the service. So he'd come to town to dig.

He used a cover story that friends of the Marine sniper would like. Dirk Springer, Pulitzer Prize winning journalist, was doing a hero piece on the great Daniel Briggs. Who'd say no to that?

Any journalist who really knows how to get a story can find the hidden buttons everyone has, and fast. With this one, Springer went with the whole enchilada, playing the Stars and Stripes bit as loud as he could. Kids needed to hear Daniel's story. Parents needed a hero for their kids. Veterans needed validation for their time served and all that horseshit. Staff Sergeant Daniel Briggs, USMC, would be that Roman candle shooting off into the sky.

But if this first foray was any indication of future success, Springer was not hopeful. Three Marine veterans sat down with him, and like lions in a cage, they stalked him, they nudged him, and finally they tore into him. They smelled a rat, and Springer's chances were cooked.

He should've known better. Marines could be a secretive lot, especially their more elite units like the Raiders and Force RECON.

But it wasn't a complete loss. In their fight they hadn't killed Springer's energy for the story. In fact, they'd done just the opposite. That told him one very important thing—that if they fought him that hard in the beginning, there must be a deeper story to uncover, and every "no" proved that he was on the right track.

"Simpletons," he repeated.

Then he smiled. Their day would come.

CHAPTER SEVENTEEN

ADAM STOKES - PARIS - 1974

His ego was as bruised as his body. And one thing he knew was that he would not call home and ask for help. He would do this himself.

A cafe waiter took pity on him. After a terse conversation with the owner, a small luncheon was provided, along with enough wine to take the sting off his wounds.

"Thanks. I promise I'll pay you back," Adam said to the waiter, a crooked ancient who might've worked at the cafe since World War I.

"*C'est bon*," the waiter said, bobbing his head and patting Adam's forearm. "*C'est bon.*"

Adam was grateful and almost let the tears come. He held them in, ate as slowly as he could since he had no real place to go, and hammered back as much wine as he dared.

He was well into his cups when two men with hard eyes came tramping into the cafe. They greeted the owner with a bear hug each, planting wet kisses on the old man's cheeks.

He shooed them away and a waiter tended to the fit-looking men like they were his children.

It was impossible not to stare. Adam tried not to. There was something in the way they chatted with fellow patrons, the way they doled out what could only be compliments to the staff. And yet, those hard eyes. More than once they fell on him and he looked away. But still, the curiosity.

He never saw the two men beckon the waiter over and point at the battered American. Adam wouldn't have understood the words if he'd heard them. The result was two new guests at his table, each bringing a wine bottle to share.

"You're American," one of them said, a dark-skinned man with arms that looked like iron ore. Adam placed his accent as Middle Eastern, though where exactly he had no clue.

The prickles on the back of Adam's neck returned. He was embarrassed to realize he was afraid. Was this round two with the thugs of Paris?

The second man, a man with a clipped British accent tuned right in. "We see you had some trouble." The Brit pointed at the cuts and bruises.

"It's nothing."

The Brit laughed. "If that's nothing, I'd hate to see something."

Adam could lie. He could say he fell down some stairs. He'd seen plenty of drunks take a dive after a misplaced step on Paris's uneven stones. But he didn't. He yearned for connection. Or maybe it was just someone to listen. Like his older brother had so many times before. The river of wine running through his blood probably helped nudge him toward the truth.

"I saw a robbery. It was an accident. I wasn't going to say anything, but they caught me. And they did this."

He raised his shirt and showed the impressive bruising. The two men nodded and sipped their wine.

"Where did this happen?" the dark one asked.

Adam told him.

The Brit leaned over and whispered in the Middle Easterner's ear. The dark one smiled.

"Do you have a place to stay?" the Brit asked.

"Not anymore. The girl I was staying with... kicked me out."

"We have a place for you to stay," the dark one said. "But first, let us finish our wine. And then, you will show us where this happened."

They drank their wine, chatted about small things, and the strangers paid for the visit, once again making the rounds in the cafe, bear hugging the proprietor and planting kisses on everyone they passed. Adam could only watch in awed confusion.

Somehow, whether it was by luck or fate, he found where the robbery occurred. Police were there, and the two men told him to stay around the corner. Adam wanted to run again. They were going to tell the police and he would be the one framed. He expected flashing lights, orders screamed in French, and a gun at the side of his head.

The two men returned, and when Adam asked what happened, they ignored his question and told him instead that it was time for a nap.

"I don't have a place to stay," Adam said.

"I told you, mate, you'll come with us. You'll be taken care of."

"Wait. I don't mean to sound ungrateful. I appreciate you two listening, offering to help me get back on my feet. But I don't know you." And then he blurted something he immediately regretted. "What are you, mafia or something?"

The two men looked at each other, shook their heads, and burst out laughing.

The dark-skinned stranger looked at him, smiling broadly. "We're Legionnaires, my good man. And tonight, we show you what Legionnaires do for their friends."

CHAPTER EIGHTEEN

BRIGGS - ROSEMARY BEACH, FLORIDA

Anna did a pass through the rented carriage house and came back to lean a hip on the tiny dining room table. “I’m not sure what I like more, the framed shell hula skirt that looks like chain mail or the king-sized bedroom nook that might’ve been modeled after a private meeting room in a Chinese madam’s retail outlet.”

“It’s eclectic. I like it.”

Anna shrugged. “I didn’t know you’d become a connoisseur of fine things. Rosemary Beach ain’t cheap.”

“Being friends with Cal Stokes has its benefits. And rib me all you want, but you’ve got a lot more of a fine life than I do.”

There were few people in the world he could talk to like this. And now that he thought about it, maybe Anna was the only one. What was it that put him at ease with her? She was gracious in every way. Elegant, beautiful, and wicked smart.

“I always knew you’d find your way into my world, Mr. Briggs,” Anna said, playing the southern belle. “But you had a question. And if I know anything about you, it's that getting down to business is always high on your list of priorities."

And it was. But in that moment, when he looked at her, he wished they could talk about what normal guys and gals talk about—movies, old friends, their shared past. But that wasn't them. That wasn't their life.

He sighed deep inside. Back to business.

"Right. The Russian. Tell me what you think of him."

"How much time do we have?"

"As much as we need."

Anna nodded, gathering her thoughts.

"You want concrete or truth mixed with possible fiction?"

"I want to know what you think."

"Okay. First, let's start with the rumors. I heard that he's immortal, that he's found the fountain of youth. That he can wrestle polar bears and tear the hearts from lions. Some say he's the world's first trillionaire, that he controls every drop of oil leaving Russia and every scrap of food leaving peasant farms. Here's what I know to be fact: He's a dangerous man. His background aside, he's figured out how to corral a populace who made it very clear they did not want to be corralled. He's captured the imaginations of Russians young and old. National pride is rising everyday though Russians are in the same spot they've been in for decades. Yes, the rich keep getting richer, but he has a firm thumb down on that lot, too. He's not afraid to threaten, bribe, or outright kill if it suits his needs. But, in my opinion, that's not the worst of it. We've had despots before. You walk down any street in the world and you'll find a murderer. No, what impresses me about the man, what keeps us watching, is his ambition. Could you imagine when the Berlin wall fell, when the Soviet Union collapsed, that a supposedly democratically elected president would find a way back into office the way he did? And the moves he made both domestically and overseas, they show he has imagination. And it is his imagination that keeps me up at night. It's the reason we've been so careful. It's the reason we stay clear of our homeland. Every operation, every coup, every plot against him has failed."

"Why do you think that is? He's not untouchable."

"Oh?"

"I'll tell you the story later. What I want to know is why you put him on that pedestal. Why is he different than any other tyrant in the past hundred years?"

Anna raked her fingers through her hair. "You'll think I'm crazy if I say it. You want concrete."

"Like I said, I want to know what you think."

Anna's lips pursed and Daniel remembered the child he'd met years ago, the precocious teen who wanted to see the world and see it on her terms.

"Okay, this is going to sound a little woo-woo, but I think he's got some kind of good luck charm, some voodoo, like he's always ten moves ahead of Lady Luck herself. I can't explain it properly. It's just what I've seen."

Daniel wondered how deep into the despot disposal game Anna and the Fund had gotten. Anna and her people were refugees running from the motherland. What was their motivation, other than the need to reclaim the land of their ancestors? Had they tried to assassinate the man?

Daniel took a breath. "Let's assume he's somehow blessed. He could be. I've seen and heard stories, too. It's not like he's iron tight with his security. So how come no one's gotten to him? There are plenty of people who'd like that to happen. He comes across as a friend, a confidant even. A man of the people. So, what is it? What's the power keeping him going?"

"If it weren't so blasphemous to say it, I'd say it's either God or Satan," Anna said.

Daniel knew that was always a possibility. He'd seen much to back up that hypothesis.

Anna went on. "But are you asking because of some act he's committed against America? Or is it directed at your friends?"

"I wouldn't say he's committed an act."

"Not yet."

"Sure," Daniel said. "I guess at this point it's more of a feeling."

"One that Cal shares?"

"Yeah."

Anna tapped her forehead and then her heart. "I know you wouldn't be asking if you didn't believe there was a legitimate threat. Let's go with that feeling, let's work on this together, and see what that two-faced jackal is up to."

CHAPTER NINETEEN

YEGOROVICH - MOSCOW

"You have your orders. I look forward to seeing the results."

President Konstantin Yegorovich walked from the roof knowing the man sitting stock still next to the roaring fire wouldn't fail. Not an impossible task. He was the president, after all, and what the president wanted—especially this president—he got.

"You have a call waiting in your office, sir," one of his secretaries murmured as he fell in stride a step back to the left.

"How have you been?" the president asked.

"Very good, Mr. President."

"And your studies?"

"I am flattered that you would—"

"Don't do that, Leonid. It shows weakness. Wasted words and stumbled pleasantries are for old nannies and feckless men. You don't want to be a feckless man, do you, Leonid?"

"No, Mr. President."

"Good. Excuse me, please."

He waited for Leonid to depart. Once alone, he picked up the receiver. "Tell me."

"There's been movement with the Fund."

He'd been after the traitors since coming to office the first time. Slippery devils they were, hiding behind foreign benefactors, always playing their games at Russia's expense. That was Russia's money, *his* money. And he would get it.

"Tell me quickly. I have dinner plans."

This particular dinner included a brash Olympic diver who'd taken to social media to promote women's equality. The president didn't mind equality. He embraced it. But the underlining message that Russia was somehow evil would not stand. He would talk to her, make sure she understood her place.

The man on the other end zipped through the report. His brevity was more than pleasing.

"Very well. Monitor the situation. I'll be in touch with follow-up orders."

What were the stinking traitors doing this very minute? He would very much like to know so that he might talk to them, then kill them, and take every ruble, euro, and dollar they'd ever squirreled away. With that level of money came a higher echelon of power that the Russian very much wanted. Needed. Required for his very existence.

If he was going to beat the Americans, he would need every penny he could steal.

CHAPTER TWENTY

STOKES - PARIS

They took their time. Cal didn't give trust lightly and he could see that his uncle was very much the same. They went on walks. Sometimes they talked, sometimes they admired the city in silence. But when they did talk, Cal felt his past returning, like he was getting a second shot with his father. It would never be a replacement, but at least it was something. And right now, that something was what Cal needed.

"Boulangerie or cafe?" Cal asked when he joined his uncle on the deck.

"Neither. I've got someone I want you to meet."

"Okay. When do we leave?"

"She's coming here. I'm sure she'll bring food with her."

There was no deeper explanation. Uncle Adam seemed lost in his thoughts, so Cal took up a chair beside him and watched the tourists swarm through Pont Neuf.

"Bonjour!" came a voice from the river bank.

"And there she is," Uncle Adam said, rising to lower the

gangplank. Cal joined him. The woman waiting on the other side of the slip of water had gray hair poofed out like a stick of cotton candy. She held a cloth grocery bag in each hand and wore a smile that had probably brightened a thousand lives.

"Bonjour, Mary," Uncle Adam said, walked to the other side to kiss her on each cheek and grab the groceries. He motioned for her to come aboard first. She scooted carefully, her advanced age evident.

Cal offered her a hand. "Bonjour."

"Bonjour," she said. She gave him the up-and-down look he'd become accustomed to from Parisian women. Nothing lurid. Just admiring.

Uncle Adam spoke to Mary in lightning French. She replied, and they went back and forth like that until they were inside and Cal had locked the door. They kept chattering like hens down the ladder and into the lower living area. Cal followed, wondering when he was going to be invited to the party.

"Cal, there's a button, right there behind the stereo. Mind pushing it?" Uncle Adam asked, then went right back to talking in French. Whatever they were saying sounded good enough for a TV talk show.

He went to the stereo and looked left and right inside the little nook that housed the boat's sound system. Mostly technology from ten years earlier.

"Where did you say the button was?" Cal assumed his uncle wanted to play some mood music, or maybe it was button to dim every light in the place in an instant.

"Right behind the stereo. Just feel around a bit."

Cal peeked inside the nook again. All wires and gizmos. No button. Then he reached around the main receiver, feeling inch by inch, and there it was. He pressed it, waited, then looked at Uncle Adam, who raised a finger.

"Give it a minute."

Cal gave it thirty seconds. Thought about pressing it again, waited another thirty seconds.

Must be old French technology, Cal thought, wondering if the water had somehow corrupted whatever it was that Uncle Adam wanted flipped. There'd been more than one power outage when the washing machine, coffee machine, and too many lights were on at once.

Then it happened. Not the hum of speakers powering up. Not the slow dim of mood lighting. No, something incredible and quite out of place happened. A door, two inches thick, slid slow and heavy over Cal's head as the railing that aided climbing passengers split in a spot Cal had assumed was a shoddy joint. The door clicked into place and then similar casings closed in over each porthole along with the window that was slightly above water level. When everything was buttoned up, Cal felt like he was in a soundproof room.

He was turning to Uncle Adam and his guest when the next extraordinary thing happened. Mary, the weathered Parisian bag lady, pulled off her hair and revealed a silver streaked brown do tied in a bun. But that wasn't the most shocking. Mary looked right at Cal, and in a middle-American accent, said, "Why don't you grab us a good belt of whiskey, dear. You look like you could use some."

CHAPTER TWENTY-ONE

STOKES - PARIS

"You're probably thinking, 'what the hell is going on here,' am I right?" Uncle Adam said, making drinks for the three of them.

There was a lot more he wanted to ask, but Cal started with, "Who are you?"

The woman looked at least ten years younger now that she shed the hair and what looked like a good deal of padding under her clothes.

"I'm an old friend of your uncle's. One of his oldest."

"You're not that old," Uncle Adam said.

The woman slapped the air. "Well of course not. I feel as spry as a 40-year-old. And the getup helps."

"But you're American?" Cal asked.

"Of course I'm American." She added a little huff like she'd grown up on Broadway. "But I do love pretending I'm French, especially with the tourists."

Uncle Adam handed out the drinks and Cal found himself near guzzling his own.

"See? I told you, you needed a drink," the woman said. She took a healthy swig of her own. "Now, down to business. My name is Glenda, last name Younger. Your uncle and I met too many years ago to count. I'll admit that my one vanity is the exact number of my age, so I'll leave that out of the conversation. And if you dare ask, I'll remove every one of your teeth."

"You're a spy," Cal guessed.

She tilted her head. "Not exactly."

Cal motioned around the room that now felt more like a bank vault. "This smells like spy stuff to me."

"How much can I tell him?" Glenda asked their host.

"Considering the circumstances, I'd say everything," Uncle Adam replied, refilling everyone's drinks.

"Very well. Everything." She took an appreciative sip of her refill and grinned. "I wish I could drink whiskey in public. In Paris, if you ask for anything but local wine they'll take you to the guillotine. But I digress." She sipped again and settled into her chair. Cal couldn't help but be entranced by the woman. It was as if by clicking her heels she'd become the maestra.

"I was an English teacher in my past life. The little ones, fifth, sixth, seventh grades. I enjoyed it more than I can tell you. I lived in a little Virginia town called Mount Airy. Perhaps you've heard of it? Lovely place. Hallmark movie locale, if you catch my drift. Those were the simple days, when my hours were filled with making sure little Susie found the perfect book to launch her reading career, or getting little Benji an extra helping at lunch because I knew they didn't feed him at home. Those were my days. Noble. Caring. I loved it." She paused for another sip. "Then I lost both parents in an automobile accident, and everything came crashing down. My job. My life. My sanity. I took what little I had, packed it in a single suitcase, and hit the road. I figured I'd be like Steinbeck, traveling the backroads of America to find myself, or maybe even die like my parents. I'm not proud of it, but there it is."

Uncle Adam laid a hand on her shoulder and said, "Get to the best part, honey. You're gonna make Cal all weepy."

Glenda slapped his hand away like they were brother and sister. "Men. Haven't you learned when to let an old woman shower you with painful poetry?" She finished her drink, handed the glass for another refill, and continued. "It was a fluke really, the way I got here. I had a series of not-so-nice boyfriends. One was rich. He said he wanted to take me to Paris. I was young and high most of the time, and I'd never been to Paris. I'd never been outside of the country. So I said yes. Our budding courtship lasted all of two days in the French capital. He left me for a younger model, underage probably, and there I was, penniless, homeless, and utterly miserable." Uncle Adam handed her the refill to which she nodded. "After a week or so of feeling sorry for myself and sleeping on park benches, I decided to look for a job. I got lucky. A private school was looking for an English tutor for their high-priced pupils. It was preferred that their candidate not know French. It was a perfect match. I taught English during the day and learned French at night. I had a knack for it. Languages came easily. I spent my nights with the families of the aristocratic children. Soon I was fluent in Swiss, German, Russian, and Italian. Oh, and French, of course. I was quite on my way. It was only a matter of time before some eligible nobleman swept me up in his cloak and carried me off on a lifetime of adventure."

Glenda's eyes twinkled when she looked over at Uncle Adam. She raised her glass to him and smiled. "And then I met your uncle. And once again, my life flipped itself in an unimaginable direction. I'd let him continue the story, but I know he'll butcher it and tell you all manner of unbelievable stories. So I will tell you the truth."

"I was hoping maybe you'd just get to the point," Uncle Adam murmured over his glass, grinning.

"You hush. I'm telling the story here and I don't need any help from the peanut gallery." She directed her attention back to Cal. "But your uncle is right. I should get to the point. Decades of jabbering on does become part of your being. Damn if I haven't become that which I despise most—a Parisian!"

"I'm pretty sure that was part of who you were in the beginning," Uncle Adam said.

Glenda's glare of mock indignation made Cal laugh. He liked this woman and her eccentricities. And it was obvious that Uncle Adam liked her too.

"Very well. I do admit that I relish the part. Acting is such fun, don't you think?" She didn't wait for Cal to reply. She was on a roll. "And now, young man, I will tell you how a bunch of know-nothing hippies became spies for the United States of America."

CHAPTER TWENTY-TWO

LENA - CAMP SPARTAN, ARRINGTON, TENNESSEE

"I don't like the pistol. I'd rather have a rifle," Lena said, struggling to put the weapon into a comfortable grip. She longed for her old rifle, what with its worn stock, the trigger guard that rested so perfectly on her mount.

"You want to learn or you want to complain?" Gaucho asked. Lena could tell that the short Hispanic with a dual-braided beard really didn't care one way or the other.

"What if I said I want to complain? Would you make me do push-ups or go for a long run?"

"Why? Do you want to do push-ups or go for a long run?"

She tried to glare at him, fix him with the toughest look she could muster. But she saw the tickle of a smile on his lips and before she knew it, she was laughing right along with him.

"I'm sorry," Lena said.

"It's okay. I've been known to wallow, too. Top never lets me forget it."

Lena had come to know both men well. When they

weren't training her to death, they were offering something much more valuable: their friendship.

"Is he always so happy and peppy?" she asked.

Gaucho rolled his eyes then went back to reloading the small arsenal lying on the wood table. "Yeah. I swear if he tells me to look on the bright side one more time..."

"Tell me about it. Yesterday, after flipping me over his shoulder and slamming me onto the mat, he told me to look on the bright side, that at least I was still alive. He said it while I was dead for breath!"

Gaucho shook his head. "Top's the optimist of the team. No changing that. Anyway, look on the bright side. You're with me now."

They went back to reloading, checking each weapon, and then it was on to live fire. By the time she was well into her twentieth magazine of the morning, Lena was happy to note that this pistol, a Springfield 9mm, was beginning to feel less like a stranger.

LUNCH WAS A SIMPLE AFFAIR—SANDWICHES, chips, and a water from the chow hall. Gaucho dove in like he always did, barely taking a breath as he inhaled each bite. Lena took it slowly. There was once a time when a sandwich was beyond her means. She had an appreciation for the little things now. She figured she could spend the rest of her life eating sandwiches out of brown bags and be just fine.

"Tell me about Daniel," Lena said, poking her hand into the bag of barbecue flavored potato chips. "He seems different than the rest of you."

Gaucho let out a low belch and laid back on the grass.

"That's because he *is* different. Why do you want to know about Snake Eyes?"

Daniel Briggs was the one who'd found her. Those eyes that lent themselves so well to his call sign, Snake Eyes. She felt both fear and a deep curiosity on the few occasions she'd seen him. Fear because she saw the killer under the calm facade. Curiosity because, well, he was a mystery.

"He's a Marine, like Cal, right?"

"Yep. Cuckoo crazy those jarheads. Why they didn't get smart and join the Army, I'll never know."

This was what she'd come to know of Gaucho. Joke first. Real answer second.

"Tell me about him. Please?"

"Fine. But you should ask him yourself, you know." Gaucho closed his eyes. "Snake Eyes is probably the coolest operator I've ever come across, and that's saying something." Lena knew that Gaucho had once been a ranking member of the Army's elite Delta Force. "He's got this way about him. When the bullets fly he's the first one to react, but it's never panic. It's like he knows what's happening before it happens. It's hard to explain."

"Try to. Please, Gaucho."

He opened one eye, looked at her, and exhaled. "Okay. I'll try. But if I tell it wrong, I warned you that I wouldn't tell it right."

Lena listened because she wanted the details. She wanted to know Daniel Briggs, and whether she should consider him friend or foe.

CHAPTER TWENTY-THREE

SPRINGER - DEFUNIAK SPRINGS, FLORIDA

No more veterans, for Christ's sake.

Each one slammed a door in his face like they were allergic to conversation. Springer hated the place. Tight-lipped witnesses and expert journalism did not mix well. While he might not be patient, he was tenacious.

He trudged up to the watering hole wedged in between a laundromat and a nail salon. Traffic was light and not a single patron was inside when the dim light swallowed him whole.

"You open for lunch?" Springer asked, barely making out the shape of a woman behind the bar.

"We are. Can I get you something to drink?"

"Bourbon, straight up, with a beer on the side."

"Any preference on the bourbon?"

Springer scanned the shelves. Nothing worth his time, but he was playing a part. "I want you to strain your back reaching for it."

She looked at him for a moment like he must be in the wrong place. But she put her cleaning rags away and selected a brown liquid off the top shelf. "What are you celebrating?"

"Just passing through. Thought I'd kick my legs up for a bit."

She poured his bourbon then filled a glass with *Bud Light*. "And here's the menu. I recommend the burger and fries."

"Keep the menu. I'll take the burger and fries, please."

He downed the bourbon shot and tried not to wince. It was far from smooth. The beer helped. His burger and fries came out in record time and Springer was surprised that they were good. Definitely better than fast food.

The bartender busied herself around the room, cleaning and adjusting like a wedding party was coming. Springer took his time. No need to rush.

When she finally made it back to the bar he asked, "You're Holly, right?"

Her eyes turned slowly toward him. "Who told you that?"

"Guy over at the gas station. Said I should come here for a drink, that you'd take good care of me." He held up his hands. "I come in peace. I swear."

That settled her mood, but he could tell she was still cagey. Time to make his move. "Your grandfather was Hollister Herndon, right?"

Now she froze, hand poised over the ice bin.

"Before you say anything, I want to tell you that this isn't about you. I don't care what you have or have not done." He knew her record. An impressive rap sheet. He drew out a hundred-dollar bill and set it on the bar. "There's more."

Her eyes flickered. "What do I need to do?"

"I just need some information."

"About my grandfather?"

"About someone he knew or had some dealings with."

"What if I don't know anything?"

"Then you keep that hundred and I'm on my way."

The hundred disappeared into her black apron. "What do you want to know?"

This was the delicate part. There was only so much he could piece together on his own. He needed witnesses, or at least some level of factual corroboration.

"A few years ago, there was a dustup. A big storm. A shoot-out. Some people died. I heard your grandfather was involved." He pulled out another hundred. Holly eyed it like a jackal. "You were named after your grandfather. They called him Hollie with an ie. Everything I've heard about him was that he was a good man. A great man even. But those few years back, he helped someone. Did he ever mention who?" Another flicker. The second hundred disappeared. Springer marked that as confirmation.

Holly's gaze went to his magic pocket of hundred-dollar bills. Two more made their way to the bar. She swiped them up and said, "Granddad was a grumpy old bastard, especially toward the end. But he was nice to me. I don't wanna dirty his name."

Again, Springer raised his hands. "I promise that's not why I'm here." He didn't need to go into specifics. She was hooked by the cash and he knew it.

She nodded. "You wanna know about the Marine."

"That's right."

"How many more hundreds you got in that pocket?"

"How many do you need?"

"Five to tell you." Funny how her country accent got deeper the greedier she got.

Five was steep, but doable. "Fine. But the information needs to be worth the extra."

Now she smiled. "What if I told you I knew everything?"

"Everything?"

"The murders. The cover up. Everything."

"I'll need proof."

She nodded. "And I'll need five hundred more."

For words and proof, this was turning into a bargain. He made the five bills appear and she made them disappear. They were quite the pair.

"Now, tell me."

She settled a hip against the bar and folded her arms. "Daniel Briggs. That's who you want to hear about."

Springer nodded and did well to suppress his smile. Holly Herndon turned out to be a master storyteller, and as it turned out, quite the hoarder as well.

CHAPTER TWENTY-FOUR

FLAP - WASHINGTON, D.C.

He slipped from the intelligence briefing before any of the lawmakers could corner him. It was just another game. Politicians were easier to sway than an everyday citizen. As long as he knew what they wanted, Edmond Flap got what he wanted.

"Director Flap!" he heard one particularly pushy congressman say as he burst from the room. Flap pointed to the phone at his ear and the man backed off. Ah, technology. It could play such the ruse. Put a phone to your ear or white earpiece in your socket and *blam*, you were disconnected from ever communicating again.

He made the "I'll call you sign" to the congressman who was quick to nod like a happy puppy. Yes, the freshmen were his favorites. He liked to slip them a little treat so they thought they were special. This one was no different. He was a Democrat who leaned heavy for strong national defense. He wanted to play war, so Flap would give him a covert war, all the while playing him like a piccolo.

Not many of the staffers knew him yet, so he walked along almost anonymously. It was easy to get lost in the prestige of the place. Even though the House offices end, their endless halls felt more like a 1980s office building.

He reached his destination and did a quick gander to see if anyone followed. None. And he didn't care about the cameras. In fact, cameras were a bonus as long as you knew what to record, and Flap very much did.

The interns were out to lunch and his host was playing gatekeeper.

"Mr. Stern," Flap said, nodding to the right-hand man of the congressman who led the committee that Flap just left.

"You've got five minutes. The boss has a stop to make."

Flap thought Ira Stern calling his employer "boss" to be an interesting choice, considering the reason for meeting.

Stern led the way into the small conference room. "What's the latest? I need concrete this time."

Flap hesitated, though he very much knew what he was going to say. "It's delicate. If the president ever finds out—"

"Don't forget who got you the top spot at Langley, Flap. I can just as easily yank you out of that chair and toss you into the secretary pool."

"You're right, of course."

"Of course I'm right." Stern flexed like he had any muscle to flex. He was a wiry Jew from Boston who thought it'd be a good idea to become a Republican, despite his family's protests. And the man had a hard-on for taking down President Zimmer. "What did he say? How did he take it?"

He meant the news about black spots that were once spies dotting the planet.

"He told me to look into it. I am."

Stern slammed his fist on the table. "That coward. This is all his fault. If it weren't for his lame attempt at foreign policy, and the way he's wrecked the CIA's funding—your funding. How many so far? How many brave soldiers on the front lines have we lost?"

"Twelve at last count."

Stern shook his head like he gave a damn. Flap knew he didn't. Stern had his eyes on one thing and one thing only: power.

"You and I both know their blood is on his hands. Keep me apprised of the situation."

"Thank you for your time, Mr. Stern."

A little extra ego stroking never hurt. Flap didn't mind. He had no ego. His mission was discord. That, and wiping out any chance that his past might come back to haunt him. He had friends who were doing that very thing right now. His own personal cleaning crew.

CHAPTER TWENTY-FIVE

BRIGGS - ROSEMARY BEACH, FLORIDA

It was impossible to look at the ocean and not think of her. He'd met her by the sea all those years ago. Her innocence was as charming as her demeanor. And the woman she became made Daniel thank the heavens for the gift given to his world.

"Penny for your thoughts?" Anna said, settling down next to him and handing over a bottle of water. She cradled an oversized mug of coffee.

"I was thinking about when we met, when you were still in Maine."

Anna nodded, holding the coffee with both hands. She shivered. "Different times."

Theirs was a friendship that knew no boundaries. It was one of the reasons he cherished his time with her. She took the time to think and answer with her soul, very much like he'd learned to do. Hers was a gift given at a young age. His was a gift given through trial and pain.

"Do you think about your father?" he asked.

"Sometimes."

"What do you remember?"

Daniel liked to remember the kind pastor who'd first taken him in, invited the broken Marine into his home, despite what ulterior motives he might've had.

Anna sighed. "I remember pancake breakfasts on Sunday. I remember watching him till the fields. I always laughed when he stripped off his shirt, turned back to the house and flexed, and then dug whatever root or stone out of the field."

"There was a good man in there."

"There was. I miss him. Sometimes I wonder what could've been, what kind of a life we'd have today."

Daniel cracked open the water bottle. "I thank God every day that He brought your father into my life. If He hadn't, I wouldn't have you to keep me on the straight and narrow." He bumped her with his hip. "I hope you know how much you mean to me and how appreciative I am for the time we share."

She bumped him back. "You make me sound like a corporate trainer who came in and turned your business around."

"Well, my business was bankrupt for sure. And if you hadn't helped me cook the books, I'm pretty sure the Feds would've hanged me for tax evasion."

"Cook the books? Really?" She was smiling at him and they shared a laugh.

This was the easy life, the one he never thought he'd have. His was a life of service, and that service was to his friends, his country, and those in need. Daniel knew what his friends called him behind his back and sometimes to his face. It'd been a hard-fought peace, but well worth it. The friend at his side was proof that the best relationships were forged through turmoil and the worst of life's lessons.

Two kids ran by, barefoot on the green lawn. Their

parents appeared a moment later, the father chasing with a bucket full of beach gear and four chairs strapped to his back. The mother waddled not far behind, her belly bulging with the next of the brood. Dad was yelling for the kids to slow down. Mom was huffing and puffing.

"Come on. We should help them," Anna said.

Daniel called out to the dad. "Sir, let me help you with that."

The dad looked back, harried and frazzled, nodded his thanks, and dumped the chairs on the lawn before sprinting after the kids. Daniel gathered up the chairs and turned back to see if Anna and the mother needed help. What he saw made absolute zero sense. The mother's belongings were on the ground. Anna was standing still, looking right at the woman who seemed to be saying something. Anna cast a furtive look back at Daniel and he was pretty sure he heard the stranger say, "Don't look at him."

He took a step forward, then stopped.

There was a small pistol in the woman's hand, resting on her supposed pregnant belly, pointed right at Anna.

CHAPTER TWENTY-SIX

ANNA - ROSEMARY BEACH, FLORIDA

Anna was no rookie in the world of espionage. It was practically her second major. Her father had been a spy. A liar, really, but still a spy. Her mother was a spy as well. It ran in Anna's blood. Her position as head of the Fund took her one giant step further down the espionage superhighway.

She needed to keep the woman's attention. She needed to give Daniel time.

Who uses children? That was the first question that came to mind. She left it unasked. She instead asked the second.

"Who sent you?"

"Just keep smiling and I won't have my husband kill your boyfriend," the woman said with a smile that matched the cheery Rosemary Beach weather. At least they didn't know who Daniel was, or they might've dispatched him first. Their mistake.

Keep talking, Anna.

"Let me guess, you're Russian. Your accent is good, but

the way you round your consonants makes me want to reach for a blini."

The woman's face told her she'd hit the mark, and that meant they were in far greater danger than a simple mugging or kidnapping for ransom.

"Honey, I'm not gonna tell you a damn thing. All you need to do is come quietly. Now, in a second I'm gonna fake like I'm having labor pains. They do hurt, you know. You tell your boyfriend you want to take me to my place. You understand?" Anna nodded. "Good. Now I'm going to put this gun back under my belly, but it's still pointed at you, so don't make a wrong move or you're deader than a coon on huntin' day."

She bent at the waist and moaned. "*Ohhh!*" she said, loud enough for her 'husband,' who was still corralling the kids, to hear.

Anna was about to play along, to say that she was more than capable of helping, but the flurry of movement behind her elicited a slack-jawed gape from the woman holding her at gunpoint. Anna had no choice but to look.

CHAPTER TWENTY-SEVEN

BRIGGS - ROSEMARY BEACH, FLORIDA

He couldn't hear what the woman was saying to Anna. He couldn't see the weapon anymore, but he sensed rather than saw the tensing in Anna's body. It was like a ripple in the Force, the universe tilted just so he could feel it.

The dad and the two kids were playing chase, the key-coded gate having stopped the beach charge. But Daniel felt the occasional glance from the husband. The man's attention was not where it should be. The only logical deduction was they were working together. A first for Daniel with children involved, but he'd seen too many things in his life to let that get in the way. You flex when you need to. Adapt or die.

Daniel went for the man first, guessing that he might also have a weapon. He made like he was going toward the restrooms sitting just inside the gate, but as the playing threesome swerved across his path, he let the kids run by and he took the man out with a blow that took him straight to the ground. To whoever might be watching, it looked like an innocent collision.

Daniel followed the man down, like he was dazed. He confirmed that the man was unconscious and did a quick search of his person. As Daniel had suspected, there was a gun inside the holster of his Tommy Bahama shorts. He slid it out and was about to turn when he heard the woman yell, "*Ohhh!*"

It was part of the play. Daniel, and the entity deep inside of him that he called the Beast, knew the ploy. There was only one way to kill a ploy. Attack it head-on.

CHAPTER TWENTY-EIGHT

ANNA - ROSEMARY BEACH, FLORIDA

It was pure reflex that made Anna drop to the ground, turning as she fell. The woman above her grunted, surely confused. What Anna saw next brought back vivid memories of the past, of the Daniel she'd first known.

He ran at them, and when the woman's pistol came out, Daniel somehow pivoted, springing like a jungle cat. The first two shots spat and missed. Anna tried to kick the woman's legs out from under her, but she moved aside, ready for anything.

Daniel hit the ground in a roll and Anna saw the flash of his eyes, more animal than man. He'd gone to that place few can go.

His hands came up. Two more shots left the gun of the female assassin. Two shots missed the rolling Marine.

His did not. Somehow, impossibly, two shots left Daniel's new weapon. Two shots hit their mark. Anna saw the woman stumble back, but she still had her gun ready to fire again.

Daniel did not hesitate. Six more shots ran from the original two in her chest up to her head. She fell back, obviously dead.

Anna was on her in a second, removing the weapon and searching for more.

Daniel scooped her up and pulled her along. "We need to go."

"But we need to find out who they were."

"I think we can safely guess who sent them."

So, the Russian had finally made his play. But why now? He'd had his chance in the past. The only thing she could think was that she'd inadvertently pulled Daniel into some kind of horrible mess.

CHAPTER TWENTY-NINE

YEGOROVICH - MOSCOW

He listened. He settled his blood pressure. He listened a bit more.

"You're sure," he asked finally.

"Yes."

"You told me it would not be a problem. You said she was alone."

"We thought she was. But that is no excuse. There will be more chances."

The president wasn't so sure. The man on the other end of the call didn't need to know the details. He'd only been ordered to bring Anna Varushkin in, to bring her home where she belonged. A simple order, and one that had gone wrong.

"Were there witnesses?"

"The second operative and the children they borrowed as decoys."

The president didn't have to think on it. "Take care of the problem. No witnesses."

He could imagine what the other was thinking, that his

president was a ruthless killer. Yes, that was true. But this was war. And there were no concessions in wartime. Not even children.

"Would you like to know when it is done?"

"I want you to come tell me about it personally."

Yegorovich ended the call. No point extending a disappointing conversation. He had much to do. And there would be time for the Varushkin girl soon. Let her think that wolves prowled the streets just for her. Yes, that was about right.

CHAPTER THIRTY

LENA - CAMP SPARTAN, ARRINGTON, TENNESSEE

"Forty-nine. Fifty," Top exclaimed, stopping the last push-up in a high plank.

Lena flopped to the ground, her arms Jell-O. "I hate push-ups," she said out of the side of her mouth. It was the only part of her body that didn't hurt, though she figured they'd find a way to make that hurt too.

Top hopped to his feet like he'd just woken up from a nap. "Come on, Lena. We're not done yet."

Lena looked up at him, her chest still heaving. "You're kidding, right? I can't move my arms." She flopped them around on the ground like dying fish.

Top reached down, grabbed the back of her belt, and hoisted her to her feet. "I know it hurts."

"Do you? You don't seem to feel the pain."

Top thought on that a moment, then he broke out into one of his signature wide grins and flexed both biceps. "You think this happened overnight?"

The Marine could probably take on a rhinoceros if he wanted.

"This was years and years in the gym. Miles and miles hiking, running. Hours in the water, first doggy paddling and figuring out how to keep my non-buoyant self above water, then learning how to really swim. You think that was easy?"

"I didn't say it was easy."

"But you were thinking it. Don't assume anything, young lady. You never know what a person's been through."

Another lesson. Lena tucked it away though she was in no mood to acknowledge the gift.

"Okay. What now?" She was hungry. Starving. They'd skipped breakfast because she had a nasty habit of puking after one of these knockdown workouts. It didn't help that it seemed the warriors on Camp Spartan all ate breakfast before their morning workout.

Top was about to answer when it seemed like the entire camp had suddenly come alive with activity. Men came out of buildings and warriors appeared from the range, weapons in hand. Lena's first thought was that some silent alarm had been triggered.

"He's back," Top said, his gaze drifting over to the front gate.

A small sedan pulled past the guard shack and drove into one of the parking spots next to the chow hall. A beautiful woman stepped out of the passenger side first and Lena couldn't help but stare. Then she saw the shock of blonde hair, and Daniel Briggs got out from the driver's seat.

"Come on," Top said, pulling along Lena, whose legs had gone to concrete.

There was a crowd gathering, the troops welcoming one of their fearless leaders home. For hardened men, operators who were the tip of the top, Lena appreciated the quiet adoration being showered on Daniel, like he was some modern-day Moses. Then his eyes met hers and she wanted to run.

"Lena," he said. That voice. So calm. So penetrating. "I have a friend who very much wants to meet you." He turned to his companion. "Anna, this is Lena. Lena, meet my very good friend, Anna Varushkin."

Anna's hand was soft, but her grip was firm, like how Lena imagined a head of state to be. If this woman made jeans and a T-shirt look this good, she wondered what Anna looked like in a ball gown.

"It's a pleasure to meet you, Lena. And may I say that you are beautiful."

Lena's face flushed a hot rock red. "Um, thanks. You're pretty too." She felt all of eleven again, awkward and gawking.

"How do you like summer camp? Or is it boot camp, Top?"

Top marched over and picked Anna up off the ground into a bear hug. "Lady, do you know how much I've missed you?" He set her down and Anna didn't look a bit mussed for the ordeal. "How long are you staying? Please tell me you'll let me cook for you."

Anna's smile was genuine and kind. "Do you think I'd visit without availing myself to Willy Trent's famous cuisine?"

Top hopped into the air and whooped like a child and they all laughed, even Lena. Was this what having friends was like?

"Now, if you gentlemen would be so kind, I'd like a word with Lena, in private."

Lena expected grumbles, or maybe a smart-alecky retort. None came, and the others dispersed quietly and were on their way.

Anna took Lena by the arm and guided her toward the

running path that led up into the hills by the cemetery. When they were far enough up the trail, Anna finally spoke.

"Do you like them?"

"Them?" Lena motioned back to where they left the others. Why did she feel so comfortable while at the same time unsettled with this woman? She had that thing that Daniel had. What was it?

"Yes, the boys." Anna's laugh was light and contagious. It was what Lena imagined a princess's laugh to sound like. "I know they've treated you well."

"How do you know?" She was about to tell Anna about all the ways Top and Gaucho had been mistreating her, acting like her masters. But she didn't. They'd done no such thing. They'd been with her every step of the way, never asking her to do anything they were not themselves doing.

Anna smiled. "We're lucky, you and me. We get to be friends with some of the strongest, most courageous, yet kind people ever to set foot on this Earth."

They walked on for a time, Lena digesting and replaying every word. Who was this Anna Varushkin?

They came to the cemetery, the grass clipped to perfection and every headstone free of nature's grasp. The place was peaceful, beautiful, the perfect place to sit and think. There were over thirty headstones, some gleaming white, and others plain, shining stone.

"They take turns tending the graves, you know," Anna said, reaching down and stroking one of the headstones.

"Who takes turns?"

"All of them. Every single employee that lives or works on Camp Spartan treats this hilltop like a shrine."

Now Lena was curious. No one had told her this story, though she'd seen various men in and around the spot before. "How did it start? I mean, why do they do it?"

Anna looked at her with those dazzling eyes, eyes that had seen the world and then some.

"Why Daniel started it, of course, for his best friend, Cal. And everyone saw that and followed his lead. They take turns, although there's no schedule. Gaucho once told me there's a waiting list. Can you believe that?"

Lena shook her head. She almost didn't believe it. And yet she did. She'd seen the hearts of these men.

"Anna?" Lena couldn't believe what she was thinking. She fidgeted to get the words out. "Can you tell me about Daniel? Can you tell me why he is the way he is?"

Anna smiled, knowingly. "Of course. I'll tell you what I can. But for the rest, you'll need to ask him. And believe me, there's a lot to tell."

CHAPTER THIRTY-ONE

ADAM STOKES - PARIS - 1974

The Legionnaires did their worst, or their best depending on how you looked at the situation. From Adam's vantage point, things were good. Better than good. He kicked the prostrate man in the side and enjoyed the agonized moan.

"There," the largest Legionnaire said, delivering a blow that knocked the last conscious thief into dreamland. "Now, we get drinks, and then you tell us about your life."

Adam's relief was complete. He'd been at the bottom, bloodied and bruised, broken in a way he'd never felt. These three men, these good men, had come to his rescue. He decided he would do anything for them. Anything.

They walked, arms wrapped around one another and two-stepped as a quartet. The Legionnaires sang and Adam sang along. He didn't know the words and didn't care. A bawdy song was just what his soul needed. That and a barrel of wine to wash away the memories.

Adam watched as other pedestrians shook their heads and

then smiled as he and his friends walked by. They were like celebrities, untouchable, greeted with warmth wherever they went. They passed a cafe and every patron sitting outside raised an eyebrow and then a cup to the passing singers. Adam's heart swelled. He hadn't felt this sense of camaraderie since his days on the field. He'd missed it. It was one of many reasons he wanted to go into the Marines. He'd found his people halfway around the world, and he was glad for it.

They closed the place down and very likely put a considerable dent in the proprietor's wine and beer supply. Other patrons came and went, always casting an amused look at the four, celebrating their victory.

"They will never mess with you again," one of his companions said.

"We take care of our own," another added, and drinks were raised and downed in seconds.

Now, the owner of the once-bustling establishment, a beefy man that smelled of butter and bread, gave them each a hug and a kiss on each cheek. He spoke to the Legionaries in French and motioned to Adam who could barely stand on his two feet.

"Come. Time for sleep," one of them said, wrapping a comforting arm around the younger American.

"I don't have a place to go," Adam heard himself say. "My girlfriend's father kicked me out, remember?"

They all had another laugh at that, even Adam, who now realized that he had not been entirely truthful with the reason for his departure.

"We have a place for you, my American friend."

Adam sagged against the man and was half carried away.

They hadn't gotten far when a shrill whistle got their attention. Adam groggily turned, the alcohol having drained him of all but the tiniest spark of energy. All he wanted to do was go to sleep. But when he turned with the others, he faced one of the most beautiful women he'd ever met. She stood with one hand on her hip. The top of her blue dress cut in a V-shape that pointed tastefully to the top of her chest. And then there was the rest of her.

Then the strangest conversation Adam ever heard began as if in a dream. It felt like he'd come in mid-story.

"Leave him with me," the woman was saying, her voice cutting through the night like she owned it.

"Mademoiselle," one of the Legionnaires said, bowing. "We've had a long day. If you'll excuse us."

"Do you know who I am?"

Adam felt the pause, and the warriors surrounding him froze. One of them nudged the other. "It's her."

"What her?" came the annoyed reply.

"You know. *Her*."

Adam craned his neck so he could see the faces of the others. Much to his surprise, the mirth was gone.

"What do you want with him?" one Legionnaire finally spat out with just enough effort to make him sound annoyed.

"I don't want you to get your hands on him."

Then the woman, who Adam guessed was an American too, slipped into French and proceeded to give the others either a tongue-lashing or the most intense story ever told. All Adam had to do was notice how he was let go and the Legionnaires stepped away from him.

"Hey, lady! These are my friends," Adam protested, taking a step toward his comrades, but they slunk farther back. To his amazement, they took one last look at whoever this dame was and ran off into the night. He turned to the stranger. "Now that wasn't very nice."

"You'd be slurring another tune if you knew what they

were doing to you," she said, stepping closer. He caught a whiff of her perfume. Delightful.

"Wait, what? What are they gonna do with me?"

He tried to take a step forward and tripped, falling smack down on his face.

"Ow," he said, though the alcohol blurred the pain.

She rolled him over and placed a handkerchief on his nose.

"Hey, what—?"

Adam heard the crack when his nose went back into place and for few seconds his eyes swam in tears.

"Come on. We'll talk when you sober up."

She pulled him to his feet. Even in his inebriated state he felt her quiet strength and marveled at it. He wanted to tell her how beautiful she was, how entranced he was. All he managed was a sloppy, "Hey, what's your name anyway?"

Her smile made him inhale and this time he felt the pain in his nose.

"My name is Virginia Walton, and you're a long way from home, Adam Stokes."

CHAPTER THIRTY-TWO

STOKES - PARIS

"You're telling me that the United States government recruited you, a bunch of counterculture longhairs, to spy for them?"

Glenda Younger let out a delighted laugh. "We were perfect for the job. Sure, it took some prodding. You don't just discard everything that's in your brain and blossom with new beliefs. No, America got smart, and they had spies and spy recruiters who were smart. They picked those of us who still loved our country but were disillusioned. Most of us hated what was going on in Vietnam, but not for the reasons in the history books. I ran away because I lost two little brothers. Loves of my life. Took care of them both when I was myself only a kid." She squinted at Cal. "But I'll bet you know something about loss, don't you, Cal?"

Cal nodded. "I lost both my parents on 9/11." He paused, not really believing that he was telling this woman about the darkest depths of his grief. "I lost a fiancée, a cousin, too many friends to count..." He couldn't go on.

Uncle Adam finished for him, his voice dusky. "And he recently lost another woman who was very special to him."

Glenda reached out and grabbed Cal's hand. Hers was mangled with fingers splayed in various ways. How had he missed that?

"I'm so sorry, Cal. I truly am."

"Thanks," Cal said, feeling the sting of Diane's loss again. He gulped down his drink, relishing the burn before any tears could come. "You were saying, about them recruiting you?"

Glenda let go of his hand and replaced her mangled appendage in her lap. "I see you also want to know about this." She raised the hand again so he could see. "I'm afraid that's another story for another day. Lesson: Don't get caught." But she laughed like it'd been some untimely joke. The hand went back in her lap. "Anyway, they found us and courted us. We spurned their courtship, some of us spit on them." She shot Uncle Adam a look.

He shook his head quickly. "Hey, that was you, Missy. I don't spit on strangers."

She giggled and covered her mouth. "Guilty as charged. It wasn't my finest moment. Ah, the wonderful thing wine and ego will do when mixed in great quantities. Now, to the good part, at least what I remember the most. You should have seen it when they took us back stateside. Why, I could've knocked the powers that be over with a kiss they were so shocked. But much to our recruiter's credit—"

"His name was Mr. Banks," Uncle Adam said. "We never saw him again after that."

"I'll let you be and not whip you for interrupting me because you're about to get me a fresh drink. Yes, your uncle remembers correctly. Our recruiter defended us and that made us want to prove ourselves all the more. Not a one did we lose in training, a feat not easily accomplished. I think it had to do with the fact that we were outsiders, in it together. Do you know what I mean?"

"I think so," Cal said. "Your bond made you stronger. You looked out for one another and never let the weakest fall back."

"I like this young man," Glenda said, accepting her fresh drink with a wink. "I won't bore you with the details of our training and subsequent assignments. They aren't germane to our current predicament."

"And what is your current predicament?" Cal asked.

Glenda stared dead into his eyes. "They're killing us off one by one, those of us left."

"Who is?"

Glenda and Uncle Adam exchanged a look.

"Glenda has a theory," Uncle Adam said.

"It's more than a theory," she shot back. "It has to be her."

Uncle Adam didn't look convinced, or maybe he didn't want to believe. Cal couldn't tell which or why.

Might as well ask the obvious question: "When you say 'her' you mean..."

Glenda leveled a crooked finger Uncle Adam's way. "I mean your uncle's former paramour. A woman of such cunning and beauty that they gave her a wonderful title to go along with her successes. The Duchess."

"She's dead, Glenda. You know that," Uncle Adam said, his eyes on the floor.

The crooked finger shot in the air. "Aha! And that's where you're wrong!" She reached into the folds of her dress and produced a phone. "I have pictures. She's alive alright. And she's working for them."

Who was them and who was the Duchess?

Uncle Adam snatched the phone and scrolled through the

pictures. "This could be some other woman. It could be a sham."

He tossed the phone onto the couch, but Glenda wouldn't let him off the hook. She was on her feet now.

"You need to pull your head out of your boxers, Adam. This is no game. You tell me right here and now why in your heart of hearts you know this is not Virginia Walton."

Uncle Adam didn't immediately answer. When he did, the words came out sharp. "I know it's not her because I killed her with my own two hands."

"Well then, Adam," she said calmly, "we need to find out who this woman is, because I think you're the next target on her list."

CHAPTER THIRTY-THREE

STERN - WASHINGTON, D.C.

Stern wrung his hands after leaving his boss's office.

"Old fool," he murmured, making the only intern in the office look away. Stern didn't care. This job was a stepping-stone. A necessary one, but nonetheless a temporary stop on his rise to the top. "No one disturbs him, you hear me?" His barked order triggered a vigorous nodding from the intern. She'd be gone in a week. The other interns walked all over her. Weak, thought Stern, grabbing a folder from his desk and marching out of the office.

The hallways of Congress were bustling, and Stern fed off the energy. He had no real place to be except away from his boss and his pussyfooting ways. The idiot had no inkling on how power ought to be wielded. In office for close to thirty years and still he acted like a rookie. "Old fool," Stern murmured again, nodding to someone who waved hello.

Stern came from hard-working stock. Jews who left the Old World smack dab in the middle of the roundup for the camps. His grandfather was a mean old cuss, but he'd bribed and bartered to get his entire family, fifty-two members, to America in three separate waves. His grandfather had then set out to carve his name in Brooklyn history, opening a bagel shop in his first year and then delis all over the city. He was a household name in the working class, so much like the don he'd become, he ushered his many friends to vote for whatever politician he dubbed his ticket.

And so, the Stern family slithered into politics, though Ira's father, a taciturn man with a better eye for cold cuts than political contenders, almost lost it all. That was the day 9-year-old Ira Stern knew he was going to Washington.

"You have to stand up to them! You make us look weak, boy!" his grandfather, Fyvush Stern, had railed against Ira's father, Yoel Stern.

Yoel Stern stood there taking the berating like he always did. Ira couldn't remember a single time he'd seen his father raise his voice. It embarrassed the youngest Stern more than he could bear.

And that's when Ira burst into the room and raised his hand. "I'll do it, grandfather. I'll take care of the family."

Fyvush opened his arms for his grandson. "Yes, Ira, I know you will." He looked up at his own son, a sad anger in his voice. "You stick to the business. I'll teach young Ira what it means to be a Stern."

From that day on, until Fyvush Stern's death, Ira and his grandfather had been inseparable. Years later he saw the movie *The Godfather*, and he couldn't help noticing the similarity in the way the great Don Corleone and his own grandfather acted. There was one large difference. Where Don Corleone could make men bend with a whisper, Fyvush Stern ruled his kingdom with a loud fury that made men scatter.

Ira Stern learned every trick, every turn, every way of deceiving his enemy. It wasn't until after his grandfather's death, a tragedy that struck Ira hard, that the only living male heir of the proud Stern patriarch severed his New York ties and made his play for Washington.

And for close to a decade he'd wheeled and dealed. He knew more about his opponents than they did about themselves. Test him on the most junior and obscure representative from Dubuque, and Ira could rattle off more than a name, he knew details, leanings, proclivities. He was a political encyclopedia that was at this very moment not being utilized to its fullest potential. His aged mentor sitting in the office he'd just left had something to do with that oversight.

"You're young, Ira. Give it time. Washington will be here when you finally get your legs."

Get your legs! The old fool! Ira Stern had more legs than any politician in the building. Put Stern up against any of them in a debate and he would win. He knew it.

One thing he hadn't decided was where exactly he would aim his trajectory. Congressman was too small. He could go home and run his way up to governor. He'd have the blessings one day. But it was too soon.

No. He had to make moves now, here, in Washington.

Ira Stern blazed through the halls of Congress, a man on an invisible mission. To anyone who might catch a look at his face as he breezed by, they would notice the sly grin tugging at one side of his mouth, a grin that would spread ear to ear when he got what he needed from Edmond Flap.

CHAPTER THIRTY-FOUR

ANNA - CAMP SPARTAN, ARRINGTON, TENNESSEE

"I like her," Anna said, stepping over a log as she went deeper into the forest, a squirrel with stuffed cheeks darting away at her approach.

"I knew you would," Daniel said. "She reminds me of you."

"I don't remember being that stubborn."

Daniel chuckled. "I do. Remember when you skipped town, thought you'd save the world all by yourself? It brought us closer, or don't you remember that?"

Anna did and she'd never regretted it, though it had landed her in water hotter than a witch's cauldron. "How could I forget? You befriended a wayward drunk. I'll never forget our first adventure together."

Daniel pushed a branch aside so she could keep going. Always the gentleman, even in the wild.

"And Lena? What's she got to do with your current adventure?"

The talk she'd had with Lena was illuminating on many

counts. She saw through the tough facade of a young woman forced to grow up on her own. There were wounds under that hide that still hadn't healed. They might never heal. The father Lena had mourned for, then found again, and lost a second time, turned out not to be her father at all. Anna told the girl about her own father, his treachery, his unhealthy relationship with Anna's mother. Yes, they had much in common, and that made Anna want to protect the girl, help raise her if need be. Or, as much as you could raise a young adult. Lena was naive in so many ways. She'd never had a boyfriend, hadn't really had any companions her own age. Hopefully, that would change soon.

"It's Cal's decision. He needs to make the call on Lena."

Anna stopped and looked at Daniel. "Are you sure about that? I don't see Cal here. It looks like he's left you and the others to make the call."

"It feels like you're mad at Cal. Wanna talk about that?"

Anna hadn't realized that her fists were clenched. She unclenched them and stuck them in her pockets. "I want to make sure she's taken care of, that's all."

"So does Cal."

"Does he?"

Daniel did that thing where he looked right through her.

"Stop it," she said. "You're doing it again."

"Doing what?"

"The thing with your eyes. I'm not in the mood." She turned away, continuing down the path.

"Anna."

Daniel hadn't moved. He was still standing there, waiting for her to come back.

She breathed a heavy sigh. "You need to tell Cal that Lena needs help. She needs all the help you can give her. I'll do it too. Anything she needs."

"Anna."

"What? You sound like a parrot."

He grinned. Anna almost tripped over a branch laying across the pine needle path.

"Watch your step," he said.

"Would you stop looking out for me already?"

Where had that come from? Anna stopped, turned to face him. "I'm sorry. I just... I don't want to see her lost again. She acts tough, but she's still a little girl. You see that don't you?"

"Of course I do. I'm not gonna let anything happen to her."

Anna's mind flipped to Diane Mayer. Daniel had said he should've been more careful. That Diane's death was his fault. Not even he was perfect. Anna didn't want Lena to be next.

"I'm sorry."

He smiled. "You said that already."

Serene, smiling Daniel Briggs in the middle of the woods. Was there a place he didn't look like he was in complete control, one with the world and everything in it?

"Sometimes I wish it was the old you," she said. "You could get riled up and really pissy with me. Then I remember what you went through. What I went through. Will there ever be an end to the pain? Do you think there's a chapter in our story where we all retire to the beach and live in perfect peace and harmony until we die quietly in our sleep?"

Daniel walked to her now, the calm reaching out over the shrinking space between them. It was a balm on her battered soul.

"I have every faith that we'll end up happy and in a place that knows no pain or suffering."

"You mean heaven," Anna said, reaching out and taking his offered hand.

"I don't know what I mean. I just know it's there."

Anna was not without faith, but she wasn't close to the realm in which Daniel lived. "How do you know? Do you see it?"

Daniel closed his eyes, breathed in deeply. Eyes open again. "I have to believe."

"You're talking in your riddles again, Mr. Briggs. Believe in what? Heaven? Hell? God? The devil?"

Anna yearned for the peace that seemed to float down over Daniel's head when he spoke next. "I have to believe that I'm right where I'm supposed to be, that this is all happening for a reason. Because if I let myself worry, if I try to twist the actions of others to my own design, I find only misery. And because you know me the best, you know that misery is something I've spent half my life fighting."

"So you're saying you won't play the Ouija board with me tonight?"

That made him laugh. "How about a rousing game of Uno instead?"

"Deal. Can I invite Lena to play?"

"I'd be offended if you didn't."

And with that they continued their hike, Anna once again hoping that this time with Daniel might never end. But she would keep that little secret to herself.

CHAPTER THIRTY-FIVE

SPRINGER - DEFUNIAK SPRINGS, FLORIDA

"You come back whenever you like," Holly Herndon said, her voice a purr as she stroked a long nail along Springer's jawline.

"Next time I'm heading down south, you'll be the first one I call."

She grabbed the back of his neck and pulled him in, her mouth next to his ear. "Why don't you go down south, again, right now?"

He was able to pry himself away without being too forceful. "Next time," he said, kissing the palm of her hand. She shivered a little too energetically for his taste.

Holly blew him a kiss as he pulled out of her driveway, his trunk containing bits of evidence he might need to convince his editor to publish every word of his story. And it was turning out to be a good one. Then there were the side perks.

Holly Herndon had the look of a washed-up handmaiden in the dull light of an empty bar, but when the clothes were stripped and she strode right at him, she was a flaxen-haired Venus in moonlight silver.

Springer licked his lips at the thought. Yeah, the side perks were nice. But he wouldn't be back. At least not soon. You wave a title, a few awards and some cash around, and Springer knew there wasn't a modern town that didn't have the easy lay he liked.

But the scent of the story was on him again, and with his sexual appetite satiated, he could go days without physical touch or much sustenance. He was like an endurance athlete hunting the top prize.

He took his time leaving DeFuniak Springs. There were places to see. The old homestead where the late, great Laney clan had lived. All dead now. Springer drove by the charred remains of the old house, the fields overgrown and on the verge of being retaken completely by the trees. A mother deer and her fawn hopped across the dirt drive, giving him a long, careful look before loping on their way.

He went from the Laney's property to the site of the final battle. Even Holly hadn't known how many men died. To hear her tell it there was a battalion of men buried somewhere nearby. From what Springer could tell, there'd been roughly twenty. Maybe that many dead. Maybe that many involved. He'd probably never know the true number. The whispers of the dead faded well in these parts.

Springer tried to imagine it, two forces colliding. Good vs. Evil? He didn't care. It was an epic battle on American soil. The bodies were dead and gone, sure, but some memories still lingered. He could feel it.

The real treasure sat in Springer's lap. He'd only had a chance to peruse the journal on a quick run to the bathroom between marathon sessions with Holly. It turned out that the sex-starved bartender's grandfather, Hollie Herndon, kept a journal. She said it helped him with his Alzheimer's. She said she found it after he died. She said a lot of things. Too many really, like she wanted to impress Springer so much that he'd whisk her away from her Podunk town. Not a chance. But he'd keep the journal. It cost him, but money wasn't on his mind. Not now. Not when the ghosts of the past lingered nearby, like they wanted him to tell the world of what they'd seen.

Yes, he felt them here, those restless spirits. If Springer had been a religious man, he might've said a prayer for their souls. But he wasn't, so he didn't. But he did hope that their suffering, and what Hollie Herndon had called "the Beast Daniel Briggs" would soon come out to play. Because that was where this was going. The hero-turned-murderer. How many more stories would Springer find along the way?

He drove away from DeFuniak Springs a hopeful man.

CHAPTER THIRTY-SIX

STOKES - PARIS

When Glenda Younger said they were going on a stakeout, Cal assumed they'd be huddled in an alley or maybe a European-sized car that was too small even for a single, emaciated clown. Wrong. Sure, they were sitting in the dark. Sure, they had to take turns being on watch. But that was where the hardships ceased.

"Another touch of cocktail, my dear?" Glenda asked, raising her head from across the room. Cal could barely make out her silhouette in the room fit for a queen. Glenda said it was one of her apartments. How many she had she didn't say. But by her mannerisms and casual way she made her way from room to room, there were ten. Cal figured this was maybe a small weekend getaway for the aged spy.

"I'll have another," Cal said, not taking his eyes from the screen that broadcast what the high-powered tele-lens was broadcasting from across the street. Uncle Adam appeared and grabbed Cal's glass for refill duty.

"Glenda, I have to ask, is this place really yours?" Cal said.

He heard her snort from across the room. "And whom might you think it really belongs to? My rich lover from the Middle East?"

Cal wouldn't be surprised. Lady Younger seemed to be full of little treats. "Maybe."

"Well, my dear, I can assure you that the place is mine. I've been fortunate, and lucky, many times over."

"Don't let her fool you, Cal. She's a whiz at business and I'm pretty sure she's seen every inside trade on the Paris Stock Exchange since Nixon left office," Uncle Adam said, returning a full glass to Cal's hand.

"Oh, don't be jealous, Adam. I merely learned that the espionage business is not only well put for the sake of our nation, but it serves as a fertile grazing ground for tasty tidbits that might or might not help a wily old woman make an informed decision on which stock she might choose to gamble upon."

Cal Stokes had plenty of his own money thanks to the forethought of his father. There were days when he dreamed of giving it all away and taking off down the road on a rebuilt motorcycle. Then he'd get a whiff of the good stuff, stay at a spot like Glenda's apartment, and he'd throw up a word of thanks to his father, who undoubtedly wanted him to be happy and make whatever decisions he chose to make.

A form appeared on the edge of the screen and Cal leaned in. At first it was just a flicker, like a glitch in the lens. That was impossible because the rest of the screen was Super HD clear. Cal zoomed in on the spot. "What the..." They'd perfectly positioned the camera. There was no way around getting full exposure. But there it was. Someone had slipped right through the telephoto net.

Cal opened the laptop next to the screen and rewound the feed. Just a blur, but still there. He zoomed in closer. Closer still. Then he saw it. The flick of hair, gray and cut to shoulder length. The jawline that was unmistakably feminine. Uncle Adam and Glenda were behind him now looking over his shoulder.

"Is it her?" Glenda asked.

"I can't tell," Uncle Adam answered. "Can you rewind again?"

They watched the clip at slow speed.

"She's good. Very good," Glenda admired, sipping her champagne.

"There. Stop it there."

They all stared at the screen and it took the definition a moment to clear. That's when they all saw it, the faintest of smiles. And Uncle Adam said, "It's her. I can't believe it's her."

CHAPTER THIRTY-SEVEN

BRIGGS - CAMP SPARTAN, ARRINGTON, TENNESSEE

He found them at the cemetery, each with a gardening tool in hand. Anna had Lena laughing. Daniel didn't want to disturb them. They looked like sisters, something neither had ever had. What a gift.

"I think someone's spying on us," Anna said, winking at Lena and turning to smile at Daniel.

"How did you know he was there?" Lena asked, genuinely curious.

"I know things about Daniel Briggs that Daniel Briggs doesn't know about himself." Anna laughed like a mighty villain, fists on her hips for the full effect.

"She's got me there, Lena. Anna's seen me at my worst," Daniel said, sitting down next to the two and clearing a stray strand of grass from a headstone.

"Did you know him?" Lena said, meaning the man buried beneath.

"I did. Brian Ramirez. He was a corpsman in the Navy. That's a—"

"I know what a corpsman is," Lena said. "It's like a medic in the Army, but corpsmen act more like Marines than sailors."

"That's right. How'd you come to know that?"

"A magician never tells."

Daniel remembered that the young woman had been mentored by Marines in the past. Snipers, no less. Friends of her father's. Friends who'd been duped by his past acts of heroism.

"What did I miss?" Daniel asked.

"Oh, I was telling Lena about Paris."

"Yeah, Anna says the city is huge, and that there's a bunch of underground tunnels with skeletons, and that the food is amazing."

She sounded much younger than her nineteen years. Maybe it was the moment and the excitement. Maybe it was the fact that she had never had a chance to be a child.

"It's a great place," Daniel said. "Did you tell her about our little adventure in the City of Lights?"

Anna shook her head. "Figured I should stick to the lighter fare for now."

"Wait, you had an adventure in Paris together and you didn't tell me?" Lena's face twisted in mock indignation. "I insist that you tell me every dirty detail right now." Her mouth slipped to a pout, but her eyes shone with curiosity.

"You want to tell the story, or me?" Anna asked.

"You're a much better storyteller," Daniel said.

Anna tipped her head in thanks for the compliment. "Very well."

She put a finger to her lips. Then she must have remembered who they'd been with at the time. Cal and Diane. She shot Daniel a look. He shrugged by way of reply. Best not to keep things from the girl.

Anna nodded and continued. “It was supposed to be a vacation, but as always happens with Cal and Daniel, our vacation turned into a fight for our lives...”

Lena didn’t say a word as Anna relayed the tale. The vacation-turned-chase sounded so much better coming from Anna. Daniel enjoyed the retelling and picked up on a few details that he’d forgotten.

When Anna was done, Lena jumped in fast, the words tumbling from her mouth. “I can’t believe you guys did that. And Liberty! She’s a hero too. I mean, I knew she was amazing, but to stop a bomber like that! She must have a sixth sense or something. Have you ever thought about that?”

“I think at the time we were happier to walk away with all our fingers and toes,” Anna said.

Lena exhaled like she’d just eaten a hearty Thanksgiving meal. “Is it always like that with your friends?” she asked Daniel.

“Sometimes.”

“Sounds like you guys go looking for trouble.”

“Sounds like you might know a thing or two about looking for trouble as well,” Daniel said.

Lena shrugged and looked away like it didn’t matter. Daniel thought she wasn’t going to answer, that she was prepared to keep dodging like she’d recently done. Then she turned back and looked him straight in the eyes. “It seems to me that you’re a magnet for action, Daniel Briggs. I don’t think you go looking for it, but somehow it always finds you. Why do you think that is?”

Daniel answered truthfully. “I think I’m supposed to be right where I’m supposed to be.”

Lena thought on that hard. Then she said, “If that’s the case, what will it take for you guys to trust me?”

“What makes you think that we don’t?”

Lena rolled her eyes like it was obvious. Daniel wasn't going to make it easy for her. She had to say the words. "Fine. I wouldn't trust me either. Not after the thing in Canada. Not with the thing with that man... my father. But I've had some time to think. And I think that I can prove myself to you. Ask Top. Ask Gaucho. I'm pretty sure they can tell you I'm a good person, that I'm in the process of earning your trust. And I'm not a kid." She threw that last part in almost desperately.

"Why do you have to earn my trust? What about Cal? What about the others?"

Now Lena looked at him with one of those 'do you think I'm a simpleton' stares. "I'm pretty sure I've got it right. I've seen how things work around here, how the others look up to you. If you say you trust me Cal will go right along with you.

"You're not wrong."

Lena clapped her hands together in triumph. "Awesome. So tell me what I need to do. I'm tough. I'll do anything, I promise. Just say it."

Daniel paused. "I told Anna not to tell you about it yet, but we had a little run-in with some friends down in Florida. I was wondering if you might like to listen to the story, and after you hear it, I'd like to see what you think we should do about it."

Lena rubbed her hands together. "I'm all ears, Mr. Briggs."

Daniel nodded to Anna, who once again rolled right into storytelling.

CHAPTER THIRTY-EIGHT

ADAM STOKES - PARIS - 1974

She was a marvel. When Virginia Walton wasn't sweet-talking art dealers along the Seine, she was bare-knuckle bargaining with vegetable stall merchants who thought they'd get a franc or two up on the pretty lady and her American friend.

"How do they know I'm American?" Adam asked one day. Virginia motioned from his head to toes, as if that was enough. "I swear, it's like I'm wearing a stars and stripes tattoo on my forehead or something."

"It's in the small details," Virginia said, sucking the marrow from the cigarette in her hand.

Virginia didn't say much, and Adam had no idea why she'd taken him in. There were mornings when he thought about going to find his Legionnaire friends. They were much better company when it came to conversation.

But something about this woman intrigued him. She was beautiful to be sure, but not in any modern way Adam Stokes had ever seen. It was as if Virginia Walton had been plucked from the royal court in Egypt or maybe Ancient Sumer. It was the regal look that did it, capped by the imperious way she tended to look at people.

"Where are you from anyway?" he asked, taking a cigarette when offered. He'd gotten used to the habit. And besides, if he didn't smoke it seemed like one more reason to paint him as an American.

"Toledo," Virginia said, still scanning everything but Adam.

"As in Ohio?"

Now she looked at him.

"You don't get around much, do you?"

"I get around," he said defensively. "How did you get from Ohio to Paris?"

"The way most people do. By airplane."

Her answers could be maddening, but much like the cigarettes, he was getting used to them.

"You could've come over on a ship, then taken a cab from the port."

She nodded, adding nothing. There were times when he wondered whether she was bored with him, that she'd toss him back to the streets in seconds. This was one of those times. Adam didn't like the way it made him feel.

"Why did you take me from my friends?"

"I didn't take you. You came willingly."

"Did I?"

"Well, you fell first. Then I fixed your nose. Then you came with me."

Adam felt a vibration of anger run through his head. "You can be a real haughty princess, you know that?"

"So I've been told."

They sat there for a while, sipping their coffee, Adam trying to get past the awkward interaction. Virginia carried on like nothing had happened. Adam was about to press again when she spoke.

"They were going to make you a Legionnaire," she said. There was a stamp of finality in the comment.

"What's so bad about that? I was going to be in the Marines." He couldn't believe how juvenile he sounded when he said it, like a child asking for a consolation prize. He tried to cover it up with, "They were tough and they took care of me."

She snorted. Adam found that he liked the sound. It was the first human thing to have come out of her.

"Oh, they were going to take care of you all right." She stubbed out her cigarette and shook out another. "They're not okay, Adam Stokes. It's the end of the month. They had a quota to fill. You were going to fill that quota."

"Fill what quota?"

A long exhale. "They're Legionnaires. They belong to the French Foreign Legion. Their job is to rope people like you into indentured servitude. I saved you from that."

He still didn't understand. She didn't know him. Maybe the French Foreign Legion was exactly what he needed. He'd show his family, the world if he had to.

"You think I couldn't cut it?" He wanted to tell her how tough he was, how courageous he could be, how physically fit he was when he wasn't sipping coffee and smoking all day.

She scowled at him. "If that's what you want, be my guest. I won't stop you." She tapped her new cigarette against her palm. "But if you want to really make a difference, and not spend the next three years as cannon fodder for the Legion, stick with me. I've got something."

So many questions ran through Adam's head that he

couldn't choose which one to spit out. The one that finally made it out of his mouth was, "Why me?"

Now she smiled a smile so brilliant, so cold, so ruthless and inviting, that it made Adam suck in a breath.

"I see something in you, Adam Stokes. Let's hope I'm not wrong."

CHAPTER THIRTY-NINE

FLAP - LANGLEY, VIRGINIA

Another folder added to the pile. He was making quick work of the mess left by his predecessor. The man was a slob. He left the place in shambles, only providing the most minimal turnover he could get away with.

Flap didn't mind. The paperwork was easy. Always had been. For him it was like crocheting was to grandmothers, or what rakes and sand were for Buddhist monks. It got Flap out of the daily grind, put him into the zone where he could think. He'd devour report after report, making notes if needed, all the while charting paths in his head. It was a gift he barely acknowledged. It just was who he was, like his near-eunuch lifestyle. Woman interested him, for sure, but he'd made a decision long ago that women, booze, money—anything that involved entanglements—were not going to get in his way.

So he kept on filing, kept on cleaning. If his secretary poked her head in to ask if she could help, he turned her away. Not unkindly. Flap wanted her to like him. A man in his position needed to be liked by his secretary. She might come in handy someday, and Flap was all about squirreling away little gifts until he needed them. That was yet another lesson he'd learned after his long fall. Prepare for doomsday.

His desk finally cleared, Flap got up from his ergonomic throne and walked to the expansive windows. He'd never had a thing for trees. He'd been a rat running through cities since he could remember. Being out here reminded him that he was no longer in the dead center of the action. Flap soothed that disparaging thought by remembering what he did have. He had an endless supply of contacts, spies, moles, secrets, and weapons at his disposal. All he had to do was reach out and press a button for the action to begin.

No need to rush things. He'd waited and he'd wait some more.

Flap wondered how the reporter was doing. There hadn't been a peep from Springer since he'd left. It would've been easy to sic a tail on the guy, but Flap had done his homework. When Springer was hot on the trail, the talented reporter went radio silent, not unlike Flap's other resources.

In time, Springer would return, carcass in tow. Flap wondered if the man would ask for money, maybe a boost with his overlords, or whether the right to publish such a story was all he really wanted. The career spy figured it was the last, though Springer's growing drug dependency might skew things. Not that Flap cared. If there was a way to manipulate a situation, Flap wanted to have it in his death grip.

A rare smile formed on Flap's lips when an odd thought sprang to mind. The elder Stokes. The reason for all his planning. In torpedoing Flap's career, Stokes had really done the opposite. He'd reignited Flap's desire, like a lion losing its pride and having to fight back, fang and claw, until he regained his place on that rock. Flap sometimes wondered if there was an afterlife. He was not in any way religious, spiritual, or scared of death. No, he wondered because he wanted Colonel Stokes looking down and watching his every move. If that were the case, Flap fully expected Stokes to know what was coming next.

Yes, yes, yes. If only he could see Calvin Stokes now, soak in the cocky eyes that would be there when his very own blood and bone took the ultimate fall. Because the fall was coming, and the crosshairs would soon rest firmly on the image of Stokes's son, Cal. And then Flap would dance with the devil on top of Stokes's memory, and take a nice, steaming piss on his grave for good measure.

CHAPTER FORTY

ANNA - CAMP SPARTAN, ARRINGTON, TENNESSEE

"I'm going to Moscow," Daniel said, the same way he might say he was going to the gym or the grocery store.

It took a moment for Anna to process. "Moscow? I hope you mean Moscow, Arizona."

"There is no Moscow, Arizona."

"You're not going." She tamped down her anger as best she could. "Daniel, why on Earth would you even think of doing such a thing? Have you forgotten about Florida?"

Daniel threw the stick and Liberty chased it into the long grass. "I haven't forgotten about Florida. That's the reason I'm going."

His perfect ease at saying something so reckless, so ludicrous, was threatening to upend Anna's day.

"I told you," she said. "My people are doing what they do best. We'll find out who sent the assassins. Only then will we make a move."

Daniel cocked his head ever so slightly to one side. "You're not my boss, remember?"

He was teasing her and she was in no mood to be teased. Diane was dead. Cal was in Paris. Lena followed her around like a lost puppy and now Daniel was going to Moscow? No. She would not stand for it.

"I know I'm not your boss. I know I can't tell you what to do. But these people—"

"They're *your* people."

"I'm an American," she said. "Same as you."

The mirth left his face. "That's not what I meant... I'm sorry if it sounded that way."

"I know that's not what you meant, dammit!" She clenched her fists and hit them on her thighs. She couldn't remember the last time she lost control. It wasn't in her nature. It was in her past. Gathering her calm, she faced him full on. "Look, that man is a lunatic. A verified, bona fide, dictionary-definition of a card-carrying lunatic. He doesn't care about anything or anyone other than himself and the power he can stuff in his pocket. Do you know how many of my friends he's had killed?" When Daniel just stood there, not answering, her temper flared again. "I can't lose you! Don't you see that?!"

She wanted to run. Run like she'd run as a child into the woods or to hide in a barn. Anything to get away. Maybe that's what she really wanted. She could get away, leave everything forever. She had the money. There was even a second who could take over in her absence. Get away and stay away. Maybe Daniel would come with her.

But when she looked at him, she knew the truth. Daniel would never run and neither would she. They were built of the same stuff, and for a purpose greater than themselves. He was older, wiser in some ways, but Anna had always wondered if there wasn't something Daniel was missing by leading his simple lifestyle.

She reached out and took his hand. "I'll go with you."

"Anna—"

"Before you say no, hear me out, okay?"

"Fine."

Anna closed her eyes and settled on the truth, the one she'd hidden away and promised herself she'd never let out. But this was Daniel. How could she keep the truth from him of all people? The answer was simple: She couldn't.

So, she looked into his eyes and told him the truth.

CHAPTER FORTY-ONE

BRIGGS - CAMP SPARTAN, ARRINGTON, TENNESSEE

"Daniel?" Anna said. "Did you hear me?"

Of course he'd heard the words, it was impossible not to. They were the words he'd been dreaming of for years. They were the words that ran straight to his heart, seeped in, claimed their spot, and set up camp.

For the first time in a long, long time, Daniel was at a loss. He stared at Anna, let his mind wander down the dream-scape. She'd said she loved him. Not a friendship love, not a platonic love. A *love* love. For a man who on most days felt every twist and turn of the universe before it happened, those words, the words themselves, were no surprise. It was the timing that flustered him. Flustered was another thing that hadn't happened in forever, not since the days when the beast had roamed free.

"Daniel," Anna said again.

He was scaring her. He could see that. And even though he wanted to reach out his hand and tell her that it was okay, that he felt the same way, a fear deep in his soul crept out and told him the old untruth: "You are unworthy." He tried to blink away the thought.

"Daniel, what's wrong? I'm sorry. I shouldn't have said anything. It's just that..."

He reached out and took her hand. "I'm sorry. I didn't mean to scare you. You took me by surprise. I never thought I deserved you, always thought you'd end up with someone better. Some well-to-do politician who's changing the world one important bill at a time."

"You know I could never do that. That's not who I am," she said.

The fluster was back. This wasn't him. This wasn't his voice. "You really do deserve better," he said.

"What are you talking about?" Anna said, the concern on her face scaring him.

Fear, the next slide down the slippery slope.

He grabbed onto the excuse, the only one he could think of—the words were pathetic, childish, and not his own. "Lena's waiting for me and I have a plane to catch in two hours."

Her disappointment and shock were plain. He walked away but felt like he should run. Run now, run forever, run as far as he could go. Don't even look back.

Daniel Briggs knew something very well. He knew something deep inside of him had opened. And if he didn't find the solution, his life would spiral down and back to oblivion.

CHAPTER FORTY-TWO

VOLKOV - KIRILLOV, RUSSIA

Alexander Volkov, Alek to his friends, had to sip carefully from his vodka. The monks of St. Benedict were proud of their handmade liquor. It was good, to be sure. It was powerful. Volkov needed to spark every one of his senses to full capacity.

He'd found early on in his spying days that men and women of the cloth were perfect informants. Those wearing traditional garb, as the men were who surrounded him tonight, typically garnered respect and were given a wide berth by the general population.

He was in Kirillov unofficially. Technically, he was on vacation. Under the surface, he was meeting with one of his favorite spies, the head of the monastery who had already downed a jug of homemade vodka. He was a gregarious party-goer who could rub elbows with Muscovite officials or the lowly beggar who came to the monastery for food each day. But under the laughing facade lay a man who'd forged an iron will. No less than three times he'd been dragged to the

Lubyanka. The third and final time that Volkov had met him, they shared a deep connection. One that neither man had known until their second meeting. The first had been an inspection. Volkov had once been tasked with not only training but overseeing some of Russia's most talented interrogators. He'd been one of the few to give the green light when harder tactics were to be used.

It was on one of his inspection tours that he'd met the laughing monk who sat across from him now. He'd been much thinner then, mostly because he'd only been given limited rations for thirty days, and yet he had not broken. An impossible feat, and one that had pulled Volkov in more by curiosity than by his job. In their second meeting, they'd realized that they were from neighboring towns in Belarus. That's when things got interesting because despite what his handlers in Moscow thought Alek Volkov was, he was really a man with deep ties to his homeland of Belarus and a leader in a quiet insurgency that had grand designs for the leaders in Russia. The bond had grown slowly over time, each man wary of the other. Volkov because of his own reputation, the monk because he trusted no one but God. They were fast friends, and the vacation had been more of a celebration between friends, a camaraderie built over even tougher decisions.

"To you, Alek," the monk yelled, raising his glass in the air, sloshing some of the vodka onto the table.

Volkov raised his glass and smiled at his friend, "You as well, brother."

The monk smiled conspiratorially and whispered, "Home."

"To our home," Alek mimicked, and they both drank from their glasses.

The monk downed his glass, gave a long, satisfied belch,

and said, "Alek, why is it that you never seem to change? Why, you look as young as when you were thirty."

Volkov laughed. "And you look like Methuselah's tired, older brother." It was an old joke, one that made no sense, but one they'd always shared, which was something that Volkov rarely got to experience, especially these days. Too many missions, too many plans. Zero fellowship.

He was refilling his own glass when the phone in his pocket buzzed. He pulled it out and read the message carefully.

"I know that look," the monk said. "You're leaving, aren't you?"

If Alek could tell the monk the truth, the man would probably smile. "It's back to Moscow for now," Volkov said. "But before I go, how about one more drink?"

Vodka flowed, and the monk's laughter filled the room. But Volkov's mind was focused on one thing.

Daniel Briggs was coming to visit, and Volkov had an inkling that all of his plans throughout the years might suddenly come to fruition. Who could have known all those years ago, when his mentor had laid the reins in his hands, that an American might be the answer to all their problems?

CHAPTER FORTY-THREE

ADAM STOKES - PARIS - 1975

It had been close to a year since Virginia Walton had nabbed him from the Legionnaires. In the beginning, it was thrilling, even funny then. Like the first time he'd been to Disneyland. The world she talked about was full of spies and their evil counterparts. She never sensationalized, as far as Adam could tell. In the beginning, she'd used him as a runner, depositing letters at the post office or dropping a note in a random trash can.

His duties increased as time went on. Sometimes he'd accompanied her to meetings. She never let his hair get too long and always reminded him that he needed to stay physically fit. They spent days in the countryside, running long, looping paths. She was as gifted physically and moved like some silent fish through turbulent waters, streaming in and out of crowds undetected, unseen. It wasn't long before he got his steam back and could outrun her. But that was merely due to his physical makeup. It had nothing to do with her lack of determination. And it was that very determination that reeled him in wholesale. She'd been a beautiful novelty in the beginning. Now, she was his entire world.

And as the months passed, he began to chafe at her coldness.

One night after a bit too much wine, he tried to drape an arm over her shoulder. She shrugged away from that one, deftly snatching a pack of cigarettes from a friend across the table. Every subtle move he put on was parried by the expert swordsman that she was.

He worked harder, ran faster, stopped smoking cigarettes for a time. He even gave up wine, but that seemed to anger her, and she chided him for it.

"Wine and Paris go hand in hand. You have to look like you fit in."

He almost got up and left then and there, but he remembered what she often said about a temper. A temper was of no use to a spy in the field. Any man or a woman who could be controlled by their anger was no spy at all.

Adam Stokes had never been in love, but he was pretty damn sure he was in it now. Ankle deep, then up to his throat. Pretty soon, he was swimming in Virginia Walton, taking in lungsful of Virginia Walton, even though Virginia Walton treated him like no more than a servant.

And oh, how the Parisian men loved her. They flocked to her night and day. And each new suitor drove another stake into Adam's heart.

It was almost Christmas, and cold winds whipped through the city. Even the most Bohemian of war protesters huddled in groups wrapped in coats and blankets, their faces covered in scarves.

Adam was on recruiting duty, though he didn't feel like talking. The clean-cut American routine was getting old. Why couldn't he dress like someone well-to-do, like Virginia did? She'd said they all had to play their part. Try to recruit another clean-cut American, or maybe even a Brit.

But recruit them for what? They were an elusive gaggle of acquaintances who sometimes talked about the downfall of America or what the Soviets might do next. They were all political in their own way, having come to Paris either by chance or by force. They were draft dodgers. Virginia told Adam to stay clear of them. He didn't know why, and when he asked she didn't answer. He didn't even know who they might be spying for. He knew only that she had him in the palm of her hand.

And if she told him to drive five hours and jump off a cliff, well, he might just do it. That was the insurmountable power of Virginia Walton. Even then, her name was growing on the streets. And soon the Duchess was known from hostels to castles. And still, Adam wanted her fiercely.

They were sitting in a one-room apartment, a place they used for impromptu meetings. Adam didn't know where she lived. He'd found a cheap place down the street.

"How many did you get this week?" she asked, making notes in a small journal.

"Just one, but I think you'll like her."

She looked up from her note-taking. "Only one? I told you, time is short."

He hated the way she talked to him. "Time is short, for what? Dammit, you never tell me a damn thing. Maybe if you told me what was going on, we could—"

She held up an imperious hand. "It's for your safety."

It's what she always said. And it felt more like she was trying to play mother hen and keep him under wing than it felt like she was telling him the truth. But he was done with it. He got up from his chair and looked down at her, eyes blazing.

"I'm sick of this, Virginia. You said we would make a difference. All you have me doing is recruiting people I don't even like."

He wanted her to yell at him. Scream at him, even. But all she did was cock her head and look up at him.

"Are you finished?"

His clenched fist could have broken through brick, but her power over him calmed him. He took a seat again and fumbled with the bottle of wine. He poured the blood-red liquid up to the lip. He didn't say anything else until he drained the entire glass and again refilled it.

"There," she purred. "Feel better now?"

He could have thrown the wine in her face. At least that's what he told himself. But he knew deep down that if he did, he'd be cast out. As much as his pride wanted him to go, he knew he was stuck. She had him.

"Tell me about the one you found," she said. "What's his name?"

Again, just like her. Right back down to business. Good ol' Virginia Walton in her prime.

"It's not a he, it's a she," Adam said, sipping his wine now, allowing the liquid to course through him. He needed that warm glow, needed to run from the anger.

"And what, pray tell, is her name?" Virginia asked.

"Her name is Glenda Younger. She's quite a hoot." He'd cozied up to the eccentric American because he knew it would infuriate Virginia.

Glenda Younger was the polar opposite of Virginia Walton, all bubbles and smiles. Glenda was youthful innocence to Virginia's matronly calm.

"Glenda Younger," she said. "Have I met her?"

"Yeah. You met her last week. Remember? The rally at the palace?"

Virginia's eyes narrowed, then went wide with acknowledgment. "You don't mean the girl with the wild hair?"

Adam smiled. "The one and only."

"Why she's a complete kook. I don't know why you waste your time on her."

But Adam knew something that Virginia didn't. Under the colorful facade, Glenda Younger was smart. Whip smart. He put her through a couple of mental tests, and she'd come out better than any of the others, even himself. He liked Glenda immediately.

"Well, she's your problem to deal with, if she makes it. And I would like to emphasize the word 'if.' She is your problem. Do you understand me?"

Adam's grin went even wider. "Loud and clear, Duchess."

Oh, how Virginia's eyes went cold now. It was fine for the streets to call her that. Not okay for Adam Stokes to say it.

"You call me that again and I'll—"

Adam raised a hand like Virginia had a minute ago. "Now, now, your ladyship. You know what they say about temper."

Ooh, how she seethed. For a second, he really thought she was going to blow her top. But she didn't. She kept it all in, Virginia Walton-style. The anger seeped from her body and she grabbed the bottle of wine, surprising Adam by drinking straight from it. After the long pull, she wiped her mouth with the back of her hand. She tilted the last drop of the bottle onto her tongue and looked at him.

"Go get another bottle. We're leaving."

"Where are we going?" Adam asked, thrilled by the confrontation. He could feel the electricity in the air, but none of it prepared him for what she said next.

"You're taking me to bed."

Adam Stokes wasn't about to say no.

They spent their first passionate night in bed, even though he knew what she was doing.

She was enticing him down into the spiral of the Virginia Walton vortex of evil. Once there, his soul would be consumed, and whatever was left of him would be lost to her will and her ego.

CHAPTER FORTY-FOUR

YOUNGER - PARIS

Adam Stokes was going to kill her. She'd left Cal and him at the apartment. They'd been sleeping and she was on watch. At least she'd had enough foresight to leave a note.

They'd found a wisp of the Duchess. Glenda knew that meant all kinds of emotions roiling around in Adam's head. Those were emotions that would only get in the way, so Glenda knew that she had to act first.

She took the long way through the city, always checking to see if she had a tail. By now, she could practically smell them—they were blocks away. Her craft was well-honed, and she was proud to think that even at her advanced age she was still very good at what she did.

Paris was very much her hometown just as Mount Airy had been her mother's. She thought of her mother now. A quiet woman, respectful wife, never showing much emotion to young Glenda. Maybe that's why Glenda ended up the way she did—full of love for the world and the human beings in it.

She said prayers for all the spies she'd outed. She respected even the people she killed, for she believed it was right to do so. When she wasn't making her millions or playing the spy game, she was giving away money, helping others. She was proud that there was a growing number of poor immigrants who were now attending universities because of her help. She knew from experience that education, the right kind of education and the right kind of love, were better weapons against extremism than a thousand Tomahawk missiles. At least that was her opinion. She'd done her homework well.

When she finally tucked herself into the little nook next to the cathedral, she knew it was only a matter of minutes. Her intuition paid off, for there, walking straight down the street in regal glory, was the Duchess, Virginia Walton.

It had cost many pretty euros to get this information and she hadn't even shared it with Adam. The emotions were too deep in that relationship and that was why Glenda was here. Was she taking a chance? Of course, but she'd taken many chances in her life. She wasn't stupid.

There were half a dozen weapons on her person. When the Duchess got close enough, Glenda stepped from the shadows.

"It's you," Virginia said, stopping feet from the cathedral entrance.

"Who did you expect? Charlie Chaplin?" Glenda threw back.

Virginia exhaled. "You never took this business seriously, but with all your chatter and fluff I'm surprised you're still alive."

Glenda shifted just so, the pistol in her hand pointed at the target. "And look at you, Mrs. Lazarus. You're supposed to be dead. Care to tell me that story?"

Then came the old Duchess smile, all cold and slithery like a snake that's wrapping around your neck. "I don't have time for your nonsense," she said.

"Too busy killing our old friends. What do you have time for?"

The smile left Virginia's face. "You don't know a thing about what I'm doing, what I've had to do."

Now it was Glenda's turn to smile. "You always were good at playing the 'poor me' routine. Even though the others never saw it, I saw right through you. The spoiled protégé who got everything she ever wanted. I'm sure this mess you're in now is quite your own fault."

"You have no idea what I've seen. What I've been through," Virginia said again. She calmed herself, but Glenda could still see the edge. Much more on edge than she used to be. How many years had it been? Twenty? Thirty? No, it had to be more. And still Virginia had the perfect chin, that regal nose, those beautiful eyes. She could see why men had always been in lockstep with the woman, but it took a woman to know a woman and Glenda had seen right through this woman's facade years ago. There was a weakness there, a need to overcompensate for some past wrong. Maybe she'd made a mistake. Maybe she'd been mistreated by her father. Glenda might never know. What looked like confidence to most looked like overconfidence to Glenda. It reeked, like cheap perfume.

"You killed Bo Tipton and the others, didn't you?" Glenda said.

She didn't really expect an honest answer, but was glad when Virginia said, "Of course I did. Who else would you think?"

Bo had been one of Glenda's closest friends. One of Adam's too. He had the warmest of hearts and an extreme love for nature. Glenda hoped he was flying with angels now.

"Tell me who you're working for—the Russians?"

Virginia didn't answer. Just looked at Glenda with those piercing eyes.

"I asked you a question," Glenda said.

"And I told you, it's none of your business. You haven't understood that since the beginning. Always poking your nose in places it doesn't belong. I should have gotten rid of you years ago."

"I'd like to see you try it now." Glenda's finger tightened on the trigger.

She could take this woman out right here and now, but she needed answers. And if she was being honest with herself, she had not completely planned this out. She'd come to find the killer of her friends. Really, she'd come for the love of Adam Stokes. It was a love that she'd buried for decades. Never once uttered a syllable of it. She admired him for so many things, but she knew that the woman standing in front of her had broken him. But really, why had she come? Just to give Adam a chance with his own nephew? He had the rest of his life to heal, to find his place in the world again. And it was because Adam Stokes had been a broken man for many years, a broken man that Glenda often had over for dinner just so she could check in on him. She'd spent Christmases and Thanksgivings with him for the same reason.

And to Adam Stokes, Glenda was a younger sister, always ready with wine and food. But Glenda had done it for one reason and one reason alone. She loved the man. And she would be damned if the Duchess came back to stomp on his heart—or worse, to kill him. She knew in that moment that Virginia Walton would never talk. She would never tell the truth. So there was only one thing to do.

Glenda had every compulsion to shoot the woman. The trigger squeezed, and then a shooting pain went through her back. The weapon clattered to the ground and she fell to her knees. There was a ringing in her ears. And she thought she heard the chiming of bells. And when she looked up, Virginia Walton was looking down at her, shaking her head.

"Should have minded your own business," said the Duchess.

Two men emerged from the shadows, each holding long guns with suppressed barrels.

But Glenda wasn't through.

She pretended to fall forward, and when she did, she lashed out with a stiletto knife in her left hand.

Virginia grunted. She couldn't get back to her feet. She was on the ground, watching the thin line of blood on the knife. She could no longer move.

"What do we do with her?" one of the men asked.

"Leave her," said the Duchess.

Glenda smiled when she registered the hint of pain in the woman's voice. Maybe she hit an artery. Maybe she sliced the Achilles tendon. Maybe, just maybe.

But now, the world was drifting away. And before the next bullet came and ended it all, Glenda said a silent prayer for her one and only love. That he would soon find his way. And that he would kill the Duchess in the process.

CHAPTER FORTY-FIVE

STOKES - PARIS

It had been two days since Glenda's disappearance when her attorney called and asked Uncle Adam for a private meeting. Adam was having none of it. He spat a few French curses through the phone and then took a breath and listened. His only reply moments later was a grunt, and he hung up the phone.

"She's dead," he said to the floor, "and she left everything to me."

What followed was a two-day brooding session that was worthy of the Stokes name.

When Uncle Adam finally emerged from his cabin, he told Cal everything he knew—where the body had been found, and the fact that Glenda was much wealthier than he had even imagined.

"I'm giving it away. I don't want any of it," he said.

"Let's not make any decisions quite yet," said Cal, figuring it was his turn to play Mr. Reality. "If you're anything like me, you're prone to snap decisions."

Uncle Adam's eyes pierced into him. "I don't make snap decisions."

Cal held up his hands. "Look, I understand, probably more than anyone in your world would. She was your friend. She obviously cared about you, or else she wouldn't have left you her entire fortune. Do you really think she would've done that if she wanted you to give it all away?" He wasn't sure if the comment was sinking in or not. "Tell me what I can do, a call or two and I'll have some of my best men here."

"No," Uncle Adam said. Again, the stamp of Stokes finality.

Cal didn't get much sleep that night. And when Uncle Adam went topside, saying he needed to get some air. Cal offered to go with him.

"I'll be fine," Uncle Adam said, and disappeared into the darkness.

Hours passed and still no Uncle Adam. Cal tried to call, but there was no answer. He chided himself for not following. For all Cal knew, his uncle, his only uncle, was now dead.

He could call his men, of course. Daniel and the others would be here as quick as they could, but what could they really do? Cal was on thin ice with the president and the last thing his country needed was to have to clean up some little mess in Paris. The old Cal wouldn't have thought about it. He would've made the call, or at least he would've hit the trail. This new Cal, once again aching with the pain of loss, sat in his indecision and stewed.

Uncle Adam reappeared later that day, his mood heightened.

"I almost had her," he said, motioning for Cal to come below deck.

The switch was flipped and the boat was buttoned up in

secrecy. Uncle Adam was taking off his coat when Cal noticed the man's shirted arm.

"Is that your blood?"

"No."

"What the hell happened?"

"Just a little scuffle. I'm fine." He pulled down his sleeve to prove it. No wound, someone else's blood. But whose? The one they called the Duchess?

Uncle Adam started pacing back and forth, ticking off thoughts with the fingers of his left hand. "I should've known it was the Russians," he murmured.

"The Russians?" Cal said.

Could this be about him? He had his own beef with the president of Russia, and there was a thing with the man from Belarus, Alexander Volkov. Was this about them? Were they the ones killing American spies?

"How do you know it was the Russians?" Cal asked.

Uncle Adam didn't immediately respond. He kept pacing back and forth, back and forth. "I had to kill one of her team. He talked in the end, though. It was touch and go for a minute there, but he finally talked. Tough son of a bitch. That's how she liked them—tight-lipped and tough as nails. Just wait until I get my hands on that sour witch. I'll kill her again."

Cal Stokes was no stranger to death and killing, but this was Paris, a city he didn't know well, and in his uncle's near-manic state, Cal wondered how much planning had been done. He had to find out. "The man you killed—can they trace him back to you?"

"Of course they can." He looked up at Cal. "But not who you think. Not the authorities. And the place I left the body... well, let's just say the authorities will let things lie when they visit that particular neighborhood." This was Uncle Adam's playground, so Cal had to trust the man.

Trust. Such a simple word and layered with so much reality. They had trusted Glenda not to go off alone. Why did she? Why did she get herself killed? If they took out this Duchess, would it end everything, or was she a single pawn out of many? The way Adam and Glenda spoke of her, she was more like a queen than a pawn, and the way she had eluded their surveillance, she was definitely a pro.

Cal was about to stop his uncle and ask all the questions running through his head, because he needed the truth and wanted to be of some help, but the phone in the room rang and Uncle Adam fetched it.

The conversation was sharp and terse. Seconds later, the phone was back in its cradle.

Uncle Adam's eyes blazed now when he looked at Cal. There was determination there, fire. Cal recognized the look —vengeance. And he wasn't at all surprised when his uncle asked, "Who do you know in Moscow?"

CHAPTER FORTY-SIX

SPRINGER - OLD ORCHARD BEACH, MAINE

Springer was getting tired of these old, small towns where everyone knew everyone. He wondered if in the old days it used to be easier for journalists. If you lived in a small town, you wanted to be known in a big town. Pulitzer got him nowhere, and he wasted hundreds of dollars before someone pointed him in the right direction. But the direction went to a small farm that was no longer a farm. It had been redeveloped into one of those starter home communities, one where half the front yards were overgrown, and the other half were well tended. Small children played in playgrounds and backyards, and any whiff of the scent that Springer had had coming to Maine was now gone.

Daniel Briggs had spent time in this town and made something of a name for himself with whatever underworld characters had been here at the time. If they were still here, he couldn't find them. Now, it was looking more and more like this was a bust of a trip. At least he had enough money for a nice room on the beach.

He found a dealer with some decent stuff. Not like the stuff he got in D.C. or New York, but it was decent enough for Maine. He decided he'd enjoy his night. He treated himself to a couple of bumps, grabbed a six-pack of Narragansett from the gas station down the street, and walked the beach. It was mostly locals for a season on the wane. There was an old woman peddling bracelets who looked like she was closing up shop.

He was bored and figured he should at least do some digging. Not that he thought it would get anywhere. His mind was spinning and he had to talk to someone. The old lady would do.

"I'll be back tomorrow," she said as he came closer.

"Have you lived here long?" he asked, picking up one of the signs for her and folding it and handing it back.

She eyed him cautiously. "Lived here most of my life."

"Have you always worked on the beach? I love your work, by the way." He didn't give a damn about bracelets and paintings, but she brightened, as he knew she would.

"This was just a habit that I picked up from my granddaughter."

"Does she live in town, too?"

"No." The woman looked wistfully down the beach. "No, she moved away a long time ago to L.A. To become an actress. I haven't seen her in two years."

"That's a shame. Pretty town here. Wish I could stay longer. Say, what did you do before this, before your hobby?"

"I was a teacher, thirty years. I used to volunteer at the church, too, but I'm sure you don't care about that."

But he did. The little tinkling of curiosity banged in the back of his mind. It was a long shot, but still a shot. "You don't happen to remember a pastor? He's on an old farm. I think there was a red top on one of the buildings. He had a young daughter."

The old woman's eyes brightened. "Why, of course I remember them. He was my pastor. And Anna, she was just the sweetest thing."

Springer's calculating mind chimed. Sometimes it was the lucky louse who got the best stuff. "You don't say. He was an old friend of mine. I was going to look him up while I was here."

All the brightness in the woman's eyes disappeared, replaced by sadness. "Well, I hate to be the one to deliver the bad news, but the pastor died a few years back. I'm not sure how or where, but it wasn't here."

Springer cursed inwardly. Any details might've helped the story. "How did you find out about his passing?" he asked.

The old woman finished clipping up her cart, filling the last of the bracelets. "Oh, the way you hear about most things, rumors and whatnot. I think there might've been something in the paper. I used to read the obits, but I stopped doing that after my husband died. You understand."

Springer nodded like he did. Sentimentality was not one of his traits. But still, he felt that there was more to the story. Something else that this woman knew. "And what about his daughter? Anna, was it?"

The woman's face brightened again. "Oh, yes, Anna. The most beautiful eyes. Smart girl, too. She used to answer the phones at the church. Had the neatest handwriting you ever saw. She was always talking about going to far-off places like Paris, London, or Bangkok. Wonderful artist."

Springer could see that she would have gone on and on about the little details that he didn't care about. Time to reel her back in.

"Do you have any idea where she ended up? With another family, maybe?"

The old woman shook her head. "No, not that I could recall. I thought that maybe she'd come back to the church. Not sure about any other family, but, well, I do remember one thing if it'll help."

"Sure, anything." Springer said.

"Well, I know they went by a certain last name. I can't recall what that is now, but a while back there was some mail that came for her and we gave it back to the mailman and he happened to know she'd taken on a new name."

The tingling anticipation ran up and down Springer's body. This was it. He felt it coming. "What was her name?"

The old woman wondered aloud. "It was something foreign, something ..." She raised an index finger in the air, "Varushkin! That's what it was, Anna Varushkin."

And just like that, Dirk Springer had yet another missing piece of the puzzle in his hand.

CHAPTER FORTY-SEVEN

LENA - CAMP SPARTAN, ARRINGTON, TENNESSEE

It had been a busy morning. She started it with a heavy workout with Top in the gym. He pounded her in pads, and she knew she'd be bruised the next day. She no longer bothered getting cleaned up and went straight to the range for a session with Gaucho. She appreciated the yin and yang of the two men, the best of friends as they were, and could now joke easily with both men. Their friendship was something she woke up each day needing, yearning for.

She was so excited when she set a new personal record—not a single target missed. And that with her least favorite weapon, the pistol. She immediately wanted to find Daniel and tell him. She still didn't know what it was about the man, but she wanted so badly to please him. And Anna, too, who was starting to feel something like an older sister to her.

She had observed the obvious connection. More so with Anna than Daniel, who was somewhat detached. That's just the way he was. But even though he looked detached, his empathy for others was right there, front and center, 24/7.

Without really knowing it, Lena had been modeling her own attitudes closely to Daniel's. She still got upset. She still had a temper. But if the stories Anna had told her were true, Daniel was as much a human being as anyone. And it was only after endless inner work that he became what he was—the calm warrior monk, the one everyone looked to. And that was what Lena wanted. She wanted to be depended on. She wanted to be part of the family.

So when she saw Daniel driving through the front gate, she was more than a little disappointed. She went looking for Anna next, but when she found the older woman, she was speaking in heavy Russian into the phone and didn't need to be disturbed. Something wasn't right.

With all her work done for the day, Lena went to the only person that was close to her age. Elijah Huckleberry worked in what the folks at SSI called the Batcave. It was a few levels underground and housed the epicenter of SSI's operations. All the computers, all the networks, all the things that Lena didn't understand. But Elijah did. Sure, some of SSI's employees shook their heads when Elijah walked by sporting the newest kicks from Kanye West, or a T-shirt and hat splashed with color. He was secure in who he was.

Lena had picked up on the fact that there might be a slight attraction brewing. Not that Lena really cared. She never really fancied boys. She'd been too busy. Too consumed with her own stuff. Boys always seemed so juvenile, so down for only one thing. Elijah was different. He was like a real grown-up, harder than most, and he always took his time to explain things that Lena would understand, and without condescension.

Once she went down to the Batcave and found him tinkering with some eight-legged robot.

"What monstrosity are we building today?" she said, her smile one of genuine warmth.

He looked up in surprise, catching his glasses as they fell off his face. "What? Oh, Lena. Hey, how are you doing?"

His getting flustered was almost cute. Almost.

"I asked what you were building."

Elijah looked down, "What? Oh, this? Just, you know, tinkering again." Lena knew that Elijah's tinkering usually meant countless hours hopped up on caffeine and would probably fetch hundreds of thousands of dollars on the open market. He would tell her what the little spider thing was in time. Right now, Lena needed answers. So she played dumb, just a little.

"Hey, do you know where Daniel was going?" Elijah tried to look cool and almost played it off, but Lena had become a grand observer of the human condition. She saw the register and saw the lie.

"Oh, I'm not sure. Maybe going to D.C."

She put a hand on his shoulder and was pretty sure she felt him shiver. "I know he's not going to D.C."

"You do?"

Lena nodded. "Look, I don't want to get you in trouble, but I want to make sure he's okay. Anna seemed pretty upset."

"She did?"

She could see the wheels spinning in his head. Elijah Huckleberry was putty in her hands right now. She had to be careful not to squeeze that putty too hard. She stared at him. He actually gulped.

"I heard he was going out of the country," Elijah managed to mumble.

"Out of the country?"

He nodded, and then in a whisper hoarse with nerves, he said, "Yeah. I think Moscow."

The word sent an electric current through Lena.

Moscow. How much pain had that city brought on her own family? A family she had never met and yet hearing its name thrilled her, and her mind cast down a path of possibilities.

"Can you find out where in Moscow he was going?"

Another long gulp. "I'm really not supposed to say, Lena. I swear you could get me fired if I said anything."

Lena threw a hip to one side. "Do you really think I would tell anybody that you told me where he was going?"

He shook his head quickly. "No, that's not what I'm saying, but you're making me confused." He took a step back like being near her was some kind of kryptonite.

"What if I said that Daniel needed my help?"

Elijah's forehead wrinkled. "Daniel Briggs needs your help? Come on, Lena."

"What? You don't think I could help him?"

He threw his hands in the air. "Geez, Lena, you really keep twisting my words. You know that?"

She could see that he wasn't completely upset, and she found that fact comforting and somewhat attractive. That still didn't mean she wasn't getting what she wanted.

"Well, I guess I can go ask Neil."

Neil Patel was the SSI legend that Elijah Huckleberry wanted to be. He jump-started the company's technical operations and it brought in hundreds of millions of dollars through software and technology advances that he himself had put together with his bare hands. Lena knew that the name Neil Patel meant much to Elijah Huckleberry.

"Wait, is Neil here?" Elijah asked, "Because if he is, I'd love to talk to him. And hey, maybe I could help."

Lena shrugged. "No, sorry. He's still out of town. But Tom gave me his number and, you know, we've been chatting."

Another white lie. She'd only spoken with Neil Patel once and that was to give him more information into her own background so that he could do some real digging. Once again, she could see the wheels turning in Elijah's head and she knew exactly where the locomotive would stop.

"Hey, listen," he said, "we're all in this together, right?"

"Right," said Lena, smiling on the inside.

Elijah flipped open a laptop and started clicking away. "Have you heard some of the stories about Neil and the trouble he and Cal got into?"

"I've heard some of them," Lena said.

"Well, if Neil Patel could get away with stuff, I guess I could... wait. Here it is." Elijah turned the laptop so she could see the screen.

She memorized the address in an instant. "Okay, cool. I promise not to say anything." She then did something completely unforgivable: she leaned down, gave him a kiss on the cheek, and said, "You're much cooler than Neil Patel, you know that, right?"

Elijah Huckleberry flushed deep crimson and before he could reply, Lena was skipping out of the Batcave.

CHAPTER FORTY-EIGHT

STERN - WASHINGTON, D.C.

He marched into the congressman's office without knocking. The old walrus looked up from whatever trashy book he was reading today. The old man loved anything by James Patterson and Ira wanted to spit on him because of it.

"Do you need something, Ira?" the old man said.

"I'd like to talk to you about the CIA situation."

The congressman's face went sour. "I thought I told you to let go of your little pet project, Ira."

Ira Stern never liked the way the congressman said his name—Ira. Like it was what you called the wart on a baboon's ass.

"Sir, I think if you take a look at my notes, you'll see that the president has been—"

The congressmen held up his hand. "We've been over this, Ira. Let it go. The president is doing what he can. He's told me himself and I believe him."

Stern somehow resisted the urge to stomp his foot like his

grandfather used to do when he got angry. "Sir, if you'll just let me explain."

Now the old man rose, something he didn't often do these days. He was a former offensive lineman from Penn State and his frame towered over the diminutive Ira Stern. There was strength there and Ira saw every ounce of it.

"I'm going to lunch, Ira, and when I get back, I expect to never hear about this again. Am I understood?"

Ira was glad there were no weapons within arm's reach because he was pretty sure that he would have done a kamikaze charge, even if the congressmen had stomped him to smithereens. Somehow, he was able to say, "Yes, sir" and move aside as the congressman went on his way.

Ira waited a full minute and then closed the door and stayed in the congressman's office. This should be his. He had the ambition that the retiring congressman no longer did. He had the will and he had the way. He could wait the year until his boss was gone. Maybe latch onto another congressman, maybe even a senator, but then the results might be the same. They all looked at him like the Brooklyn Jew that he was. And even though he was deep Republican and wanted to smash the Democrats into little pieces, they still treated him like he played for the other side.

He'd never admit that his current job had been a favor, or that he would never have gotten it if the congressman hadn't been on his last term. But it was a foot in the door. His boss, though aging and halfway to pasture, was still influential, and that influence was passed down to his subordinates. Ira had learned to use that influence, but now he realized he needed to be more careful not to use his boss's name unless it was utterly necessary.

Still, if he could be the man who took down President Brandon Zimmer, there were accolades to be had. They would look at him differently then. This was the way that he would prove himself—tear down a fellow Northeasterner and grab the trophy for the Republican Party. They would be begging for him to run Congress, Senate, maybe even the White House one day. Though, from the mess he'd seen on Pennsylvania Avenue, he didn't know if he really wanted that, but his ego did.

He went to his own office and placed a call to Director Flap. Edmond was not in the office and his secretary would not say when he would return. Ira waited fifteen minutes, then thirty, heard the congressmen return and locked his office door.

Forty-five minutes, an hour, and still Edmond Flap did not return his phone call. Patience, Ira, have patience.

Patience was one of those gifts that he worked for but had yet to receive.

There was still a card he had in play. It was like one of those jokers you normally took out of the deck before a round of Texas Hold 'em, one you only kept in play if you were crazy.

Maybe Ira Stern was a little crazy. Stir crazy for sure. Crazy for more. More power, more big decisions, more Democrats to send on their way.

At an hour and thirty minutes after calling director Flap's office, Ira Stern made another call. He had met the man during a retreat in Israel. It turned out they lived three blocks apart as kids and never met. While Ira had gone into the family business and then politics, his new friend had gone into the army. Then one night after a few too many drinks, had admitted that he was a spy for the CIA. Through the years, he'd climbed up the CIA ladder and was now in a position where he could provide Ira with a tasty morsel of intel here and there whenever he asked for one. This friend had been the one to recommend Edmond Flap and the rest of that part was history.

He called his friend at the CIA and asked for any update on the missing spy.

"I'll see what I can find, Ira. Give me a day."

Ira thanked the man, told him to say hello to his wife, and then ended the call.

There, that was better now. It was high time someone did Ira Stern's bidding. His blood pressure settled. Now, with the medicine running through his veins, he could wait.

And instead of stewing, he got back to work.

CHAPTER FORTY-NINE

STOKES - MOSCOW

He shouldn't have been surprised when he saw Daniel Briggs waiting on the tarmac. Cal had to reach back home to get strings pulled in order to fly to Russia. He assumed Daniel was there to help. Cal would never call him his babysitter, but he freely admitted that there have been times when Daniel Briggs had saved his life.

"Daniel, you remember my Uncle Adam."

The two men shook hands while Liberty nuzzled up against Cal's leg. Her tail wagged—*thump, thump, thump*—as he smoothed down her dark coat.

"I missed you too, girl," Cal said. He looked up at Daniel. "So where's the rest of the welcome wagon?"

"I have no idea," Daniel said. "This is just a coincidence."

Cal cocked his head. "I guess I assumed that you came because I called back to SSI."

Daniel shook his head and then told Cal about the dustup in Florida and the fact that every trail seemed to lead back to Moscow. Not to mention that, for all he knew, Aleksander

Volkov had been the one to know that Cal was coming. That didn't sit well with Cal. And so, when Daniel suggested that they go meet their secretive host, Cal was more than onboard.

He'd spent months thinking about the mysterious man from Belarus. No matter how much digging Neil had done, he couldn't find anything on the man. Maybe some of his history would come from the man himself.

The driver of their blacked-out Mercedes sedan weaved in and out of traffic, pushing a 120 mph at times. Daniel didn't seem to be worried, so that meant Cal didn't have to worry. The sniper was Cal's fair-weather barometer.

When they arrived at the sparkling high rise, the Mercedes zoomed into the underground lot, an impressive gate closing behind. There was a two-man security detail waiting, but they didn't go as far as to search Cal or his uncle.

The elevator went up to the tenth floor of the twenty-floor building, where more security greeted them. This time wands were waved over their bodies and when they found a weapon on Cal's person, they took it, inspected it, and looked him over. He just shrugged in return. He wasn't going to allow them to keep it. The main guard looked him in the eye, and Cal thought he saw the hint of a smirk on the man's face as he handed the weapon back to him.

Cal fully expected to walk into the house of some czar. Priceless gilded paintings all over the walls. While the apartment they entered was expansive, it was also empty. Every window was taped over with black paper, and there was a folding table in one corner with four chairs, one currently occupied by none other than Alek Volkov.

"Please join me," he said without rising as smoke curling from his cigarette created a dingey sort of halo around his head.

Cal, Daniel, and Uncle Adam sat down in the rickety folding chairs. Volkov watched them for an uncomfortable moment.

"You going to deal, or should I?" Cal said, not much in the mood for silent power games.

"How fortuitous it is that we all get to meet today," said Volkov, dispassionately ignoring the comment. "I've had a day or two to spend with your friend Daniel, and he's been kind enough to fill me in on the current troubles that he's had. But by your entrance, one can only assume that you've come to our lovely capital for another reason."

So Volkov didn't know everything after all. Either that or he was waiting for Cal to divulge the reason for their meeting. Maybe this was a perfect test for their budding friendship. It turned out that Uncle Adam was the first to make that decision.

"We're looking for a woman. They call her the Duchess."

Volkov's eyes widened ever so slightly. "I am aware of the Duchess. She's American, no?"

Uncle Adam nodded. "She is."

Volkov stubbed out his cigarette, even though it was only half-burned, and ran a long-fingered hand through his blonde hair. "By the look you're giving me, I can only assume that you also know that she's currently in Moscow. This woman, the Duchess, why do you want her?"

Cal and his uncle exchanged a look. Then Cal explained. "We believe she's behind the killing of American spies."

"Several of my friends," Uncle Adam added.

Volkov nodded thoughtfully. "I am sorry for your loss. How I wish there were ways to curtail such unpleasantries in our line of work. And while I wish I could help you, I'm sorry to say that I cannot."

Uncle Adam leaned forward. "Cannot or will not?"

Once again, Volkov nodded his appreciation of the question. "Fine distinction. But I will say that I cannot, although I wish I could. You see this woman, Virginia Walton, the woman you call the Duchess—she is involved with an operation that, would it become known, would destroy my entire cover. I've spent decades building it, and in a heartbeat it would be gone, shattered. I cannot have a part in whatever play it is you wish to put on. I will, of course, lend you any resource I can. But intelligence on this particular topic..." he exhaled heavily. "I wish it were different."

Just then there was a commotion from the door. A woman screamed indignation. Everyone's eyes went to the door. Cal caught sight of Volkov's expression—more curious than concerned.

The door opened and a familiar face appeared there. Then a second.

Blonde and beautiful Lena, and the one and only Elijah Huckleberry.

Lena's face was in a snarl, while Huckleberry's was flustered to say the least. He tripped over his own feet coming across the threshold and one of the security detail had to grab him by the back of the collar to steady him.

"My, my," Volkov said, "You didn't tell me we were expecting more company."

"Mr. Briggs, Mr. Stokes, I can explain," Elijah Huckleberry said.

Cal raised a hand. "It's okay." He looked at Lena. "What are you doing here?"

Her snarl was gone, replaced by a cute sweetness, and her words dripped with honey when she spoke.

"I thought Daniel might need some help."

Daniel was the first to laugh. "So, you thought you'd hop on a plane and fly to Moscow to help me?"

Lena shrugged like it was the most natural thing to do. Hack the system, find out where one of the bosses has been, and follow them across the world. This young lady was full of surprises. Once again, if Daniel Briggs wasn't concerned, neither was Cal Stokes.

Cal hadn't realized that Volkov had risen from the seat and had walked around the table.

"Lena, how good to meet you. My name is Alek."

"You're the one, aren't you?" Lena said. "The one Daniel told me about."

Volkov looked at Daniel, who nodded. "This is a surprise, and had I known that you were coming I would have—"

Lena interrupted, "Baked a cake?"

Volkov smiled. "Not exactly."

"Introduced me to my parents?"

His face went grave. "In due time, yes. But alas, they do not live in Moscow and the trip to meet them would be long and at this moment I cannot be your escort." Volkov turned back to the others. "I've had a moment to think, and if you let me spend some time with the fair Lena, maybe I can look into the whereabouts of your friend."

Everyone looked to Lena.

Like the self-confident young adult that she was, she shrugged and said, "Whatevs."

CHAPTER FIFTY

ADAM STOKES - NEAR LANGLEY, VIRGINIA - 1976

Three nights, no sleep.

How many times could they do that? The CIA trainers seemed to take great relish at beating down their new recruits. At every turn they called them hippies or counterculture specialists, sometimes even socialists and communists. The funny thing being that those weren't really insults. They were the truth, plain and simple. Maybe not entirely for Adam Stokes, but this was his small family now.

They were somewhere rural, bunked in a barn littered with hay and mouse droppings. It was noon and too hot to be in a barn, but Adam was too tired to walk out and find a tree to fall asleep under. They had been given a day of rest for their accomplishments, and Adam could see that the instructors were showing small signs that they were impressed. Not a single recruit that he and Virginia had brought from Paris had dropped out. Those first days had been awful—no sleep, lots of physical training. They all burned through calories while puking up cigarette tar and years of wine consumption. But that had been months ago. And with their bodies now hardened and their minds keen on the task, something very interesting was going on. They gelled and protected one another and came to one another's aid when needed.

The barn door opened and inside stepped the most senior instructor. He was a weathered man that could have been eighty or fifty. He could run for miles and climb a rope like a squirrel.

"Hey kid, you've got a visitor," he said to Adam, and he was gone, off to run a marathon before the next day.

Adam somehow pushed his weary, sweat-soaked body off the cot and trudged to the door. The sun hit him in the face when he opened it. It felt like a sucker punch to the jaw. Maybe next week when they left for the city, things would be easier, cooler at least. Adam was looking forward to it. He wasn't sure which city they'd be going to, but they had already been studying how to run surveillance, how to nab a target, and how to drop messages. He slurped it up like Campbell's Chicken Noodle Soup. But right now, all he could think about was sleep and who was depriving him of it.

But it was that sliver of intrigue that got him to trudge from the barn to the farmhouse that the instructors used as their base of operations. He heard laughter coming from inside. Strange, there hadn't been much laughter save for when one recruit fell on his face. It might've been sadistic, but the instructors were nothing but professional.

The laughing? Why the laughing? The three steps up to the stoop felt like climbing Mount Kilimanjaro. He ran through the list of people who could be visiting and came up short. No one knew he was here. He looked back toward the barn and saw a group of his peers returning from the showers. Glenda Younger waved to him and he waved back.

More laughter from inside. He rapped on the door twice as they'd been taught.

"Come in," someone said.

It was dark inside. Cigar smoke assaulted him when he stepped in. He couldn't immediately see who was in the room. More chuckles, like someone was still chewing on the last joke. And then Adam saw him—his brother, Calvin, not in uniform like the last time he saw him, but in civilian clothes that were nonetheless spit-polished and pressed.

"Hi," Calvin said.

"Hello," Adam answered back.

He looked at the instructors. One of them said, "I wish I had known this hippy was a brother of a Marine. Maybe I wouldn't have given him such a hard time."

"I don't need special treatment," Adam said, the rage quick to boil. His brother looked at the instructors who nodded and left the farmhouse. Since when was Calvin in charge? What the hell was going on here?

The door behind him closed and Calvin took a seat. "You look good," he said. "How's the training going?"

Adam crossed his arms over his chest. "For some reason, you're playing the Grand Poobah. Why don't you tell me?"

His brother's lips went thin for a moment, then back to normal. "Look, I'm not checking up on you. I promise. But it wouldn't have hurt to drop mom and dad a line every once in a while. What has it been, three years?"

Adam shook his head. "It doesn't matter. Why should they care where I am?"

"They're your parents, Adam. Give them a break, will you?"

Adam honestly didn't know why he was so upset. Maybe it was because Calvin seemed to be one step ahead yet again.

What had the guy really done wrong, but to show up and say hi?

Adam moved his hands from his chest to his pockets. "So, what are you doing here?"

Calvin's face softened. "Just passing through town. Had some time on leave between duty stations and I thought I'd say hi."

Adam grunted. "And somehow you knew I was here?"

"Look, I can't tell you how I knew you were here, so let's just put that aside. Can we talk as brothers? I've missed you."

Those three words washed the rest of the anger away.

"How are a mom and dad?" Adam asked. "I'm sure they think I'm a real shit son."

His brother chuckled softly. "Now why would you say that?"

"Come on. You said it yourself. I haven't talked to them in like three years. What kind of a son does that?"

Calvin rose from the chair. "Your world got flipped upside down, little brother. They understand. All they want is to make sure that you're safe and that you're happy. I can tell them that you're safe, if that's okay. But are you happy?"

The flood of emotion that hit Adam made him feel like he was thirteen again. "Yeah. You can tell them I'm happy and that I'm doing something that matters. Can you tell them that?"

Adam didn't know why, but that seemed important. Deep down he knew that maybe that's what it had been all about the whole time. He wanted to do something that mattered—to protect his country.

Calvin smiled. "Of course I'll tell them. And hey, your instructors say you're a whiz with a pistol. I'd like to see you shoot some time."

Adam nodded, distrusting of his own ears. He wanted to

step across that endless chasm between them and hug his brother—the man who had been his best friend, who protected and loved him.

The farmhouse door opened and none other than Virginia Walton stepped in.

"Adam, it's time to go," she said, her voice full of high and mighty.

Calvin, ever the polite one, said, "Hi, I'm Calvin Stokes, Adam's brother," and shot out a rod-straight arm.

Virginia refused the handshake and fixed him with a death stare. "I know who you are. Adam's told me all about you. Now, if you don't mind, we've got work to do."

There was no work to do and Adam knew it. They were finished for the day.

He was suddenly confused, torn. There was his brother, the one he'd known since the day he came into this world, solid and always there. But then there was Virginia—the passion, the love, the excitement. And not for the last time in his life, a decision he made on the spot would have long-ranging repercussions.

He left the farmhouse with Virginia, and without another word to his brother.

CHAPTER FIFTY-ONE

FLAP - ARLINGTON, VIRGINIA

Meetings, meetings, and more meetings. That's what his life had become. There were the meetings with politicians who thought they owned the CIA. There were the meetings with business leaders who thought they could bend the CIA to get whatever information they needed. There were the meetings with spies and there were the meetings with the uber-wealthy, some who were merely curious, others who were no doubt trying to figure out how they could bend Flap to their will. It shouldn't have surprised him, but it did. Especially the fact that anyone else in his position could use the influence to become ridiculously wealthy. Some nights he ticked back through the old CIA directors, trying to figure out which one of them had used the intelligence that came across their desk every day to build a fortune. The international intelligence that had come in reports in the past week alone could have made Flap millions. No temptation there. It was much better to be a eunuch amongst mere mortals who could be tempted by the many forbidden fruits bestowed upon humanity.

He checked his phone as soon as he got into the armored vehicle and frowned when he saw not one, but ten text messages from Ira Stern. The New York Republican was getting close to poking one of Flap's nerves. Luckily, the director of the CIA saw the would-be politician as nothing more than a disposable snot rag to be discarded after use. And what the Ira Stern couldn't seem to fathom was that he was one of myriad minnows in a shark tank the size of Montana. But that didn't mean he wouldn't have to be dealt with... in due time.

He checked his other messages and frowned again when he saw that the most important intelligence he'd been waiting for was still not there. A piece of the broader puzzle had yet to make it to his hand, but it would come. Yegorovich had pulled the trigger too early in Florida and his quarry had gotten away. Flap only had bits and pieces of what had happened. Two Russian assassins dead. No video, no photography, just a minor disturbance in a normally quiet beach town. But who had been with her? Flap didn't know and nor did the authorities. He still had to be careful on American soil even though the FBI and local police could contribute to his broader knowledge. He had contacts everywhere, but it wasn't like buying the testimony from some vendor who'd witnessed a crime on the streets of Beirut. American streets were different.

In Baghdad, you could kill a man for his business and nary a soul would bat an eye, but in America there were rules. There were laws, though Flap sometimes wondered how long those laws would last. Imagine the outrage of the populace at the news of a donut shop owner killed for her business. America was not prepared for anarchy of this sort.

Flap shook his head, getting rid of the random mental wanderings. He really should place a call to Stern. Let him think that he still had the CIA on the hook—even though it was very much in reverse. The sheer volume of correspondence showed that Stern was close to boiling and needed to be tempered. A hotheaded Stern would make a boneheaded move. His boss had already made mention of it though Flap doubted that the congressman had mentioned their private conversation to Stern.

The congressman was much like Flap, undeterred in his path, not really caring what Stern did, but still standing for what was right. He was of the old breed and would be gone soon and that was fine with Flap. He didn't care a lick for old or new breeds. He wrestled with them all. And then by wonder of wonders, miracle of miracles, his phone jangled with that familiar number.

"Director Flap," he answered.

"Sir, I have the president on the line for you."

"Please put him through. Thank you."

The president's voice came through: "I hope I'm not disturbing you, Edmond."

"No sir. I just sat through my last meeting of the day. How can I be of service?"

He heard the president exhale. "If I could only have ten more of you, Edmond. Anyway, I need a favor."

It wasn't every day that the president called to ask a favor.

"I'm all ears, Mr. President."

"I really shouldn't be asking you this, but I have a friend who needs to hitch a ride—if you know what I mean."

"Who is your friend, and where would your friend like to go?"

The president told him and Flap smiled.

"I'm happy to make that happen, sir. If you'll send me your friend's information, I'll have my people make contact."

"That's very good. Very good. Thank you, Edmond. And I know I don't have to say this, but if we could keep this between us."

Again, Flap smiled. "Of course, Mr. President. Anything you say to me stays with me unless you say otherwise."

"And you'll let me know how it goes."

"Absolutely, Mr. President. I'll be in touch."

The line went dead. Flap sat back in his seat, his body momentarily jostled by one of many constant potholes in and around the Washington, D.C. area, but he didn't care. Kindness and helpfulness brought him the answer. How novel. The note he sent was short and innocuous to all but the recipient:

"Your Christmas present is coming early. I'll let you know when I have the shipping details."

A couple of calls to set things up and Edmond Flap was in for a night of pleasant dreams, clean thoughts, and deep breaths. A big step in the right direction and a massive stone unturned. Flap wondered what plans President Yegorovich had for Anna Varushkin and what the political landscape might look like once he had those billions in hand.

CHAPTER FIFTY-TWO

VOLKOV - MOSCOW

He weaved in and out of traffic for the first fifteen minutes waiting to see if Lena would say something, anything. She didn't. Instead, she stared straight ahead, barely blinking her eyes. He knew because he checked. Complete and utter commitment to staring straight ahead was impressive.

"The last time I saw you, you were only a baby," he said, shattering the silence as he sped around a truck that looked like it had entered service back in the Cold War.

"Oh," she answered.

So it was going to be that way. That was fine with Volkov. He had patience too.

"Yes," he said, "you were the prettiest little thing. Why, I remember the first time your father insisted that I change your diaper."

Lena raised her hand. "You can stop there. I don't need to know the details."

Volkov chuckled. "Are you sure? It would tell you so much about me."

She turned now, facing him completely. The level of intensity with which she leveled her eyes was impressive. "You think I came with you to find out how nasty my diapers were?"

"Well, maybe not that detail in particular, but—"

She raised her hand again. "But nothing. Tell me about my mother." And then, as if she realized how rude she'd been, she added: "Please."

Volkov nodded, gripping a little tighter onto the steering wheel. "Your mother was beautiful. Like you. Smart—I'm assuming like you as well. She graduated from university at the top of her class, and twice went to the Olympics as a gymnast."

"What event did she compete in?"

Volkov grunted, maybe now he had her. "She was good at it all, but excelled at the balance beam and the uneven bars. She was a strong, tiny thing."

"Was she Russian or Soviet?" Lena asked.

Fine question, Volkov thought. "Both and neither. Do you know where we're from?"

"Belarus," she answered. "They were under Soviet rule, but now they are separate countries, right?"

"To a point, yes. But the Russians will never release their claim on us. Even now, our woeful leaders are trying to conduct an election and Moscow can't help but insert its will."

Lena grunted. "So, what—it's all about control, money, or resources?"

"How about all of the above," he said.

Lena nodded and let her gaze drift out the side window to where a line of school children was being marched down the sidewalk. "Tell me more about my family. And tell me why you do what you do."

He knew what she meant. Volkov had told Daniel and Cal about his position in the Russian spy agency—deep mole status—and apparently they'd told Lena. That was fine. He would have told her in due time.

And so he told her everything. How he'd been selected at a young age to ski for Mother Russia and the Olympics. How he'd been found by his mentor, Orlov. How he'd been told about their true origins, about the despicable program instilled by Hitler himself—the Lebensborn—breeding the master race. How, when those kidnapped children returned to Belarus they'd been shunned, spat on, forced to live on the outskirts of society, or killed, and how brave men and women had banded together to care for those children. And how the descendants of the organization had bloomed from tragedy and that this was the organization over which Volkov now presided.

He told her about the archaic mating rituals that had once been used, now symbolic, and how modern fertilization techniques made it so their lineage could reproduce without the awkward trappings of an arranged marriage.

"So, what, was I born in a test tube?" Lena asked.

Volkov wanted to ask her what she felt in her soul was the answer to that, but stopped himself, figuring it an inappropriate question.

"Your mother and father loved each other dearly," he said. "You were born through their love—natural conception. I considered them my brother and sister. So, when you were taken, it was as if my own daughter had been stolen. Can you imagine such a thing, Lena?"

She looked at him again, her eyes a mixture of anger and indignation. "Of course I can imagine it. The only man I knew as a father was taken from me." She paused, an obvious question brewing in her. And then, "Why?"

"Why was he taken from you?"

"No, why did he take me?"

And here was a hard conversation. Volkov had hoped they could have gotten to know each other a little better before the truth came out. But sometimes truth had a way of creeping to the surface at the most inopportune time. But Volkov was prepared as it was the story that he wanted to tell Lena ever since he found out she was alive.

"Your father was once a good man, my good friend. He was one of the best athletes and shooters I'd ever seen. But you know this, of course—he trained you. And from what I've heard, you picked up some wonderful things from this man." He wanted to ask her if she'd been treated kindly, but he figured that she had, that the man who turned to kidnapping had found his humanity after all.

"We may never know what really caused his break. We can guess that the missions got to him, or that he had some type of mental disorder. It was a long time ago. He fell in love with a girl, or at least that is what he told us. She was going to have a baby. But at some point, his mental break turned into physical abuse. This woman was not your mother, Lena. She was another of our people, someone that we never got to bury, never got to say goodbye to—and this was when his path crossed with Cal Stokes's father. It was Berlin. And out of the goodness of his heart, Calvin Stokes, Sr. tried to save this woman. And he almost succeeded. But she was killed during the rescue by a party we will never find. Unfortunately, that fact is lost to history. But the elder Stokes's action further riled your father. He hid it well for a time being. But then I found out that he had been tracking the American, using our resources for his own private, personal vendetta.

"I confronted him about it. He tried to play it off, tried to say it was part of some other thing he was working on at the time. But, he could not convince me. This was personal. Deeply personal. And he was given a warning. Remember this had been years after Stokes's intervention in Berlin. More years passed. I thought my friend had returned to us with his sanity intact. But then one night when your very own mother went to check on you, she found that you were gone, taken by this man who would soon pass himself off as your father. I have no doubt that he loved you and cared for you, but he also trained you to be his weapon. And he almost succeeded."

"He did succeed," Lena said. She was crying now, trying not to look at him. "I killed a man. He told me to kill a man and I did."

"I know the man of whom you speak, and I can only say that in killing him, you saved the life of another."

"You mean Cal," she said, sniffling.

"I do. Whatever your father wanted to do to Cal Stokes is now over and done. And you should consider your own role in his vendetta an innocent one. I've spoken with Daniel and Cal at length and they've told me of your progress. I suspect it won't be long before they ask you to join them."

She brightened at that. "They're good people, you know. I was really mad when they first got me. Like, really mad. But now it feels like the most natural thing. It's the reason that I had to come to Moscow. It didn't seem right that Daniel would just take off by himself. And I'm pretty sure Anna is upset about it."

"Who is Anna?"

Lena wiped her eye with the back of her hand. "Oh, she's only the most glamorous woman I've ever met. I'm pretty sure she's in love with Daniel, and Daniel's probably in love with her."

And just like the young adult she was, she turned a full one-eighty. "So, what do I call you anyway? I don't think I want to call you uncle."

"How about just Alek?"

"Alek," she said. "Like with a C, or with a K?"

"With a K," he said with a light laugh.

And with the formalities of their story behind them, they settled in for the rest of the ride, exchanging old stories. Lena asked about her mother, but not her father for some reason. Volkov didn't push. He wasn't ready to go there yet. He settled into his storytelling ways and enjoyed the conversation more than he'd enjoyed any conversation in years.

CHAPTER FIFTY-THREE

WILCOX - BORA BORA, FRENCH POLYNESIA

Crystalline waters stretched as far as the eye could see. Three steps out the front door and he would be swimming with tropical fish. It had been part of his daily routine for weeks, but Matthew Wilcox was getting bored.

"Bored as a gourd in a fjord," he said, lifting a tiny ceramic elephant off the end table and staring into its cartoonish eyes. "And I'm going to stab you with a toothpick, you squat little bastard." He exhaled sharply. "Nahhh, you can live. You don't even belong here. We're the same in that regard. The fauna and flora of ol' Bora Bora."

He snorted, placed the tchotchke back on the table, and tried desperately to ignore the fact that he was now attempting to converse with inanimate objects.

He couldn't be blamed for it. Up until this point, his life had been a whirl of nonstop movement. Jetting off to one country to kill a man, then off to some beautiful island like where he was now so that he could refresh, maybe enjoy some female companionship, and to plan his next kill. Only now, something was wrong, and for weeks he'd been trying to ignore that fact. One tiny, teeny-weeny, itsy-bitsy little problem. It had all started with the Arctic. A perfect plan run to perfect perfection. He'd had the Russian president in his hand. And how sweet it had been when he looked down at that piece of garbage, ready to take the final shot and blow his borscht brains all over the clean, white snow.

Matthew Wilcox wasn't a man that thought about repercussions, about what happens when you cut off the Hydra's head. If two more popped up, he'd kill those, too. Thus, he hadn't seen anything wrong with killing President Yegorovich. Good ol' Konstantin had had his fun, but was death and burial in some unmarked Canadian grave to be his fate? No siree, Bobotchka. Wilcox was subdued and then all hell broke loose.

He remembered every detail with the clarity of a man who could not forget such things, one that made it his daily duty to recall the day and refresh his hatred anew. Death was the marker of his life. Death was what got him up in the morning. Death was what paid him. Death, always death. And yet the death of Diane Mayer, though it hadn't necessarily changed something in Matthew Wilcox, had sparked an old flame, something that was always there yet trying to remain hidden: compassion.

The compassion was for his friend, Cal Stokes. As Cal wrapped his hands around his dead girlfriend, Wilcox ran off toward the origin of the sniper fire. He had the prick in his sights, and it had taken every ounce of skill in his human arsenal, wrapping his own hands around the sniper's neck, and then—poof!

Nothing.

When he'd woken up, he looked into the eyes of an old friend. Well, not a friend, but someone who he'd met casually in the Philippines. He'd called himself George then, but by now Wilcox knew the man's name was Alexander Volkov.

The swiftness with which Volkov snatched Wilcox still amazed the wily assassin. They hammered him pretty hard with questions. He dodged each one with his usual caginess. Jokes were his forte. And he liked to think that this was the reason he'd never once been touched. They left him in a comfortable room by himself with no less than four cameras staring at him. He danced before them. Taunted them with idiotic little jokes.

"Uh, now, eventually, you plan to have dinosaurs on your dinosaur tour, right? Hello? Hello?"

For whatever reason—call it luck or the fact that they were tired of his crap—eventually he'd been let go. And off he went with the uneasy feeling that for the week that he'd been in captivity, he'd been something of a spectacle, like an ideal specimen of the human species put in a private viewing room for aliens. Slither right this way and see the rare Homo sapiens in his natural habitat.

Very few things unnerved Matthew Wilcox. One, was lack of control. Two was a joke with no punchline. Three... well, whatever had happened with Volkov sent shivers down the backs of his legs.

And now, here he lingered in Bora Bora talking to ceramic tchotchkes. He wondered how many people could say that.

Five, four, three, two, one.

"Get up, you lazy sack," he said to himself, hopping to his feet, running out the open door, and diving into the ocean. He swam straight to the bottom, grabbed onto one of the wooden pylons of the house and sat there for a full three minutes. The only reason he didn't stay longer was that he heard the tinny hum of a boat coming his way. That would be breakfast—fresh fruit and a ceviche, prepared with loving delicacy by a chef who should probably be cooking in Paris or London.

He climbed up the ladder and waved to the boat as it came near. The chef herself, as swarthy as any sea pirate, held the platter up in one hand.

"You should eat more," she said, "you're getting skinny."

Wilcox patted his flat stomach. "Madam, you happen to be speaking to the ideal specimen of the human species. Besides, I'm a poster boy for Jenny Craig. They get uppity when you start packing on the pounds."

The woman shook her head and handed the platter up to Wilcox. All his favorites—plenty of pineapple, mango, an assortment of cured meats, and of course the chef's secret ceviche recipe. It was so good that he could have killed her for it. Not that he would. He was no savage. Besides, art tended to die hard along with the relatively easy death of the artist. There was something too important about that fact to give him pause. And here he was, thinking philosophically about killing a chef over ceviche.

With a deep bow, he said, "My dear, it won't be long now before I marry you and whisk you away so that you can cook for me like this forever."

The veteran chef tried to suppress a smile, but she let out a snort, "You're too much." And she waved him away and the boat sped off, on to deliver the next meal.

Once he'd finished his breakfast, capping it off with a jigger of rare rum he'd found in Bermuda, he did something that he hadn't done since that week of casual street fighting in Indonesia—he checked his computer.

There were plenty of messages, plenty of offers, updates

regarding targets he'd been tracking for months, sometimes years. What normal people didn't understand was that with a little force and maybe a few threats, there was plenty of money to be taken out there. Money Wilcox had plenty of. Now it was adventure that pulled him from target to target. But it wasn't what he wanted, as he scrolled through the files and reports whipping by on his computer. No, he wanted to know one very important thing—where to find Cal Stokes.

And thanks to some very high-tech and expensive surveillance, he soon knew where the heir of Stokes Security International was. Moscow, of all places.

What the hell was he doing in Moscow?

He checked a few more sources and sure enough, Daniel Briggs was in Moscow, too. Probably nothing to it, and probably something that Wilcox should stay out of for now. The enigmatic duo of Stokes and Briggs had caused him enough trouble for the year. He'd stay in Bora Bora for another year and then make contact again. His eyes went to the end table and settled on his little ceramic conversation partner. No, the boredom was too much. There was the pull of mystery that lured him.

And then he saw that President Konstantin Yegorovich was in Moscow.

Hmmmm...

Wilcox had special plans for that mighty prick. The Russians themselves could just as well go to hell in his opinion.

He closed his laptop, sprang to his feet, and repeated his run and perfect dive into the ocean. He let out all his air this time, sinking to the bottom. And there he sat, conditioning his lungs, tuning out the rest of the world. In time he'd go back to the surface and think about whether a trip to

Moscow might be warranted, or whether this time he might let things lie.

Matthew Wilcox was not a let-things-lie kind of guy, and the thought of that would make him smile.

For now, he sat weightless, feeling the burn on his lungs, clenching his fists.

CHAPTER FIFTY-FOUR

STOKES - MOSCOW

Uncle Adam wasn't happy with the arrangement, but what could he say? Cal and Daniel were the operators. They needed to go in, nab the Duchess, and then figure out what to do. But they still took their time.

Elijah Huckleberry monitored the location with every technological gizmo he could bring to bear. Daniel did his magic—hitting the streets, sniffing around, watching. Cal absorbed it all until he was ready to press go. Once they did, there was no turning back.

Liberty whined when Cal told her to stay with Elijah Huckleberry.

"Don't worry, Mr. Stokes, I'll take care of her," Huckleberry said.

"It's not me who needs the convincing."

"Might be good cover taking a dog along," the tech wiz added. "Plus, she can get into places you can't."

"Trust me, I thought about that," Cal said, giving Liberty

a final roughing up of the ears. "I'd love to take her, but this is Moscow, not the fields of Virginia."

The building was a Soviet-era relic that had recently been refurbished. Renovations were still happening on one side of the building, and while the taste was a bit too much East German for Cal, he could appreciate the work that had been done. It wasn't easy to turn a concrete eyesore into a modern masterpiece, which was what the building truly was inside.

Construction crews had gone home for the night. This sudden cease of machine noise, along with the absence of residents, made the place hum with a certain eeriness. It was like a movie theater that had been suddenly evacuated, all the patrons having left their things behind, the echoes of their lives still on the air. The place had a real ghost town feel, bolstered by the fact that every scan that Huckleberry did and every tingle in Daniel's unique senses told them that the building was empty.

The unit they entered, the location provided by Volkov himself, was a spacious two-story condominium. The furniture inside was still covered in white sheets and someone had left a patching job in the living room, the ladder still sitting there beneath the repaired drywall.

They spread out, taking their time, trying to detect any signs of life. Cal didn't know why, but the place gave him the creeps.

"You think this place is haunted?" Cal asked Daniel when they'd rejoined in the kitchen. "I thought I saw Khrushchev drinking a glass of kvass in the other room."

Daniel gave him one of those looks.

"I'm kidding," Cal said, unable to hide the dash of nerves in his chuckle.

"Pull yourself together, Marine," said the sniper.

They found a hiding spot with a perfect view of the front

door. Daniel unlocked the sliding glass door that led to the balcony, should they need that escape route. They were only on the second floor. A drop to the street wasn't life-threatening. They hadn't known what to expect, so they went in fully armed, prepared. They would either kill her or take her in. Cal preferred the latter.

While Uncle Adam was sure of the Duchess's involvement in the killing of American spies, Cal would rather wait and see.

An hour, then two. Nighttime was full on now. Flashy cars zoomed by below, blaring music on their way to some trendy club.

Three hours, four. Cal was about to call it off. Maybe Volkov's intelligence had been faulty. It wouldn't be the first time. That was the way these things worked.

Daniel hadn't moved. How did he do that? And what did he think about during those long hours? Cal's inner monologue went something like this: "When the hell was this woman going to get here already? The cramp in my leg is getting worse. I'm getting too old for this. I wonder if Diane was in pain when she died?" And that leveled him into an internal conversation he'd been having, whether personal connections vibed with his way of life.

He'd lost so much and yet he loved what he did, for he felt that he'd really made a difference. But was it this and only this that propelled him forward? Or had it been something else? He had to face the truth that, whether it was wiping Islamic fanatics from the face of Iraq, or uprooting crooked politicians, there wasn't much that Cal didn't truly enjoy about the life he led, and that had almost solely to do with the men around him—well, men and women now. Lena could be an interesting addition, but how close was too close? When was a personal relationship towed across that imaginary line, put into something more sacred so that when you lost that person, something in you broke forever? That's how Cal felt now that Diane was gone. He had indeed been put back together and would still hold, but that day on the ice one of those broken pieces had been whisked away into the ether. It was no wonder that those who lose many dear ones in life tend to protect what little pieces they have remaining.

It was just as he was composing his resolute vow to soldier on despite all losses when they heard the shoes—high heels by the sound of it—clicking down the hallway. There was a tense moment when the voices on the other side paused at the front door. And then the door opened. Two people appeared. The first to come inside was dressed all in black, exactly one half of her hair shaved to the scalp, wearing huge, round-rimmed glasses.

She came in waving her hands, gesturing toward pieces of furniture, yammering on in Russian. Right behind came the Duchess. Cal didn't understand a word of Russian, but he got the gist. The first woman with the shaved head was some kind of interior designer, the Duchess, her patron. The other woman was the problem. She could be subdued without much harm, but then there would be a witness. Before he could formulate a plan, the choice was made for him. Apparently, the fashionista wanted to get some air and made a beeline straight for where Cal and Daniel were hiding.

Daniel was first to move, standing with pistol raised, Cal right behind, fanning out wide so they could cut off escape. The fashionista's eyes went wide, nearly encompassing the lenses of the large glasses.

"Have a seat," Cal said, pointing to two sheet-covered chairs.

The fashionista froze. The Duchess barked out an order in Russian and the black-clad woman slowly sat. The Duchess,

Virginia Walton, did not take a seat. What she did do was remove the scarf from her neck and throw it to the ground.

"Americans in Moscow," she said. "What are the odds?"

She didn't look even a little bit scared. Her eyes scanned Daniel and Cal as if she were looking for some sort of opening. She was beautiful, the grace and wisdom of age having sculpted her face to refinement. The moniker of Duchess fit perfectly. All she needed was a crown to cap off the disguise.

"Do we do this the hard way or the easy way?" she asked.

"That depends on you," Cal said, shifting even closer to the front door.

She exhaled, "I'm too old for hard. We should do it the easy way. This one doesn't know anything," she said, pointing at the designer, who Cal was pretty sure was about to have a nervous breakdown. Her leg was going a mile a minute and there was a fluttering whimper coming from her throat.

"Tie her to the chair and do it quickly," Cal said.

The Duchess nodded, took the scarf from the floor and bound the woman to the chair, calmly reassuring her in Russian. The woman's whimpering ceased and she even seemed resolute now.

Daniel checked to make sure that it was secure and then finished the job with some duct tape from his backpack.

The Duchess clasped her hands in front of her. "There, all nice and tidy. Would you like to search me now?"

Cal patted her down from head to toe. Nothing, save for an impressively taut physique. No doubt she could give women half her age a run for their money.

"Where to now?" she asked. "America? Guantanamo Bay? Somewhere less pleasant, perhaps?"

Cal could see that this woman was a hard case, and hard cases were tough nuts to crack. "Who said we're taking you anywhere?"

"You don't look like cold-blooded killers," she said, "And besides, if you're anything like your uncle, compassion is your weakness."

So the rumors about this woman were true. She was good, and she had Cal's identity pegged. That made her a dangerous player. It also made Cal's weapon rise. He leveled the barrel at her chest.

"If you kill me, I can't help you," she said, her face expressionless.

"Help us do what?"

Now she smiled, her teeth perfect and pearly white. "Why, retrieve your uncle, of course. Why else do you think we lured you here, Cal Stokes?"

CHAPTER FIFTY-FIVE

ADAM STOKES - PARIS - 1977

They'd done well, very well. The recruits they found from all over Paris were now scattered throughout the world. They'd completed CIA training and passed with flying colors. Not a man or woman had dropped, and Adam had seen how impressed their instructors had been. He wondered if someone on high was thinking about rewriting the playbook that spies didn't need to come from Ivy League schools, that they could be plucked from just about anywhere given they possessed the right kind of raw talent. And while he took some pleasure in the fact that he had a place in their tight-knit band, he knew the woman lying in his arms was really the one to whom the full credit was due.

Virginia Walton, the woman they dubbed "the Duchess," had looked into the heart and soul of each man and woman and deemed them worthy. It was still hard to believe that she was only a year or two older than he. He hadn't quite pinpointed exactly how old she was. She was secretive about the strangest things. She didn't like to talk about her past. In fact, he wasn't sure if she'd even told the CIA the entire truth. There was something she was hiding, probably some sort of dark pain that he never really wanted to dig up. It was only in those curious moments, when maybe he had a few too many and his courage ran up, that he really wanted to know. And it was for no other reason than he wanted to protect her from it, because Adam Stokes had fallen head over heels in love with this woman, this woman who could be so cold and calculating, and nothing but business.

The first few times they'd been together, passion had been ratcheted high. It was more like the coupling of apex animals —two opposing predators that had found each other. But she'd warmed to him over the years. Sometimes she'd let slip a little detail about her past, a favorite shoe she'd worn at the age of five, a trip taken to the shore, though which shore she never said. All the while she held onto the story that she was firmly Midwest in origin, despite the fact that every mannerism she threw to the world suggested that she'd been raised and molded on the gilded streets of Manhattan.

Virginia stirred and he held her closer. He didn't want this to end. He needed the physical touch as much as he needed food. More so these days, and perhaps that was because they were spending fewer and fewer nights together. Her official cover kept growing by the day. One night, she'd have cocktails with a local business owner. Another, she was sharing a cigarette with the cousin of a prince. He could tell that the royalty was what pulled her.

It was the 1970s and the Middle East had yet to become what it would later be. Years later, Adam Stokes would look back and realize that she'd been right about them all—the Saudis and their oil money, the Afghans and their religious strife, even the Russians and their constant search for identity. His cover was much less glamorous, but still enjoyable.

While Virginia looked the part she played, Adam Stokes was still a young man, and it was hard to cover his innocence with new clothes or a different haircut. So, they played to his strengths. He took over the duty as recruitment officer, though Virginia had a say in each one. But it was good for Adam because while Virginia was away, he'd gotten to know the others, the ones that he would send off wherever Langley wanted to train them, to wherever it was in the world they would end up, and he never forgot a face. It was one of the gifts he'd come to recognize. Faces and names—two important aspects of his new tradecraft.

"I have to go," Virginia said, trying to slide out from his arms.

He held on to her tighter. "I thought you said you didn't have to go until tomorrow."

She pushed again and still he held. "I have to prepare," she said.

When he didn't let go, she pressed her thumb into a particular pressure point just inside his rib cage. He relented and let her go, marveling as she slid from the bed, her elegance even more captivating in the moonlight. She slipped into a robe and he frowned, not ready to give her up just yet.

"What do you have on the docket tomorrow?" he asked, slipping into his own robe and wrapping his arms around her again. He tried to ignore the fact that she stiffened at his touch.

"I'll be gone a week, maybe two," she said.

This was news to Adam. "Back to the States?"

She shook her head and pulled away from his embrace. "I can't say."

It was the same story. He knew they were both spies, but he wanted more. And in that moment, he was ready to do anything to get her to stay. He dropped to one knee and pulled the box from his pocket, holding it out as he opened it. "Don't go."

She'd been facing the bathroom and turned.

Adam didn't know what he should have expected, but it hurt him to no end to see that steel frown in the absence of a smile and tears of joy.

"Get up," she said.

"No. I'm serious. We should get married, run away, live wherever we want."

Her look cut right through him. "Don't be silly, Adam. We're just getting started. We don't have time for this."

"Maybe you don't have time for this, but—"

"No. WE don't have time for this. Are you telling me you want to trash all the work we've done to get here? Do you know what would happen if they found out?"

"I don't care," Adam said honestly.

She let out a laugh. "You really are crazy. You know that? This..." she pointed to him and then to her, "...this is over. You need to get a grip on what you want."

"I want you," he said, getting to his feet, the ring still extended.

She slapped the box out of his hand and the ring went skittering.

He was momentarily shocked, but somehow was able to find words again. "Just tell me why."

At least her face softened this time, actual emotion in her eyes. "I never should have let you into my bed. You don't want me, Adam. You don't want the person I am. I'm not good for you. This has been fun. It really has. But..."

His voice rose. "I'm sick of the games. Why can't you just tell me why you're this way? I thought we were going somewhere together, and now you say it's over? For what? For a job? It's all bullshit, Virginia, and you know that."

"It's not," she screamed and then quickly composed herself. "I was married. Okay?"

He could tell by the way she said it that she wasn't lying. And to him, it really didn't matter. "So what? You were married and didn't tell me. We can get past that."

"Maybe you can, but I can't. Okay?"

He reached out and tried to grab her hand, but she snatched it away.

"Tell me what happened," he said. "Why are you like this?" Her eyes looked at him and he could see the glimmer of fear, then her look went dead.

Like a robot she said, "He wasn't a good man. I thought he was. Everybody said I should marry him. It was fine. He came from money. He was good-looking. He had an important job. I thought I loved him. At least, I loved the *idea* of him. An easy life, no worries about money. We took a sailboat to a private island for our honeymoon. When I first saw it, I thought it was the most beautiful place in the world. Staff would come in the morning and leave after dinner. We were the only two people on the island after dessert. And that first night, that's when he showed me who he really was. He took me by force. And when I resisted, he beat me. Oh, but he wasn't stupid. He never hit my face. We stayed there for two weeks—two weeks of the same horror again and again. As soon the servants were gone, he would pounce. And I soon found that there was nothing I could do but take it. The less I struggled, the less he beat me. Eight months later, I had a miscarriage. I hadn't been home for more than fifteen minutes when he hit me, and this time he did hit me in the face."

Virginia drew a line down her jaw. "He broke it." Then she drew a line above her right eyebrow. "And he hit me over here with a champagne bottle."

All Adam could do was listen in slack-jawed horror.

"On our one-year anniversary," she continued, "he bought me a puppy. He thought it would be good practice for when we had a baby, only I didn't want a baby. I told him that when I lost my baby I had the doctor tie my tubes. The rage built in his face. And he was a big man, a football player. And his big hands came for me, like they always did, to my neck. Only this time, I was ready. I don't know how many times I stabbed him in the stomach. I only know that when I was done, his blood was all over me and he was gasping like a fish on the ground." Virginia inhaled, smoothing the hair at the back of her neck. "I thought I'd go to jail. I thought about killing myself. But... someone saved me. Someone gave me another chance, here, doing this. This is my penance. So you see why I can't leave? You see why I can't love you?"

Adam shook his head. "I don't care. I don't care about any of it. I'm so sorry it happened, but I can be here for you. I can..."

She shook her head and he knew it was the final stake in his heart. "I have to go," she said, "...and I'm sorry. Truly, I am."

She reached out, touched his cheek, and then left before he could say another word. She got dressed and was gone.

She left him to his brokenness, to the horrible echo of that terrible tale, and to think that there was no way he could do this job without her.

CHAPTER FIFTY-SIX

SPRINGER - LAS VEGAS

Yes, Springer had found the gold mine. The trail of Daniel Briggs ended here, but it had provided the most information that he'd found thus far. He'd come to town with only a sketch of the man that even strangers called "Snake Eyes," and now he would leave with a fully painted portrait. Well, fully painted once he'd put his own magnificent artwork on paper. He was already dictating bits and pieces on the rare chance he had a few moments in the hotel. For his entire week in Sin City, he'd spent it on the beat.

It all began with a waitress who thought she remembered a man by the description Springer gave. When he showed her a picture, her eyes lit up.

"Hey, I remember him. He got me out of this really bad jam. You see, I was dating this guy. Awful, subhuman piece of dirt. A serial wife beater. When Snake Eyes found out about it, he came by and well, he told me to leave and told the guy to stay. After three days, he called me and told me to come back. I have no idea what he said or did to that piece of dirt, but the guy was gone. It had taken less than three days from start to finish. Daniel never took credit for it, but I never saw the guy again, like ever. I mean, I heard he was still living here. He owned a house. I heard it got repossessed by the bank."

Then there was a loan shark who had the opposite kind of story. When Springer showed the man Daniel's picture, his face went pale. He pulled the gun from his waist and said, "Get the fuck out of here before I kill you." When he did a little digging on that particular loan shark, he found that years before the man—who'd once owned a chain of pawnshops—had spent an extended period of time in the ICU. The documentation didn't say why or how it had happened, just that the man had sustained, "some sort of fall."

The myth of Daniel Briggs grew with each retelling of a fresh tale. By the time Dirk Springer had conducted no fewer than fifty positive interviews, he was pretty sure Daniel Briggs was the most successful vigilante he'd ever heard of—lives saved, fortunes recovered, children protected.

That was the good side.

The bad side was husbands gone, businesses ruined, and buildings left to crumble from neglect. That was the aftermath of Daniel Briggs, and he'd only spent a handful of years in the city. It was enough for Springer.

While his interviewees would never raise their right hand in the courtroom, they knew they were protected by the solemn vow of a journalist. The only reason Springer would ever have to contact them again is if he wanted to do a follow-up.

Daniel Briggs was the underground legend that would soon hit newsstands around the world. This secret of man, a warrior who had saved so many, this hardcore Robin Hood who'd murdered, hunted, and terrorized, might seek justice or he might not. That wasn't up to Dirk Springer. His only job was to tell the story and oh, what a tale it would be.

It was his last night in Vegas and he made sure to backup and triple backup every piece of information he'd found. And then it was time to celebrate. The models showed up at exactly 11:30 p.m. They came with a sandwich bag of cocaine and a list of hot hangouts that they would be hitting. One night of celebration couldn't hurt. Then it would be back to the real world, back to the story, and back to see how Daniel Briggs would take it.

CHAPTER FIFTY-SEVEN

STERN - WASHINGTON, D.C.

Stern almost bowled over a group of elementary school children when he stormed out of the office. The teacher and guide looked at him for an apology, but all he did was huff at the children and march off on his way. He didn't care about kids. He didn't care about who saw what. All he cared about was that he wasn't getting what he wanted on his timeline, and his timeline was everything. If his grandfather had shown him anything, it was that time mattered. *Control* of time was the thing, and time was playing out of Stern's hand. He thought that after this piddling appointment with his current boss, he would have been elevated to something bigger—a bigger congressman or a bigger senator. But nobody was playing.

Nobody wanted Ira Stern and maybe that was fine. He would go home to Brooklyn and marshal the troops. There were plenty of resources and plenty of people who could hit the streets, grab the phones, give the other politicians an earful. Decades of favors were about to be collected and Ira

Stern didn't give a damn which bridge he burned next. He'd give the old fool he called his boss a piece of his mind, and he figured he might even be fired for it. But he knew the old coot didn't have the balls for it. He also didn't have the brains to see how Stern could be his ally, *the* ally, the man to further cement his own legacy. But no, his boss was a moron, a simpleton whose time had come and gone like a foul wind.

So, Stern did what he always did when he was planning. He speed-walked down the corridors of Congress, avoiding eye contact, mumbling to himself. He was so lost in his own thoughts that he almost ran straight into a guy who could have been a Washington offensive lineman. Stern was surprised when he looked up to see the president in the middle of the hallway surrounded by his security detail.

President Brandon Zimmer was exactly where Ira Stern wanted to be, *deserved* to be. Zimmer was from Massachusetts. His father had been a senator. Adding to that, he was annoyingly good-looking, always on the top of the eligible bachelors' list, even though he looked a little more weathered than when he'd entered the office. But the office did that to any man.

Zimmer looked up from the woman he was talking to, a perfectly sculpted specimen. Stern seemed to remember her name was Haines.

"Ira Stern," Zimmer said, his voice perking the interest of passersby.

Stern had to bite his tongue not to spit venom at the man. No use getting thrown in the clink by the Secret Service.

"Mr. President," he said through gritted teeth.

"I was just coming to see you."

That set Stern back. "I'm sorry. Did you say you were coming to see me?"

There was a look of amusement on the president's face. "You look like you're in a rush. Maybe another time."

There was nothing in his eyes to suggest that he would allow another time. Stern was trapped, and for what? Then he thought about the man sitting in the office he'd just left. Was this about that? About the fact that Stern had been pressing him for weeks to bring up accusations against the president?

If it was, the act of deception was monumental. Blatant treason for a giveaway to the opposite party. But still, Stern noticed that one of his legs shook and he was embarrassed for it.

"John," said Zimmer, turning to one of his Secret Service detail, "do you think you could find us a quiet place to talk?" The president then whispered something to Haines, who nodded and whispered something back.

Stern felt like they were talking about him, but that could just be his ego itching. "Can I ask what this is about, Mr. President?" he dared to ask.

Zimmer looked mildly annoyed. "I think I'll wait until we have—"

The Secret Service agent reappeared. "Mr. President, would you like to follow me?"

"After you, please," Zimmer said to Stern.

Ira Stern had no option but to follow the larger man. It was a small, empty committee room that they entered, one of the few that Stern had never been in.

The Secret Service did an extra sweep of the place and the lineman gave Stern an uncomfortable up and down look.

"Do you think you can give us a minute, Marge?" Zimmer said to his chief of staff.

"No problem. I've got a couple of calls to make. I'll see you in the hall." She left with the agents, the door slamming like a cell door behind them.

"How do you like Washington, Stern? Do you miss Brooklyn?"

What kind of question was that? Stern found it hard to find the words at first. "I like it just fine, Mr. President."

"Good, good. That's good to hear. And what about your boss? He treating you okay?"

Oh shit. Where was this going? It wasn't like the president to make house calls. "He's been very kind, Mr. President. I'm not sure I could have asked for a better situation for myself and for my career."

Zimmer unbuttoned his coat and leaned against the wall. "Your grandfather was quite the politician, wasn't he? Nothing like what we have today. More old school. Was he a mean old cuss like my grandfather? Or was he more like Marlon Brando in *The Godfather*?"

"I'd say a little bit of both, Mr. President." Stern couldn't believe he was choking out the words. It felt like blasphemy.

Zimmer nodded as if he already knew or had already experienced it. "They say you take after your grandfather. They said the same thing about me and my father. I never like when they say that. Do you like it when they say that about you?"

Here Stern didn't hesitate: "My grandfather was a great man, Mr. President. He brought our family up from nothing, gave us a place in the new world, showed me how to be a man when my own father couldn't. So yes, I'd say when people say I'm like my grandfather, I take that as a generous compliment."

"That's good. Very good. It's not every day that you meet a man who holds his family in such high esteem." Zimmer pushed off the wall and walked to the center of the room, where no doubt, countless debates raged. "You don't like me much, do you Stern?"

"Mr. President, I don't even know you."

"I know that. They say we're not *supposed* to like each other. You're a Republican. I'm a Democrat. And I've found during my time in Washington how deep those lines can be drawn. More a gap the size of the Grand Canyon than a chalk line on cement. But I made the time to come find you because my little birdies have told me that you have plans for me. Certain international and state secrets have made it to your ears. You plan to use that information against me, even though I'm doing everything I can to remedy the situation."

This was his chance. This was when Stern could speak up, when he could point the finger and damn Zimmer forever. Only when Zimmer said it, he made it sound like he really did have everything under control, that he knew everything. That's when Stern knew that Flap had told the president everything.

There was only one thing to do in this situation with this president—a very popular president, one with clout and many friends on both sides of the aisle. Stern tucked his tail.

"I'm not sure what you've heard, Mr. President, but I'm assuming you've probably played the game a few times. It was posturing, trying to make my own way in the world. It's a long way from Brooklyn, sir. You know us kids. We're always looking for a way in."

Zimmer walked over to Stern and placed a hand on his shoulder. "I don't mind posturing. In fact, I get a real kick out of it these days. But let me make one thing clear. When it comes to our troops, who are agents, men and women serving all over this planet, their safety is my number one concern. Do you understand?"

Stern nodded because it was the only thing he could do.

"Well, good. I'm glad we had this chat. Thank you for making the time. And if you happen to be on Pennsylvania

Avenue anytime soon, be sure to stop by and say hello. I'd love to give you a tour of the place." Then he was gone, leaving a befuddled Ira Stern to bob in his wake.

Weeks of planning had just been cut short. He'd been made to feel insignificant, like that time in first grade when his grandfather taught him to fight back with anything he could find, and he'd gone back to school with a two-by-four. Well, he'd deal with Flap, and he'd find a two-by-four and take out Zimmer himself.

CHAPTER FIFTY-EIGHT

BRIGGS - MOSCOW

They'd gotten the Duchess, but they lost Adam Stokes.

Cal was beside himself. He was ready to call in the real cavalry, even the president. Neil had convinced him to wait. Maybe they could work out a deal. Maybe they could trust this woman to save her own skin at least.

The problem Daniel was having was that he was as muddle-headed as he'd been in a decade. Something about that last conversation with Anna really flipped him. Gone was the clarity. Gone was the focus. Replaced by a confused mix of emotions that roiled in his stomach like sour milk.

"Hey, are you awake?" Cal asked.

"Sorry, what did you say?" Daniel said, absentmindedly stroking Liberty's coat.

"I said, we need to find him, and we need to find him now."

"Elijah's working on it."

"I have half a mind to go in that room and beat it out of her," Cal said.

The Duchess was secure in the next room. She promised to help, but only if they secured her own safety. She had yet to tell them her story even though they'd asked.

"You know you're not going to lay a hand on her," Daniel said. "So don't even talk about it."

Cal looked like he might object but turned away instead. "Fine. Let's do whatever deal she wants. I want to get my uncle back"

Elijah Huckleberry had told them that Adam Stokes had gone for a walk. When Elijah asked him if it was safe, Adam said, "I'm just going to see a friend." They weren't aware that Adam Stokes had any friends in Moscow other than the Duchess, and she wasn't exactly his friend. But there was something else there. Even in his confused state, Daniel could see it.

There was some connection between Virginia Walton and Adam Stokes—something deeper and more visceral, like a jagged magnet that cut you as soon as you were pulled close. What choice did they have? Daniel didn't like making the kind of deals that would give a woman like Virginia Walton another chance. She was too far gone.

He was about to say that they should call Doc Higgins, The Jefferson Group resident interrogation specialist. He could get her to talk. Daniel didn't get the chance.

Elijah Huckleberry burst into the room breathless, even though his room was ten feet away.

"What is it?" Cal asked. "Did you find him?"

Elijah shook his head and looked at Daniel like he was asking for help.

"What's wrong?" Daniel said.

"I don't know if..."

"Spit it out!" Cal barked. He composed himself in a second. "Sorry. What's going on? Tell us."

Elijah took a deep breath and looked straight at Daniel. "They've got her."

"They've got who?" Cal asked.

But Daniel knew. "They have Anna, don't they?"

Elijah nodded, and Daniel had the momentary impulse that maybe he would strangle Virginia Walton himself if he could only find out who had taken the woman who professed her love for him.

CHAPTER FIFTY-NINE

ANNA - MOSCOW

She'd known as soon as they'd landed that the black SUVs that circled her plane were Russian. And not the good kind of Russian, not her Russian friends. No, they were sent by none other than President Konstantin Yegorovich himself.

They tied her hands and put a black bag over her head. She tried to remain calm, counting down the literal seconds and minutes until they got to where the car finally stopped. They dragged her from it, her high heels scuffing off her feet. Damp concrete underfoot, the lingering smell of sewage and cooked onions. They took the bag from her head. The room they put her in had a single, dirty mattress that had probably been made for a 5-year-old.

The man in the mask pointed to the hole in the corner. "Piss there," he said in Russian, then he was gone.

At least she had her watch, that was much of a blessing. All she did was stare at it, count the minutes, the hours. All she could hear was the distant dripping of water, as if from some leaky pipe. Occasionally, she would hear a door open somewhere, squeaky hinges screeching in the night. And then soft footfalls. The dirty bulb overhead occasionally flickered. She wasn't going to get any rest.

A portly woman came in at exactly five in the morning. Anna had just dozed off. The woman carried a small wooden bat in her right hand and a tray in the other. She set the tray down. On it was a plastic glass of brownish liquid sloshing to and fro, a metal plate, something that looked like peanut butter pie, but was probably something much, much worse.

"Eat it," the woman said, nudging Anna with the stick.

"I'm not hungry," Anna said.

The bat poked again, "Eat it."

Anna sat up a little straighter. "I said, I'm not hungry. I want to talk to whoever's—"

The woman didn't look fast, but her swing was. It caught Anna on the fleshy part of her left arm. She gritted through the surprise, staring up at the woman.

"Eat it," the woman said again.

Anna shook her head slowly from left to right.

The bat swung again, and this time Anna caught it in both hands, more luck than perfect timing. The smack stung her hands, and she thought that maybe a finger was broken. She held on, trying to get to her feet, trying to wrestle the weapon from the woman's grip.

Anna had trained. She was strong, but she was no match for the jailkeeper. A soggy boot caught her in the abdomen and then a left hook caught her in the cheek. Still, she held onto the bat. A knee to the ribs was what finally did it, blasting all the air from her lungs. She curled up in a ball and tried to protect her face, but the woman bent closer and poked her again with the bat.

"Eat it," she said.

Anna shook her head.

The woman knelt down, her left hand grabbing Anna's neck. The bat traced Anna's lips and pressed in, forcing her jaws open. And the beefy hand came in with something awful. It was like year-old liverwurst drenched with bat dung gravy.

"Eat it," the woman said, and now Anna had no choice but to comply. The older woman had her pinned down. The stabbing pain in her ribs made it hurt to breathe, and the sting in her cheek coursed down her jawline.

She chewed the food and accepted the splash of brown water. It tasted weak and dirty. Likely a watery tea of very low quality. She was made to sit up, hold the plate herself, and scoop it into her own mouth. She felt like a 2-year-old being told to eat her peas.

When she'd finished the pile of glop, she handed it back to the woman.

The woman shook her head. "Eat it."

Anna didn't know what she meant. The plate, she means for me to lick it. She tried to hand over the plate again.

The woman stuck out her tongue and mimicked licking the plate. "Eat it."

She had no choice. She licked the plate clean and she drank the rest of the filthy water.

Now the woman collected the plate, the glass, and the tray. She gave Anna one last look, the flabby smile on her malevolent face showing off an impressive array of accordion yellow teeth, and then she was gone.

And thanks to her trusty watch, Anna found that it only took two minutes for the food to send her running to the foul-smelling hole in the corner.

CHAPTER SIXTY

YEGOROVICH - MOSCOW

He was surprised to see how young she looked. Beautiful for sure, but young. Too young to be holding so many billions in her hands. And something about her made him salivate. It was the twin aspects of her beauty and... something more. Something beneath the beauty. Not within her, but within the future that this capture portended, for there was the very real possibility that her capture might lead to him building the army he'd been wanting. He'd wanted something off the books and completely mercenary that also would give him power. He could quite literally kill anyone he wanted and be completely unattached to it. Yes, that made him salivate, more so than her beauty. True power.

He'd live in a cabin far off in the woods with nothing but an iron stove. The gold, the perfumes, and the ever-flowing champagne were all pleasant accoutrements to his current station, but he didn't really care about them. Not like the others did, the hangers-on that always wanted to whisper in his ear. Well, let them whisper with champagne breath. He wanted something bigger. He wanted total and complete control. And this woman, this Anna Varushkin, would be the one to give it to him.

He had the old jailer with the babushka bring in a table, two chairs, and some decent cutlery. When the table was set, he made his entrance. She didn't rise, but merely looked up at him from her stinking mattress. He'd been in places far worse. He had been a captive himself on occasion. It was one of the prices you paid for being part of the intelligentsia of Mother Russia.

"I thought we'd enjoy some dinner," he said, taking a seat and unfolding the napkin in his lap.

She didn't move, but continued staring at him. The lack of sleep and awful food couldn't do much to diminish her beauty. It made him wonder what she looked like when she really took care of herself.

"Please, come join me," he said.

She rose carefully, though he could see that her legs were shaking. She did a good job hiding it and walked to the table as if she were walking into a fine restaurant—something in New York or Paris.

He got up and held out the chair. She stiffened but took the seat. He smelled her hair as she passed, catching the whiff of sweat, fear, and dank imprisonment. What a shame. He retook his seat and snapped his fingers. The old jailer returned with a bottle of wine—crisp chardonnay that he'd selected from his own collection. He poured two glasses and lifted his own.

"What shall we toast?"

She surprised him by lifting her own glass. "To your death," she said in perfect Russian.

Yegorovich noticed the old jailer twitch, but she didn't move their way. He'd gotten a full report of the first meeting and watched it on video. The jailer had done her job, but he hated to see such beauty marred by bruises.

"To my death then," he said, clinking his glass against hers. "May it come in many, many years." He grinned and sampled the wine, marveling at its taste. Finer things were not beneath them, but they were just icing on the cake, not the cake itself.

She drank the entire glass and he refilled it. He was more careful on his second glass, sipping as he watched her.

"I'm sure you know why you're here," he said.

She'd regained a bit of her composure, perhaps the effect of alcohol coursing through her lovely veins.

"I came to Russia to visit a friend and your thugs picked me up at the airport. I demand to speak to the American ambassador."

He *tsked* the silly comment away. "How silly. The American ambassador is a buffoon." He took another sip of his wine, thinking that maybe he'd have to ask the vintner for another case. "Even if he knew you were here, there is nothing he could do."

Dinner was presented by his private butler, a man he nabbed while on vacation in New Guinea. The man could make stale toasted rye bread taste like caviar, a true magician, and tonight he did not disappoint. By the time he was done setting platters on the table, the small space was overflowing with rare meats of every kind, and vegetables—some roasted, some grilled, some sautéed. Butter and garlic were in abundance.

He could see right away what the sight of the food did to Miss Varushkin.

"Please, help yourself," he said.

Anna didn't hesitate. She speared a filet minion with a fork and cut into it quickly, only regaining her manners after her third bite. He watched—a princess humbled to peasant status. Oh, what imprisonment can do. He could keep her here for months, break her down bit by bit. But he was becoming an impatient man.

So many plans and not enough money of his own to see those plans through. It was all tied up, tracked by the Americans and the British and all their feckless friends. But here before him was a source of true wealth. Something untraceable, something that would be his and his alone.

"Tell me about the money," he said. The jailer was gone and Yegorovich knew that the video was turned off as well. This was a conversation "off the record," as the Americans say.

"What money?" she said, taking a scoop of roasted potatoes and plopping them on her plate.

"The Fund," he said. "I know you hid it. You took over for your grandfather, Yorgi. You said you've stashed away a fortune. You are a very wealthy woman."

She ate the potatoes in silence for a moment, no doubt searching for the perfect words befitting a capable traitor of her stature.

"Let's say I did have the money of which you speak," she said. "It wouldn't be mine. It would belong to the poor souls who fled our country—men and women that you drove off instead of embracing them. Instead of using them for their talents, you wasted an opportunity. But as I said, this is all speculation on my part. I've never heard of this fund and I don't know a thing about you."

Yegorovich selected a prawn from the table and pried off its head, watching the juices dribble onto his plate. "I have all the time in the world to listen to your tales. I know who you are and I know what you control. I'd much rather make this as painless as possible. You could be here for years, or you tell me what I need to know, and I'll make your death quick, painless, and with a soldier's honor."

Her eyes narrowed on him. "A soldier or a spy?"

He laughed. "Is there a difference?"

Now she laughed. A beautiful sound.

"You don't know what it means to be a real man," she said. "Or a true warrior. You're just a thief and I hope that on the day you die, they burn your body and flush your ashes down the toilet."

She had fire, this one. "You might not care for your own well-being, but what would you say if I told you I know the whereabouts of your friend, Daniel Briggs." He watched her stunned face for a moment and smiled at the effect his words were having. "Or is he more than that? Your lover maybe? Let's say I killed this Daniel Briggs. Would you tell me your secrets then?"

Her silence was all the answer he needed. It was only a matter of time.

CHAPTER SIXTY-ONE

LENA - OUTSKIRTS OF MOSCOW

Alek Volkov was the perfect host until he had to leave from time to time, either for phone calls or the occasional in-person meeting. Every meal together—breakfast, lunch, and dinner—they talked about many things. His childhood, his upbringing, his time as a spy. He asked her about her childhood. She found herself freely talking to him. She told him about how her then father had called her Little Rabbit, how he cared for her, taught her how to shoot, how she kept the house, and how they went for long walks on the farm.

"You should keep those memories," he said once. "Do not downplay their significance in your life."

It was still a struggle though, for the man who had been her father was not really her father. He'd kidnapped her, raised her as his own and trained her to be a killer. She was pretty sure any other girl her age would be in intense therapy or committed to a mental institution by now. It's how she knew she was made of tough stuff. She saw that same tough stuff in Volkov. He told her of the missions he'd conducted, the friends he'd lost, the near-death experiences that would send most men to the bottle or the grave. And he spoke of it all so openly, like he wanted her to know every bit of him.

In turn, she felt the same way. So much so that when he returned from a rather extended meeting—he texted to tell her he'd be late for lunch—she knew something was wrong. She'd come to read his emotions, even when he tried to hide them.

"Sorry, I'm late," he said.

"Would you like me to put lunch on the table?" She liked cooking for Volkov. He told her to call him Alek, but for some reason she preferred Volkov. It sounded more Russian, more their line of work, like a code name out of some spy movie.

"There has been a development," he said, shuffling the key fob in his hand.

"Is it Daniel or Cal? Did something happen?"

"No, no, they're fine."

"Do they still have the Duchess? Virginia Walton, I mean." Again, the name the Duchess felt like some serious spy game, something too far above the purveyance of a 19-year-old.

"They still have her and... well, she's not speaking."

She could tell that he was trying to find the right words to regulate the fear that would soon hit her. But she was no child, and indeed had not been one even when she was one. "Just tell me," she said.

Volkov nodded. "Your friend, Anna, she's been captured."

He was right. The fear scraped at her insides.

"What happened?" she asked, trying in vain to keep the terror out of her voice. Anna was her friend. Anna was someone who she wanted in her life. "Who could have done this?"

"We think it was Yegorovich," Volkov said, "Though I haven't confirmed it yet."

"We have to do something," Lena said.

"We will, once I have confirmation."

"Then get the confirmation," she said.

Volkov nodded, then disappeared to his office, closing the door behind him. He did this so she couldn't listen, and it angered her.

She paced back and forth, fearing the worst.

Not Anna. Why?

It should have been Daniel. Not that she *wanted* it to be Daniel, but at least someone like Daniel could take care of himself.

When Volkov finally emerged from his office an hour later, she was frantic for news.

"What did you find?"

"He has her," he said, fishing a pack of cigarettes from his pocket.

"Do you know where?"

"Not yet," he said, "and I don't think I can find out without giving myself up."

Lena wanted to tell him to screw his cover, that Anna was way more important than that. But she knew deep down, from all the conversations that she and Volkov had, that to sacrifice himself and everything he'd worked for meant that many more would suffer.

They talked through options, but none hit the mark. Lena suggested they call Daniel, but Volkov said he had tried and that there had been no response.

Cigarette after cigarette went through Volkov's lungs as they talked past lunchtime, spit-balling ideas. He was going to open a fresh pack of cigarettes when he paused. And Lena knew that he'd come up with a solution.

"What? Tell me," she said.

"No, it's dangerous. We can't do it."

"Yes, we can. With your resources and my skill, we can do anything."

Volkov grinned at that. "While I appreciate your confidence in me, the idea that so conveniently popped itself into my head does not require my direct involvement."

"Then... what? How can we help them?"

Volkov's face went serious. "*You*. You are the answer Lena. But if you're caught, we lose you again and there's nothing I can do to stop that."

Waiting was not something she'd been raised to do. "I don't care. It's worth the risk. She'd do it for me."

And Lena knew that to be the case. Anna had taken Lena under her wing. Now, Lena would repay that kindness.

"Very well," Volkov said. "Let me tell you what I had in mind."

CHAPTER SIXTY-TWO

WILCOX - RUSSIAN AIRSPACE

He did a set of fifty push-ups in the spacious center aisle, then flipped over and did a hundred crunches for good measure. He then segued into a five-minute yoga routine, all the while processing what he'd already decided. The tropics, the beautiful water, and all the answers the seclusion brought were precisely why he picked up meditation years before. It was why he liked to sit in silence and absorb the world whistling around him.

Every few minutes there was a new update from his vast network. The picture on the ground was pretty bleak for Cal and the gang.

For anyone else, Wilcox might've flown on, maybe hit Beijing, maybe chat with monks in Nepal. He could go anywhere. He had all the resources he needed. And yet, the best resource he had was right here—his brain and his body. And he wanted to use those two things for one thing only—to help his old pal Cal. Their last reunion had been cut short. He genuinely liked the man, despite the fact that Cal fought for the good guys 100 percent of the time and Wilcox fought for, well, Wilcox.

More times than not, however, he was doing the right thing on the spiritual calendar of his choosing. Wilcox felt that kind of connection with Cal Stokes and that's what had led to his decision to come to Russia. He'd made some pretty high-profile kills in the past year or two here. Crooked politicians, crooked *Russian* politicians were like cockroaches to Wilcox. He wanted to crush and smear their guts all over the concrete, but there was no time for that now.

So here we go, off to save the day again, a modern-day Lone Ranger. Or was he more like Lassie? Lassie, quick! Timmy's getting waterboarded in an underground shithole prison! Quick, Lassie, get in there and slaughter all the guards! Lassie would save the day for sure.

There were palms to be greased and all the little details of his craft to sort out. It was good to be at work again. Even better because Wilcox knew it involved killing Russians.

CHAPTER SIXTY-THREE

ADAM STOKES - MOSCOW

Before this, he'd felt good for his age. While not necessarily spry, he could still bend over without wincing. This is something that even his 20-year-old body would have had a hard time doing.

The first day, they beat him at regular intervals. Whenever he expected a question, none came. Only flying fists, feet, and elbows. One sadistic prick liked to use his head. It felt like a concrete sledgehammer. He'd been knocked unconscious too many times to count. And he had to give it to the Russian thugs, they knew the limits. They knew just how far to push the physical form.

Sometimes, they woke him with a bucket full of ice water. Other times, it was smelling salt. One time, he woke up to Mr. Headbutt urinating on him.

He'd lost all track of time. There was no way to see whether it was night or day. Sometimes they brought him food. Sometimes they didn't. He was thirsty. And while his body was wracked with pain, and he'd been trained for this sort of thing, he knew that something else was coming. They were prepping him, softening his defenses. And Adam Stokes knew that in this game, especially with Russian interrogation, the prisoner always broke. Unless, of course, the prisoner could find a way to kill himself. Adam Stokes was not going to go there.

The wooden door was thrown open, jarring him from his restless sleep. Three of them, this time. The kicks came hard and with pinpoint accuracy, especially when he curled himself up into a ball. There were grunts, but no words. One of them picked him up, slammed a fist into his belly, and dropped him back down to the ground.

He cast a cautious glance up. Luckily, his eyes still worked. He saw them staring down at him, chests heaving from the exertion. At least that was something. One of them, the guy on the right, skinniest of the three, reached into his pocket and produced a set of brass knuckles. Those were going to hurt. The man sampled the knuckles on his opposite hand. Once, twice, three times. He was all pro. He motioned one of his pals to pick up Adam.

Adam was all rag doll, now. Even if he wanted to fight back, his body wouldn't allow it. Probably better to go slack. Maybe they'd drop him from the dead weight. Adam thought he saw someone shuffle by the open door, a guard or maybe another thug going to put a beating on another prisoner.

The figure was soon forgotten when the brass knuckles pummeled him. One particularly brutal hit took him in the hip and made him scream out loud. He hated that sound. It showed the weakness coming out. They dropped him to the ground as if the scream had been the magic word.

They stared down at him again, Mr. Brass Knuckles replacing the useful tool in his pocket. And then something fascinating happened. The man who would beat Adam

Stokes, the man who was so proud of his professional work, smiled as his bald and tattooed head split open. The axe came down to the man's nose in a burst of blood and brain and bone, and he fell to the ground. The other two had barely enough time to whirl around when they were chopped down just as quickly.

Adam couldn't see who it was, but he heard the bodies hit the floor. The blood gushed and pooled. And then there was another form standing over him.

Adam blinked rapidly to clear his vision.

There was an old man, and then another joined him. They were dressed in janitor's clothes, and they each held an axe, the blades coated in blood.

"I don't think he remembers us," one of the men said in pure, streamlined American English.

"Well, I'm offended," the other one said. His twin. Yes, that was it.

Now, the faces so familiar... but from where?

He knew he recruited them way back when he was only a child. At least, that's how it felt. His brain was so muddled from the blows and the dehydration.

"I know you," Adam said, his voice no more than a croak.

The twins, yes, they were twins from Oklahoma. Or was it Texas? Their mother emigrated from Russia. Her father had been a professor. No, a physicist. Yes, that was it.

"It looks like he remembers us," one of them said, and Adam remembered his name. Max. And he looked at Max's brother, Phillip, and Adam Stokes's heart leapt. Old friends, and when he stood and attempted to hug them, they reached out for him. And thank goodness they did, for as soon as he had his feet planted, he fainted off to nothingness.

CHAPTER SIXTY-FOUR

ADAM STOKES - MADRID - 1978

It was his first vacation in years. This time in a rundown hovel that should have been condemned. Sure, he traveled all over the world for business and stayed in some of the nicest hotels ever built, but there were plenty of crappy ones, too. This one was a fine example. He wasn't about to complain. A vacation had been suggested by one of his superiors, and while Adam had scoffed initially, now he was glad for it. Three weeks off and nothing to do but wander Madrid.

He ate tapas until he felt like he could burst. He walked it off, replaced it with wine, then walked some more until three or four in the morning. It gave him plenty of time to think. Such were the demands of his line of work. His network of underappreciated spies was growing. He knew that it was only a matter of time before they hit real pay dirt.

Every now and then he came across herds of American tourists backpacking through Europe. It was hard not to size them up. Ah yes, she'd be able to hold her own in Switzerland, and this one here—her boyfriend?—had the right build for Belgium. He forced himself to turn off that part of his mind. There were plenty of kids who would answer his call. His spiel was perfect, though it was never the same.

He knew how to find a sense of belonging or an under-appreciated level of patriotism in a near-socialist. He befriended them all and funneled them back to the States when the background checks came through. Sure, sometimes he had to push. Many of them had records, some as anti-war demonstrators, others as pure misfits. Just as Virginia Walton had taught him, he found their hidden talents. He saw that a shy, unassuming coed from Duke had the amazing ability to recall anything she said or heard, and that's really what he needed.

He didn't need operators, per se, he needed passive intelligence-gatherers, people that could fade into the shadows if needed, or flaunt themselves down Main Street without a care. They were actors one and all and he was their director. Along the way, they'd become his friends. He thought of many of them as he walked the streets of Madrid. He wondered if he'd see many of them again.

Mostly though, he thought of Virginia. He still loved her.

There had been a couple of relationships since, but nothing that stuck. They were more flirtatious flings than true romance. No, she was the one that he thought about when he went to sleep, and the one he dreamed about as he tossed and turned each night. If he had been honest with his superiors, he would have told them that his sleep had gone to crap since Virginia left.

He worried about her. He missed her. She'd left a hole that only she could fill and no one-night stand was coming close to filling anything in Adam Stokes's heart.

He dodged a careening moped carting three teens who

were each waving football flags. *Soccer*, to use the base American term for the game.

If he had not stepped up on the curb to get out of the way and then turned a certain way in doing so, he would have missed her. There she was in the window of a bookstore, sitting in a battered leather armchair reading a book. She looked lovely and forlorn.

He thought about moving on. First, he walked around the corner and watched her from there. She was as beautiful as ever. Her hair had changed to fit the times. Always stylish was the Duchess. The proprietor of the bookshop came to check on her, and she smiled up at him, probably telling him that she was fine, that this one book would see her through the day. It was probably Voltaire. She loved Voltaire.

He kept telling himself that he needed to go in and say hello, that maybe their love could be rekindled. But then he remembered what she had told him at their last meeting, and the way she looked at him like a broken doll that could never be put back together. He wanted to help her. He wanted to be with her. He wanted to hold and inhale her.

He wanted her to be his, and he hers. But for some reason, he didn't move.

The next day he followed her. Twice he thought she'd seen him, but his craft had immensely improved. One hour he looked like a college student, or like a businessman going to work. The next, a drab bookkeeper. And on it went, and on he followed her.

She was staying in a small apartment in the center of the city. He watched her that night from a rooftop across the way. There were no visitors, no phone calls, just Virginia and a book. He kept telling himself to get the nerve to go knock on her door. But what would she say?

It was on the third day that he knew he would confront

her, if only to make sure she was okay. At least that's what he told himself. When he went to make his move, she was sitting in an open-air cafe, nibbling on something that looked like the Spanish version of quiche. A woman appeared and sat down next to her. The visitor could have been from any one of the fair-skinned countries of Europe, nondescript as she was. Adam was too far to hear what they spoke of, but he suspected they were speaking in Spanish. Work for Virginia most likely. The conversation lasted no more than ten minutes, and then Virginia moved on. This time strolling through the university like she owned the place. She entered the university library and he followed.

The next visitor was another woman, this one more striking. Tall, blonde, and as highbrow as they come. Adam watched them through the stacks and then realized that he recognized the woman. Impossibly, she'd been part of a report he'd read before leaving for Madrid. He liked to school himself up on any contacts or spies for the opposing side when he went to a new city. This woman, though she was blonde in this library, had been raven-haired and a bit stooped in the picture he'd seen of her. As she turned, Adam Stokes was sure it was her.

What was Virginia doing meeting with a Russian?

He could have confronted them right then and there, but he took the coward's route. He told himself it was his job, placed a call, and was told to wait by a certain pay phone. Ten minutes later there were a series of checks to confirm his identity and he was patched through. He told the voice on the other end of the line what he had seen, who he had seen, and why he thought headquarters might find it interesting.

Adam was told to come back to the same pay phone in an hour. He did, and this time was met by three operatives. They'd been sent by Langley to do a deeper search. He was told to go back to his apartment and wait for further word. Adam suggested that he be part of the operation but was told politely that it was out of his hands, and so he waited. He thought it was stupid that he had done this, that he had put the CIA on Virginia's tail. Virginia Walton was one of the best he'd ever met, if not *the* best. Her confidence, her skill, all-natural and only enhanced by the training that Langley had given her.

It was a complete surprise when two days later none other than the station chief from Madrid visited Adam Stokes and gave him the news.

"She's working for the Russians."

Just like that, Adam Stokes's life got turned upside-down again.

CHAPTER SIXTY-FIVE

YEGOROVICH - MOSCOW

Yegorovich needed time to think. And when he needed time to think, he liked to get away from all that was unholy about his office. And that meant no assistants, no phones, no anything.

The place was dirty, but it was a house that had been vetted and secured many times over. They wouldn't let him stay for long. That still amazed him. He was the one in charge. He was the President of the Russian Federation and still the paper pushers of his country dictated his schedule. He pawned it off as much as he could, but there were still times when he needed to show his face, when his own physical force needed to be demonstrated. But now he would get at least half a day to himself.

Anna Varushkin hadn't said much that was of value, though he knew without a doubt that this Daniel Briggs, whoever he was, was important to her. That had been plain to see. Edmond Flap had yet to present the full details on this Briggs character other than to say that he was somewhere in

Moscow and had gotten his hands on the Duchess. He was a minor player. Yegorovich let Flap play his games, especially if he kept providing the information like he had for all these years. What Flap had failed to provide was intel that Cal Stokes was in Moscow. And for the time being, Yegorovich would be unaware that the American's uncle, a born-again Parisian, had escaped a rented detention center. The place was leased out to visiting entities from other countries, covert players who needed a place to have private discussions with foreign nationals. But that was outside of Yegorovich's current purview.

He spent the first hour thinking. He spent the second hour sketching. It was an old habit. As a child he'd wanted to be an artist. It was something he still did when he needed to think. It unhinged a part of his brain that simply sitting would not do. He was putting the finishing touches on the remembered face of Calvin Stokes, Sr., when the emergency phone rang. He looked down at the picture of Stokes, the man now long dead, though he wished it wasn't so.

Yegorovich grabbed the phone and answered, "What is it?" News of a nuclear holocaust would not have surprised him. It was always a possibility, especially with those crazy Pakistanis always rattling their sabers or those insane North Koreans. He was getting tired of dealing with that possibility. But it was no nuclear holocaust that came across his emergency phone.

"Mr. President, I'm sorry to disturb you."

"That's okay. I assume it's important." It had to be. No one would have bothered him otherwise. Konstantin Yegorovich was not a man to be bothered.

"Mr. President, it's..."

"Just spit it out, young man."

"There's a woman, an American. She'd like to meet you."

"You were told not to disturb me."

"Yes, Mr. President. I understand. But I was also told that if there was ever a young woman who matched this particular young lady's description, and this person wanted to see you, to..."

Now Yegorovich understood. He had very specific tastes. They ran contrary to his taste in wine. Younger than thirty was good. Younger than twenty even better.

"Who is she?" Yegorovich asked.

"Her name is Amber Larson, Mr. President. She's in training to be on the American Olympic ski team, though she says her family was from Russia." Ah, athletes, Olympic athletes, now *they* were specimens.

But there was so much work to do. He was torn. All work and no play, as the Americans say. "Very well. When can you bring her?"

The man on the other end brightened, "We can have her there in ten minutes, Mr. President. How would you like her dressed?"

Sometimes he liked to take his dates on short trips, maybe a visit to the opera or the ballet, though he hated such things. No, what he wanted today was someone more down-to-earth.

"What does she want?" he asked.

"They told me you would ask that, Mr. President. I believe she would like to explore the possibility of becoming an athlete for Russia."

"And you've checked her credentials?"

"Yes, Mr. President."

"Very well. Bring her. Have her wear something casual, formfitting, maybe something to go with the occasion."

"Understood, Mr. President."

Yegorovich hung up the phone and went back to his sketch. Though by the time he got back to it, he was unhappy with the way he'd formed Stokes's eyes. They weren't right, not brooding enough. He crumpled up the paper and threw it in the fire.

A car pulled up ten minutes later. Yegorovich watched as the shock of blonde hair exited the car. He answered the front door himself. He was all smiles when he saw she was dressed in training attire, perfectly formfitting. And my, was she young.

"You must be Miss Larson," he said in English.

"Yes, Mr. President, but you can call me Amber."

There were some nerves there, but still much confidence, something that stirred his sexual desire. He held onto her hand. "Have you eaten?"

"I wouldn't say no to dinner, Mr. President."

"Please, call me Konstantin."

"I could eat, Konstantin."

"Then I shall cook for you. Please come inside."

The kitchen was well stocked and he was no novice at the stove. She told him about her family, about how her father had come to America after the Soviet Union collapsed.

"A sad time for our country," Yegorovich interjected. "But with sad times come opportunity, no?"

They talked through dinner and one of the guards brought dessert, something Yegorovich had ordered from his favorite restaurant. A cream-filled pastry that she said melted in your mouth. Yegorovich was pleased. She was beautiful, confident, and smart. And she possessed a certain mystique that drew him closer to her.

Normally, he would assert himself, use force if need be. But this one took the reins. She might just be a fan, someone who'd like to tell her grandkids that she'd once had a fling with the Russian President. That was fine with Yegorovich. She had been searched from head to toe, and she was much smaller than him, so she was no threat. He kissed her first on the cheek. And when she didn't flinch, he kissed her once on the bottom lip.

"That's nice," she said, stroking his cheek. He liked that she didn't ask for anything, that she hadn't talked favors. At least not yet. It might come later, but she seemed to know the game. She seemed to know what he wanted. There was just enough cat and mouse. Not too easy, but not too hard.

Before long, they ended up in the bedroom. She would have been already showered. It was something he insisted on. He liked them clean.

He excused himself, showered quickly, pleased at the excitement coursing through his body.

When he re-entered the bedroom, she was under the sheets, obviously naked. He turned out the lights and slipped in next to her. She held him at arm's length for a moment. He would have bowled right in, but she said, "I don't want you to think that I do this all the time."

"Are you about to say that you're not that kind of girl," he asked, teasing. He could see her smile in the darkness.

"Oh, I am that kind of girl, Mr. President."

And then he went to her. But before he could wrap himself around her and take her for his own, something smashed into his head once, then twice. And as the red darkness closed in at the edges of his vision, he saw her rise. She was still clothed. And he thought he saw her pick up a phone. He wondered about it idly as he passed into unconsciousness.

CHAPTER SIXTY-SIX

VOLKOV - MOSCOW

The advance team had done the hard work. Guards had been subdued and he'd been able to sneak in without a soul knowing he was there.

He'd given their impromptu operation a one-in-three chance of succeeding. So when he'd got the call from Lena, he'd been surprised, but happy. It was the ultimate Hail Mary, kidnapping the Russian president. But it was the only way, if they were going to find out where Anna Varushkin was being held. Volkov's informant said that Yegorovich had special plans for Varushkin and special plans coming from Yegorovich meant nothing good. So now, he was risking everything. His mission, his life, his cover, everything. Lena was waiting for him in the bedroom, standing next to Yegorovich's unconscious body with a marble statue of Lenin in her hand.

"He's still breathing," she said, "I had to clock him twice."

Volkov checked the president's vitals. Still breathing, still a strong heartbeat, though the man might have a concussion. That was the least of Volkov's worries.

He pulled his backpack off, dipped in and pulled out two masks. "Here. Put this on."

She did what she was told, and Volkov slipped his back over his face. "Come on. You get the arms and I'll get the legs."

The advance team was taking care of the guard. Volkov wanted them nowhere near Yegorovich. They didn't need to know the whole story because they didn't know who Volkov was.

They got Yegorovich downstairs and out the back door to the waiting vehicle. There they tossed him inside and covered him with a blanket. Volkov injected a sedative that would keep the man asleep for at least as long as it would take to get back to the safe house.

"Get in, I'm driving," Volkov said.

Everything had gone perfectly, and that made him uneasy. Nothing ever went perfectly.

They went down a side street, a long way back to the main road, and he thought they'd made it. Not to safety, but at least away from the scene of the crime. He pressed on the gas and that's when he heard it. The squealing of tires. He looked in the rear view and saw a caravan of SUVs coming their way.

"Hold on," he told Lena, flaming on the gas and vaulting the vehicle forward.

He could outrun them. At least that's what he told himself. He made a few turns and he thought he'd lost them. But whoever they were—the president's men no doubt—they found them again. The SUVs sped across a field with weapons pointed. They would be precise in their firing, for their president was somewhere inside.

Volkov didn't trust the common Russian soldier, but he knew that the elite sniper was a staple of such security squads. The first confirmation came in a single round, blasting out the front right high beam. By the sound of the impact, it would probably have been a smaller caliber weapon. Something more mobile, something that could be taken in a hurry. Thankfully, nothing like the American 50 caliber round. Best to lose them.

Another shot splintered the front windshield. Then he saw it up ahead—the road he'd passed on the way in, jammed with construction traffic. That's where he would lose them. And if anyone was waiting up ahead, he would see them. But the chasers were converging.

Another shot hit the front windshield again. It was getting hard to see. Volkov pulled a hard right, scraping along the side of a delivery van who honked as the smaller sedan flew by.

In and out of traffic, past flag markers, past cranes.

He figured they were home free. It was an impossible shot. No way the SUVs could get through. It would take them time, and in that time Volkov and Lena would be gone.

But they must have had their best in that chasing vehicle because a round went through the back windshield, through the driver's seat, and hit Alexander Volkov in the back.

He tried to hold onto the steering wheel with his now useless right hand, but he was fading.

As Lena reached over to steady him and right their driving path, Volkov cursed himself for being so reckless. Everything in his mind went blank. Then there was nothingness.

CHAPTER SIXTY-SEVEN

LENA - MOSCOW

Somehow, she was able to get control of the wheel and scoot over to Volkov's lap and press her foot on the gas.

He was bleeding a lot. To make matters worse, she thought she saw Yegorovich moving in the back. He was murmuring something, and there was nothing that Lena could do. She had to get them out of there. She didn't know where to go, so she went straight, and then she took a right, and then a left, completely clueless. Soon, traffic thinned, and suddenly she was on open road. She pressed the gas as far as it would go. The engine squealed high in complaint.

"Volkov, you need to wake up," she said. But he didn't answer her. He just kept bleeding. So much blood. It was on her back and running down her leg.

Then she saw them behind again in the rearview—one, two, three, four black vehicles.

She'd come too far. There was no way she was going to let them take her. But what could she do? She was in a strange city on top of a man that was bleeding out, driving a car that she wasn't familiar with.

The road veered right. She took it at close to 100 mph. It didn't matter. They were still coming.

Yegorovich was murmuring louder now. Had Volkov not given him enough sedative? Or was this a side effect of the drug?

"Volkov, wake up dammit! I need you."

Still nothing. Just the blood sticking to her leg, dripping into her shoe.

Blue and white lights blared on a hundred yards ahead of her. It was the police, and there was nowhere to go. She screeched to a stop, then leaned over and fumbled in the glove compartment. Maybe there was a weapon. Nothing. Maybe in Volkov's pocket. No, just cigarettes and another set of keys.

The police cars were coming straight for them. She would either be killed or thrown in prison and no one, not Daniel, not Anna, not even Cal, would know what had happened to her.

The police cars were coming fast. She held onto the steering wheel with her foot pressed hard on the brake. Then at the last second, they swerved around her. And to her utter amazement, the five cars lined up across the road. Uniformed men poured out, long weapons in hand.

And when the SUVs came, they were no match for the police.

The night sky lit up with grenades from a launcher and took out Yegorovich's security detail in one swift massacre. And then the slaughter was on, full bore. There was nowhere for the survivors to go. It was done—quickly and efficiently.

Lena realized too late that she should have taken that as her cue to go. But Volkov needed help. She was no doctor.

Sure, she knew how to put in a couple of sutures, but that was it. Police were coming her way now. She made her decision. She put the car in park, opened the driver's side door, and stepped out with her hands raised.

"I need help! My friend is hurt!"

She squinted at the men who approached her. They were too old to be in uniform. They looked more like retirees who decided to dress up for Halloween. Cops and robbers in the nursing home.

A man approached, his face disfigured, and in the flashing lights she could see it was destroyed by bruises and cuts. And as if there hadn't been enough surprises, the man spoke to her in English.

"Are you Lena?"

She nodded dumbly.

The man pointed to the car and the others, ordering them to pull Volkov from the driver's seat. Another team checked on Yegorovich and transferred him to one of the police cruisers.

"I don't understand," Lena said, her voice a breathless hiss. She was sure she was going into shock.

"It's okay, honey. I'm a friend," the man said.

"Who are you?" Lena asked, her hands shaking.

"My name is Adam Stokes. I'm Cal's uncle. And you look like you've had a long night."

Lena laughed at that. "You don't look so hot yourself."

He shared her smile. "Come on, let's take care of your friend. Then we can take you to see the others."

CHAPTER SIXTY-EIGHT

FLAP - WASHINGTON, D.C.

The pieces were coming together very nicely indeed. The woman, Virginia Walton, the one they called the Duchess, was an interesting find. She'd had a brief but storied career, and it was only because Flap was now director of the CIA that he even found out about her. The fact that she had worked for the Russians back in the 1970s didn't mean a thing. It was one of those fortuitous coincidences that told Edmond Flap he was doing the right thing. His connections with Russia were strong, and while he thought the country itself was a complete mess, even a complete mess could be of some use. Besides, the president of Russia himself was Edmond's friend. Or at least an ally. Flap didn't have any friends. Never wanted them. Friends were a liability, and in his line of work, a liability was a death sentence.

With the access he had as director, he dug as deep as he could on the Stokes clan. Lo and behold, he found out that there was a brother. The man that had almost tanked Flap's career, Calvin Stokes Sr., had a brother, and not even Cal Stokes the younger knew it.

So, he'd activated good ol' Uncle Adam's ex-flame. The woman he thought was dead, but who had been saved by the French Intelligence Service via a merchant who had fished her from sin, patched her up, and given her to the government. She had gone through a series of masters. They ended up living a quiet life in the French countryside. Her file said that she raised goats, and that she'd become quite the purveyor of an expensive cheese. But her past always called her back. Little missions here and there, far away from anyone who'd known her from her former life. But it was Flap who brought the Duchess back full glory. Not that she even knew who he was or that he was involved, because that was the way of these things. Better to have an intermediary on top of that, lest Flap's own hands get dirty.

He watched from afar as she picked apart the network she'd spent building in her younger days. She was good. Very good. She lived up to her name. And when she lured Adam Stokes from his hole, Flap knew he'd made the right decision. Because Flap was out to ruin any last living relative of the Stokes clan. Death was too easy, too quick, and too good. He'd had to toil for years to get his life back. Now he was ready to spend years—the rest of his days if he had to—ruining the Stokes name.

He led their stalwart party to Moscow. Sure, Adam Stokes had gotten away and the whole thing was turning into quite the mess, but that was fine with Edmond Flap. Let everyone else run through the muck. He'd spent his time there. This was part of the grand story, the opera of his life. Of course, Konstantin Yegorovich knew that Flap had something going on in Russia. But while they were allies, they never told each other everything unless there was a pointed question, and then their agreement was to tell the truth. Yegorovich had never asked, so Flap had never told. He'd given a little whisper about Daniel Briggs and his connection with Anna Varushkin, but that was it.

Yegorovich didn't give a damn about Adam Stokes, so he didn't need to know about Adam Stokes. Besides, the Russian president had some sort of incongruous respect for Calvin Stokes, Sr., and that had cascaded down to his son Cal. Despite the fact that it was Cal himself who had ordered Yegorovich's kidnapping months before. But like the true adventurer that he was, Yegorovich took it in stride. Though it was only one more reason why he should respect Cal Stokes. Once again, that was fine with Edmond Flap.

It had nothing to do with what he had in store. But he needed to talk to Yegorovich, and the man wasn't answering his phone. Probably off with one of his young conquests. He liked to do that from time to time, especially when he was stressed. He never showed it to the public and definitely not to the sycophants around him, but Yegorovich trusted Flap enough to reveal his stress to his old ally.

Maybe that was it. Maybe Yegorovich was off getting his ashes hauled, or maybe he was having a conversation with the soon-to-be-famous Anna Varushkin. That one was a mystery. The fact that she controlled the assets and the votes of so many Russian expatriates was impressive.

He tried calling Yegorovich again, but there was no answer. He'd wait until the morning. There was no rush. He simply wanted to make sure that the chase for the missing Americans was strenuous, but not too strenuous. Let them fight but let them get away. It was one of the few things Flap had ever asked of the Russian.

But in this, he was wholly sincere. Like a request from a veteran cardinal, Flap would see Stokes's clan back on American soil. And that was when he would start tearing them apart. No doubt Dirk Springer would be back soon, and he'd have yet more ammunition to ravage Stokes's friends, but for now there was still time.

In rapid succession, he got three texts from one of his deputies. Ira Stern was complaining about him again. He'd already heard about the conversation that Zimmer had with the Brooklyn native. While he really didn't care, Flap didn't want Stern's idiotic moves to get in his way.

Always the patient man, Edmond Flap finished his tea, took a quick shower, and headed to bed. There would be time to deal with Stern tomorrow. Maybe Yegorovich would call during the night. Either way, Flap's dreams were calling.

Each night, a tale of the downfall of Stokes clan unfolded in the lagging moments before sleep. His dreams were sweetened all the more.

CHAPTER SIXTY-NINE

ADAM STOKES - PARIS - 1979

Adam Stokes couldn't remember why he'd volunteered for this job. He had insisted, and why? There were plenty of others that could do this.

It was all because of his feelings, because of his attachment, and because he couldn't let go.

Virginia Walton was where the surveillance team said she was. Sitting in the park under the willow tree. She had her shoes off and she was reading a fashion magazine, a cigarette dangling from two fingers. If he didn't know her, he would have thought that she was beautiful—stunningly so. But he knew her, had explored every inch of her, and for the past year, he'd studied her every move. It was part of his job, but it felt more like it was part of his life. And to think it was all in service of getting over her.

"Hello, Virginia," he said, and he was pleased to see that she was mildly startled.

"You've gotten better," she said, quickly composing herself.

It was dusk. Night was falling quickly. Most Parisians were heading home to prepare dinner or to prepare for a long night out. They had the park to themselves. That was by design.

"You're looking good, Adam," she said.

She didn't rise to embrace him. And maybe that was better.

"You really should have called," she said. "We could have had dinner or maybe caught a movie."

"I don't have your phone number anymore," he said, sitting down on a spot on the stone wall where he could see her every move. Better to be careful with this one. She more than likely had two or three weapons on her person. Adam Stokes was no rookie. He'd seen his fair share of violence, having trained with the best.

Now *he* was one of the best. It was something that he knew, something he'd worked hard at. And one of the big reasons he'd worked so hard was the woman sitting across from him.

"How did you find me?" she said, sounding like she really didn't care.

"A mutual acquaintance," he lied, glancing around to make sure they were truly alone.

No wandering eyes across the water. He should have known. This had been one of their spots, a small retreat inside the bustling city.

"Why did you do it, Virginia?"

Her beautiful eyes looked up at him and he felt that familiar twinge of longing. She still had that power.

"I don't know what you mean, Adam. Can you be more specific? If you're talking about why I left you, I thought we already had that conversation. I have led a checkered past. You don't want a person like me in your life."

"I don't feel that way about you anymore." Again, a lie. "I'm talking about the Russians. When did they get to you?"

"Well, I don't know where you're getting your intelligence, but you're mistaken. And besides, that sounded like a threat."

"It was just a question, Virginia. Why can't you truthfully answer the question? They know everything. They sent me here to bring you in."

Her eyes went cold now, but she didn't back down. Tough to the last.

"If they know what I've been doing," she said, "then why do they need to bring me in?"

"So you're not denying it."

She laughed in his face. "They're using you. You know that? God, you're still as naive as the first night I met you. I don't know why I helped you. You should have died on some African battlefield field with those stupid Legionnaires. Look, world, Adam Stokes still thinks that he's Superman!"

He knew she was trying to bait him, but he was past that. He got up and walked toward the water. "Tell me why, Virginia."

She sucked in a huge lungful of smoke and breathed it out, then rose and came to him. "Does it really matter? I assume they're watching us right now. I assume they're probably recording every word I say."

"It would help your situation," he said.

"Oh, you don't say. Tell me, when has the truth ever helped people like us? You told me you loved me. And look what happened to you."

He told the CIA everything—the relationship, how it had started and how it ended. So he didn't care who heard.

"Everything's a smokescreen with you, isn't it?" he said accusingly. "I'll bet you've never had a sincere relationship in your life. I'll bet every boyfriend you've had was a conquest.

Every relationship you've ever been in, from friends to family, was just a stepping stone. Have I guessed right?"

"You don't know anything about me, Adam. And for the record, I did have friends. People that I trusted before *he* ruined everything. So no, now I don't trust anyone. I live for me and I really don't care."

"You cared enough to save me," he said.

"I was on recruiting duty and you were just another recruit."

"I know how you felt about me." And he wasn't just saying this, he'd felt it. He'd seen it in her eyes on those rare occasions when he'd gotten her to relax. She'd been with him, truly. "So why did you do it?" he asked again. "How did they get you?"

Virginia sniffed the air and flicked her cigarette into the breeze. "You live in a black and white world. I learned long ago that there's more gray here than we'll ever be aware of. I've learned to play in that gray muck. And if you're truly wondering, if whoever's listening to us right now is wondering, they didn't come to me. I went to them and I'll tell you why. The idiots in Langley are way behind. Change is coming. The United States of America is trying to be a positive example for the world. They don't want to play in the pigpen anymore. No. They want everything to be folded up in a pretty, pink envelope. Well, that's not the way you do this. The Russians, now, they *know*. They know how to play the game. So, I went to the better player. And in case you're wondering, the deal was never about giving secrets away. But I have done things for them. In exchange, they've done things for me. So really, I'd say I'm more of an independent than one who works for any one particular country.

"That's treason, Virginia."

"Sue me," she said, pulling out another cigarette and lighting it with a match.

He let her inhale and passed a minute without a word. He looked over at the water for a moment. Then he asked her, "Can I have one of those?"

She lifted the pack and he went to grab for it. But when he did, he passed the package and grabbed her wrist instead with one swift move. To any passerby, it would look like two lovers embracing. He pulled her into his stomach, held her there, and marveled at the fact that for the first time ever, she looked scared. And that look, instead of pleasing him, broke his heart all over again. What could they have been in another life?

But they'd each made their own decisions. And now here he was sent by the CIA to kill the woman he had fallen in love with.

She gasped once—just once.

"Aren't you going to say you're sorry?" she said, her eyes tearing—he suspected—from the pain of the stiletto in her abdomen.

"I'm not sorry," he replied.

Her eyes fluttered, but she regained her focus. "Good. Then that means that you learned something after all."

They were close to the edge now, and he didn't even have to push her. She just slipped from his grasp and slid under the water. She was gone, forever weighted to the others.

Adam walked away from the scene, taking Virginia's purse with him. He flung her cigarettes in after her. What a fitting end.

Every day he remembered. And every day he relived it all the while trying to assuage the feeling that he'd committed some sort of mortal sin. In reality, he'd done a deed for his country, for the safety of his fellow spies, and for the good of the world.

But if that was so, why then could he not shake the weight of guilt from his soul?

Because he was a man in love?

CHAPTER SEVENTY

STERN - GEORGETOWN, WASHINGTON, D.C.

He only came back to his apartment to sleep. He took all his meals out, so he only needed a bed and a place to sit and read. But what he needed tonight was sleep.

Everywhere he turned, it felt like doors were closing. Zimmer and that idiot Flap were conspiring against him. He blamed Flap for giving him the information that started it all. He blamed the president because, well, he was a Democrat and he belonged to the other side. Ira Stern vowed that if he was ever in office, he would never work with anyone from across the aisle. That wasn't how it worked, at least not how he'd been raised. His grandfather had always told him never to change horses.

He grabbed a bottle of water from the fridge and then used the bathroom. It was still early and he could hear people out on the streets. He would have to put in earplugs, even though he was probably tired enough not to need them. When he emerged from the bathroom, clad in the pajama bottoms that he kept under the sink, he was surprised to see a familiar face looking at him from across the bedroom.

"What the hell are you doing here?" he asked.

Flap was sitting in the corner, the dim light overhead, highlighting his face like an Alfred Hitchcock movie. In fact, in that moment, he looked very much like that old storyteller and Stern had to shake his head to dislodge the memory of growing up and watching those damn movies with his grandfather. They always creeped him out.

"We need to talk, Ira."

Flap rarely used Stern's first name. Stern thought about calling security, but then realized if Flap had gotten in, security was probably neutralized. He had no doubt that Flap had hidden his own storied past, though, on occasion he looked more like a bumbling professor than a career spymaster. But tonight, Ira Stern did not like the look on the CIA director's face.

He tried to push his concern aside by saying, "It's late and I need to get some sleep."

"Sit down, Ira."

"You can't tell me what to do."

"I said, sit down, please."

Again, thoughts of Alfred Hitchcock came to mind. A ridiculous thought flooded into his brain that maybe birds would fly out of the ceiling. That was nonsense.

"The congressman will be hearing about this," Stern said, trying to sound confident and feeling anything but.

"The congressman knows I'm here," Flap said.

How was that possible? Then he remembered. His boss had a long relationship with the CIA. But why here and why now? Ira Stern did not like having visitors in his personal space, as the lack of furnishings could attest. He was not much for hosting.

"Sit down, Ira," Flap said, his voice as cutting and as clear as Stern had ever heard it.

He found himself sitting down on the edge of the bed and had to hold his knees apart after they knocked together, his nerves rattling inside.

"I thought we had an agreement," Flap said. "I provided you with certain information and you promised to behave. You said you would take your time. But all I see sitting in front of me is a spoiled, impatient brat, and I'm tired of getting phone calls and texts because of your ill-timed deeds."

Ill-timed deeds? Who was this guy?

The Brooklyn in Stern rose up. "Look Flap, I told you exactly what I was going to do with the information, but I don't know why you're surprised about what I've been up to. I'm sure if the president knew what *you've* been up to, then he'd have a few words to say to you. Maybe I can invite him over to your house when you're getting ready for bed."

Immediately, Stern knew he'd gone too far. Something changed in Flap. Stern couldn't quite put his finger on it. It was like a decision had been made. Patience had been on the man's face a mere moment before. Now it was gone.

"I'm sorry to hear you say that Ira. I so hoped that we would continue to work together. There were many things that I could have shared with you. We could have helped one another, but now..." The words drifted into the air and sat there. Stern wanted to pluck them and shove them back down Flap's throat.

This was all wrong, all wrong. He needed to get Flap back on his side. He needed—

Something grabbed him around the throat. An arm. He looked up at the face of a bullish man with dead eyes and not a hint of remorse. Stern tried to speak. He tried to struggle with the grip.

Flap stood up from the chair and walked over. "Such a waste," he said, shaking his head. "You look like you want to say something." He motioned to the dead-eyed man and the pressure receded, thankfully.

Stern coughed a few times.

"What did you have to tell me?" Flap said.

"I wanted to tell you that I promise not to say anything. That I'm sorry. That we should start over and you're right, we can help each other. I know I can help you."

Flap stared at him with those all-seeing eyes.

This was a different man than Stern had worked with before. Gone was the facade. This man promised one thing and one thing only. Doom.

"If you believe in a God," Flap said, "you should pray to him now, because they won't find your body and they won't get to say farewell."

Stern tried to scream when the hands clamped down harder and harder. He thought his neck would snap, but it didn't. The pressure was expertly applied. As he struggled in vain, Flap walked from the room, never once looking back. The last thing Ira Stern ever saw and heard was CIA director Edmond Flap's leather shoes clacking out the door.

CHAPTER SEVENTY-ONE

YEGOROVICH - MOSCOW

His sense of smell came back first. It reminded him of his childhood, when his grandmother would cook for him on the weekends, his parents having deposited him there so they could go off and do whatever it was that they did. He remembered now that his grandmother would wake up early and make all of young Konstantin's favorite treats.

He thought that's what he smelled now, and he wondered if he was dreaming. The spike that was causing his head to split with pain told him he wasn't.

"He's waking up," a female voice said in English.

He knew that voice. How did he know that voice? His brain was all fog and he couldn't process where he was. Even when he opened his eyes and his vision blurred.

"Where am I?" he croaked. The words came out in Russian. Even though he was fluent in English, he couldn't seem to find those words yet.

"What did he say?" a male voice asked, again in English.

He found the words. In English, he said, "Where am I? And who are you?"

He wasn't afraid. He hadn't been afraid in a very long time. If it was his time to die, so be it. He tried to sit up but found that his hands were bound in front of him. He still couldn't see and was embarrassed when he moaned when he moved. The pain was a searing halo around his head.

"Get him some water," the male voice said.

Again, a familiar sound. Then it came back to him. The young woman, the American. At his place, naked in bed. Only she wasn't completely naked...

"You're very clever," he said, speaking to the woman. "I would ask how you knew where to find me, but I suspect you won't tell me."

It wasn't the girl who answered. It was the male voice.

"Do you remember me?"

Yegorovich let the voice settle on his mind. The muddle was going away, and now, yes, he did remember.

"Young Calvin Stokes," he said, though he could only see the silhouette. "I apologize. My vision seems to be 'on the fritz' as you Americans say. Tell me, is this the last time that we'll be meeting in such a way? If not, I really must have a conversation with my security staff. First Canada, and now this."

"We're looking for a woman called Anna Varushkin," Cal said.

Yegorovich laughed. "Ah, so this Daniel Briggs must be your friend." The pieces were coming together. What a coincidence. There was no sense lying. "Miss Varushkin is my guest. In fact, we've recently had a very interesting conversation."

"You need to let her go," Cal said.

"And why would I do that? You can kill me, Calvin, but

that would go against your code, wouldn't it? What would your father think?"

His eyes had cleared now. He could see Cal standing across the room, arms crossed. Another man stood next to him with blond hair tied in a ponytail. This must be Daniel Briggs. And then the girl, still beautiful, but her eyes different now—hard, serious, trained on him. He directed his attention to her.

"My dear," he said, "you really must pursue a career in acting. With your skills, there's not a single director that wouldn't be honored to have you."

She didn't reply. What fun was that? When it was obvious that no one was going to join in his banter, he looked back to Cal.

"Honestly," he said, "this was not the brightest move. Even you can see that. Ah, but you were desperate, were you not?"

Another man entered the room then, his face swollen and showing signs of a recent hand-to-hand sparring match. Yegorovich did not recognize the man, not until he looked closer, and then he inhaled sharply.

"It couldn't be... is it you? Back from the dead?"

Cal answered for the man. "This is my uncle. He was one of your guests, too, and I assume you were going to tell me that you didn't know a thing about it."

"But I did not."

Cal and his uncle looked at each other. His uncle then tossed a second confusing question Yegorovich's way.

"How long have you been working with the Duchess?"

"The Duchess?" Yegorovich asked, searching his mind, wondering what the man was talking about.

"Her real name is Virginia Walton," the uncle said, stepping forward. Whoever had marked his face had really done a number on the man.

"I don't know this Duchess, and I don't know this Virginia —" He paused. "There was a woman, back in the eighties, maybe. No, that isn't right. The seventies, I think. She was rumored to be an American spy working in Paris, but she died."

Again, Cal and his uncle exchanged a look which said that Yegorovich's answer had not cleared up their confusion. They'd thought that he, president of Russia, had been controlling this woman. He understood that now. And when he thought about it, he seemed to remember hearing more about this woman. That she'd worked with the KGB. Yes, that was it. That was the connection. But she'd died, didn't she?

His four captors stood together, whispering, the girl occasionally looking back at Yegorovich. He felt confident they would not kill him. But he knew that some form of payment would be extracted. He would get his due in the end. But payment was a two-way street. He would exact his toll as well.

They all turned around to face him, and the man with the blond hair spoke for the first time. This man's eyes bore into the Russian like a dark screw to his soul. It made Yegorovich feel as though he was marked for death without any compromise.

Briggs pulled a pistol from his pocket, walked up to Yegorovich, and pressed it to his forehead. "Tell us where Miss Varushkin is. Because the only code I have is loaded into the chamber of this weapon."

"Kill me and you won't get what you want. Let me live and maybe we can work something out. A deal, perhaps."

"No deals," Briggs said.

But Yegorovich knew they needed him. And with that

knowledge, he could stall. He could take the pain until he could take it no more. It would either be an experience to learn from or the last great adventure of his life. Either way, the smile he flashed at Briggs was genuine, and when he said, "shoot when you're ready," he fully meant it.

CHAPTER SEVENTY-TWO

ANNA - MOSCOW

The old jailer was back, wooden bat swinging at her side. She brought lunch now, or was it dinner? Anna didn't know. She lost all track of time. She'd taken to counting the pockmarks on the ceiling and then the bugs that scurried along the floor. She also told herself stories. Remembered her childhood. Remembered the conversation she'd had with Daniel. If only he was there now. If he was sitting in the same cell, even shackled to the wall, she knew she would be okay.

But now, after the visit with Yegorovich—when had it been? The day before? Longer than that? Things felt inevitable. She thought about killing herself. If only there was a way to do it. She could taunt her captor and maybe piss her off so much that she would beat her to death. No, that was no way to go. She had to hold out hope. But hope was in short supply.

"Eat," her jailer said.

Anna knew better than to object. She was tired of the beatings, and while the food was terrible and would only sit in her stomach for mere minutes, it was a small price to pay. She could only hope that some part of the food was giving her nourishment.

When she was done, she handed the tray back to the old jailer, who left promptly, only to return moments later, backing into the cell like she was pulling a cart. But there was no cart coming in after her. There was a man in a Russian uniform following right behind.

"Turn around," the man said in Russian, and the jailer did. And when she did, Anna saw that there was a gun in the man's hand. He poked his head around the older woman, saw Anna, and winked.

What in the world?

Then, without further ado, the pistol was raised and came down hard on the back of the jailer's skull, knocking her senseless. One more rap to the head and she was down for the count.

"My, my, my...look at where they've put you," the man said.

Was it her mind tricking her or was he speaking in English?

"The Russians have some of the crappiest accommodations. I should know. I've stayed in some of the nicest ones. You ask them to roll out the red carpet and they'll give you a moldy blanket that was just draped over a horse." He chuckled at his own joke and offered her a hand.

Anna wasn't sure if she should take it.

"I promise I won't bite," he said. "I'm here to help you."

"Who are you?" she asked.

He did a pirouette on one foot. "You don't like my disguise? I'm sure they've told you about me."

"I don't have any idea who you are," Anna said truthfully. Something about the man's nonchalant behavior made her think that maybe he was crazy.

He huffed in frustration. “Well then, I’ll just have to have a chat with them about that then, won’t I?” He stood up straight, put one arm across his belly, and then bowed. “Matthew Wilcox at your service, madam. Now, if you’ll gather your things, you need only touch my robe and you shall be upheld in more than this.

She stared, disbelieving.

“Oh, come on,” he said with a roll of the eyes. “That’s a quote from Dickens. I swear, folks these days have zero culture. Very well. Take my hand and I’ll get you out of this Russian shithole and back to real civilization. Better?”

It all made sense then. Wilcox, the assassin that Daniel had told her about, the one who had caused so much trouble for Cal.

“Did Daniel send you?”

Wilcox snorted. “Are you kidding? That goody-goody? They don’t even know you’re here. I’d rather it be a surprise when I bring you in. Maybe I’ll wrap you in a nice red bow, put you in a pretty, pink dress. Of course, we’ll have to clean you up before that, but that shouldn’t be hard to do.” He held out his hand. “Now, madam, if you would be so kind as to take my hand, our pumpkin chariot awaits.”

Because she really couldn’t quantify what was happening, she said nothing, took the man’s hand, and went with him. As they made their way out of the small detention facility, she saw the dead bodies strewn around like so much refuse.

All the while, Matthew Wilcox whistled a nameless tune, looking very much like the cat that had captured the canary and killed its entire family in the process.

CHAPTER SEVENTY-THREE

LENA - MOSCOW

It was impossible not to be happy.

Anna was back. She'd been escorted in by that strange man, that Matthew Wilcox. Anna and Daniel were sitting in chairs facing each other. He had her hands in his, and she didn't want to disturb them. It was a miracle really. This crazy Wilcox who'd come in a Russian uniform, spouting German of all things, playing Adolf Hitler. He'd really put on a show, and then escorted Anna in like he was playing the classical theater. How strange.

Volkov was now in safe hands. They said he was on the mend, but it would be a long recovery. The bullet that hit him had torn into a few vital organs. But at least his cover was not blown.

There was still the lingering question of how they would get back to the States.

But with Cal and SSI on their side, Lena was sure they'd figure it out. The big question on everyone's mind was what to do with Konstantin Yegorovich. The Russian president had seemed right at home with them. She'd taken no less than three showers to get the smell of him off her. Never once had he tried to make another move. It was like everything that had transpired between them had never happened.

That was how Lena knew that this man was ruled by one thing and one thing alone—his own ego. He showed no fear and acted as if he'd planned the entire thing. He hadn't even blinked when Anna reappeared. In fact, he looked smug. He was in the other room now, and there was no way that he could get out. Daniel had personally seen to that, adding a sedative to the mix just in case the Russian tried to make a move.

"No, dammit!" Cal said loud enough for all of them to hear.

Wilcox turned to Daniel. "Will you speak some reason to this guy? I swear. He thinks we live in some fucking fairytale where he's the knight in shining armor and the Wicked Witch of the West can be doused with water and never come back."

"He thinks we should kill Yegorovich," Cal said,

"I agree." Anna said.

Daniel looked like he couldn't decide. And that was very unlike the Daniel Briggs Lena had come to know. Something had changed in him and Lena didn't know what. He was obviously happy to have Anna back, but there was some hesitancy there. Like he really couldn't make a decision. Even though everything she knew about him was that he was possibly the most decisive person on Cal's team.

"Do you know the shitstorm we'll unleash if we kill him?" Cal said.

"Shitstorm? I love shitstorms," Wilcox said, raising jazz hands in the air. "I've got enough umbrellas for all of it. I vote bring on the shitstorm."

"While I don't appreciate the levity," Anna said, "I think that being rid of him would solve a few of our problems."

"Snake Eyes," Cal said, "will you please put some common sense back into this conversation?"

"We should think about it," Daniel said. "Cal's right, this is bigger than just us."

"You don't know what he's capable of," Anna said. "I've seen him."

"I don't doubt that," Daniel replied. "But my gut says that this is a little blip on his path. If we let him go—"

"We are not letting him go," Wilcox said. "The first time you guys did that, I was okay with it. I mean, it took me a little while to get over it, but I got over it. Now you've got the guy on a silver fucking platter and you want to let him go again? I'm with Anna. I've seen what this prick has done. I say we cut off his head and bowl it down Main Street, Moscow. That'll send a sign that you don't fuck with the good ol' US of A."

Cal threw his hands up. "You've got to be shitting me. You are ten kinds of insane, you know that?"

"Don't I get a vote in this?" Lena asked. "I think Cal's right. We need to let him go. There'll be another opportunity in the future. I know it."

She didn't tell them that she had a very bad feeling about killing men. Not that she herself wouldn't, but she'd had a vision that had shaken her. She'd imagined Elijah killing the man, a rightful killing for sure. Then the man's death unleashed a horde of demons that overwhelmed them and choked the light from the sky and blotted out their world and enveloped them all. She didn't know where that vision had come from, but she knew enough to trust it.

It took another hour to convince Anna. By the time they had, Wilcox had left in a huff.

"He'll be fine." Cal said with a dismissive wave. "He'll stew for a while and treat us like he's a snubbed feline. But he'll get over it."

But Lena wasn't so sure. When she looked at Wilcox, she saw only discord. The man seemed to thrive on chaos. He drank it with breakfast and then stirred it into his dessert at night. She'd have to find out why Cal and Daniel let him live. But that was a question for another day. Today, they had to figure out how to let Yegorovich go.

And how the hell would they get home?

CHAPTER SEVENTY-FOUR

SPRINGER - ARLINGTON, VIRGINIA

His new penthouse apartment was perfect. He'd taken on a loan under the assumption that he'd get a fat check very soon. There was a Pulitzer to plan for, not to mention a book deal. Already thinking farther than that, a TV series or maybe a movie, he had the context to make that happen. There was one actor he knew of who salivated at the thought of working with a Pulitzer prize winner. Funny how people were pulled in. And he, Dirk Springer, would pull them in any way he could.

The apartment was only half full of furniture. None of the stuff from his old place had come. Everything was new. He had a designer working on everything with a minimalist modern take. He'd been very specific with his directions: "I want women to love it," he told her, and apparently that's all she needed. That, and the many checks he had already written her.

For now, it was borrowed money, tomorrow it would be deposited cash. He'd emailed a story to Edmond Flap early in the day. He was excited, giddy. Some of it was his fresh dose of drugs. Mostly it was the story. He loved it when other people loved a story of his. And this was a great story. An epic one, one that his peers would read and wish they had written. It was so unbelievable that it could have been fiction. There were still a few holes to plug, but that's what Flap was for.

He figured the CIA director would lend him a hand smoothing out the details. They had a date, 8 p.m., early enough so that Springer wouldn't be too drunk. Plenty of time to find a young thing later and bring her home.

Flap arrived right on time. The cocaine in Springer wanted to remark on the director's shabby attire, but he bit his tongue.

He spread out his hands to the room. "What did you think?"

"Where's your bar?" Flap asked.

Springer pointed to the butler's pantry next to the kitchen. "Just had it stocked."

"Well, I think this is cause to celebrate."

So he liked it. His spirit did leaps inside. "Get anything you want. Any of the expensive stuff, whatever."

"I'll have water, maybe a little wine. But you, you deserve something special," Flap said.

Springer's smile went ear to ear. The director of the CIA himself wanted to pour him a drink. Well, how many reporters could say that? "Then I'll go with champagne. There's a bottle in the wine fridge."

"I'll get it," Flap said. "You go sit down."

Springer was so giddy that he wanted to tap dance. He heard the champagne cork pop. Moments later, Flap returned with the champagne in one hand and a bottle of cheap beer in the other. He handed the champagne to Springer.

"To your story," Flap said, raising his beer.

Springer for the life of him couldn't find the words to reply, so he clinked his glass against the beer bottle and turned it upside down, pounding the entire thing.

"Do you mind if I get another?" Springer said.

Flap shook his head and found a seat.

When Springer returned, he saw that Flap was holding a stack of papers. "I hope you don't mind. I printed out the story. I thought we might go over a few details."

Springer didn't mind at all. He'd canceled his plans just to stay here and discuss where he'd gotten every morsel of information. He'd tell Flap how he'd pieced the complicated web together.

Flap asked, "I assume you haven't given the story to your editor yet like we discussed?"

"No, no, not yet. There are some things I want to run by you. I want it to be absolutely perfect when I give it to that old bastard."

Springer didn't really have anything against his boss. He had been a little tight on per diem, but he felt like calling someone an old bastard.

"Why don't we go outside?" Flap said. "It's lovely out tonight and I'd like to see the view."

Springer barely heard the traffic far below. They were a good ten stories up. And while he wasn't much for heights, the commanding view made him feel like he was on top of the world.

"So, tell me," Flap said, "how far do you think you'll take the story?"

Springer had already thought it out. "Well, I might turn it into a longer thing for magazine publication. Maybe a book, TV, movies." He saw the look on Flap's face. "Wait, I thought you were cool with all that."

"Oh no, it's fine. I want you to get all the accolades. You

deserve it. Really, you do. You're a master storyteller, Dirk Springer. Every award you get ought to be set on one of your many shelves. But there's only one problem."

Springer's throat constricted. "Problem? What kind of problem?"

"Have you thought about what Daniel Briggs will do when he finds out about this?"

"I figured he'd probably be arrested, tried for treason or whatever the hell the government does."

Flap nodded and walked to the edge of the roof, peering down. That wasn't a move that Springer was going to follow, heights and all that.

"Not a big fan of heights?" Flap said.

"Not really."

"Funny you should rent this penthouse, then."

Springer shrugged. "Yeah, pretty funny, right?" He tried to laugh, but all of a sudden he wanted to shiver. Had he had one bump or four? Was it the champagne going to his head?

"Dirk, you should come see this." Flap motioned him over.

For some reason, Springer's feet moved one in front of the other. What the hell? Soon he was standing right next to Flap, reluctantly looking down.

"Quite the view, eh?" Flap said.

He wanted to move back but couldn't. "Yeah, it's great. But I'm not really a fan."

Flap looked up at him. "You should jump, you know?"

And for some reason, Springer had the impulse that he *should* jump. He took another step closer to the ledge.

Flap grabbed his arm. "Hold on a minute. Do you feel it?"

Springer's heart hammered in his chest. "Feel what?"

"What I put in your drink? It's pretty ingenious, really. Completely undetectable. Stolen technology from North

Korea. Can you believe that? A drug that can convince a person to do anything you want, and it came from the hermit kingdom itself." He shook his head in wonder. "It's the first time I've used it myself. How do you feel?"

"Not good. I can't—"

"Control yourself? Good, good. That's excellent feedback, Dirk. I appreciate it. And I do appreciate your work. But this story can't come out, at least not yet. And I have a feeling that left to your own impulses, you'll go against my will. Is that correct?"

Springer didn't want to nod, but he did. He couldn't help himself.

"That's what I thought," Flap said, and he took a step back. "I've got work to do, so we should go ahead and get this over with."

Springer wanted to run. He wanted to run so fast and so far that he could have passed through a brick wall. But he couldn't move. He was stuck in that spot just by Flap's suggestion.

And as he stood there, his mind caught up with his body.

Suddenly everything that Flap said made sense. It wasn't smart to release the story right now. They should wait, it would be a better time. All Flap was doing was telling him the truth, common sense, in a way that Springer had not been able to see. But he saw it now. This was the way it should be.

He felt much better now. His heart no longer galloped. Instead it beat at a steady fifty a minute.

"You look like you feel much better," Flap said, smiling.

"I do, thank you," Springer said, meaning every word.

"Good. Very good. Now, if you'll do me one last favor, Dirk."

"Sure, anything." He didn't know why he'd been so worried, so scared. Flap was his friend and they were going to work together. Maybe he'd get another Pulitzer, or maybe not. Who really cared? As long as he could be friends with Edmond Flap. Maybe they'd go on vacation together. Maybe get an office together.

"Did you hear what I said?" Flap said, and Springer realized that it wasn't the first time Flap had tried to get his attention.

"I'm sorry, I think I was daydreaming."

"Mm, another side effect of the drug. I'll have my people look into that. Now, as I was saying, it's time for you to jump, Dirk. Don't you agree?"

Springer nodded his head. Of course he agreed. This was his good buddy, Edmond Flap.

"Want me to do it now?"

"Yes, that would be fine."

"Okay, then. I'll see you in a minute."

And then he turned, and without any further hesitation, leapt feet out and straight down ten stories.

Smiling all the way, wondering for those few seconds what he and his good pal Edmond would do next.

The wind ripped at his lungs. It was delightful.

CHAPTER SEVENTY-FIVE

FLAP - THE WHITE HOUSE

"You're telling me that this woman, this Duchess, was working all on her own?" the president asked. "What was her motive?"

"We're still looking into it," Flap said. "It seems that she had some deep-seated grudge, potentially against the agency, America, or all of the above."

Zimmer grunted and looked back down at the file. "And you say Cal's uncle used to be involved with her?"

"Yes, sir. Oh, I don't think there's any need to worry. You vetted the younger Stokes yourself. As for Adam Stokes, though he's been living in hiding for all these years, everything we've found suggests that he's being completely honest with us."

Zimmer was scanning the file for the third time. Flap wondered if the president was looking for irregularities, or maybe he was questioning his friend Cal again. Zimmer had explained that their relationship was complicated. They'd had their ups and downs, and now the file on his lap added further mystery.

"I can't believe Cal didn't know about his uncle," Zimmer said.

"I hope you agree with having both of the Stokes men as part of the debriefing process. The woman would only speak with them in attendance, especially the elder Stokes."

"That's fine. That's fine. Whatever you think, Edmond." Zimmer finally looked up from the file. "And what about the Russians? What are you hearing about the mess that Cal left behind?"

He said it in a way that made it obvious that many messes had been left in Cal Stokes's wake, and that Zimmer had almost gotten used to it.

"It seems as though the Russians are playing it off as some terrorist attack. They even launched a few raids in Chechnya."

Zimmer nodded. "I guess my Russian counterpart doesn't have to worry as much about keeping his public appeased." He closed the file. "And how is Konstantin doing. Two brushes with Cal Stokes, and he still seems to be in good spirits."

Flap shrugged. "I don't know the man, Mr. President, but everything we've been able to gather seems to agree with your assessment."

"I can't say I'd have the same attitude if I had been kidnapped twice," Zimmer said. "But hopefully that doesn't happen. Now, first I'd like to thank you for taking care of the situation." He patted the file on his lap.

"It was my pleasure, Mr. President. Anything you need, you know where to find me."

Zimmer handed the file back. "The second thing I wanted

to talk to you about was President Yegorovich. How many dealings have you had with the Russians in the past?"

"A few, sir."

"Good. You can look into what the real fallout of this mess is."

"Our analysts are already working on it, Mr. President. Should have a full report within the week."

"Good. Thank you, Edmond. And may I say again how appreciative I am of the job that you're doing."

Flap smiled and wondered what Zimmer would think if he knew his own CIA director's true motives. Not that he ever would, because Edmond Flap kept everything close to the vest.

Everything.

CHAPTER SEVENTY-SIX

ANNA - CAMP SPARTAN, ARRINGTON, TENNESSEE

They'd made it back to the States without incident. Everyone except for Virginia Walton and Adam Stokes. Cal had just arrived from Paris and taken Lena out for a day of shooting.

Anna had come to her favorite spot at SSI headquarters—the cemetery. It was so quiet, peaceful, and the sun seemed to shine just right when she was there. Her wounds were healing, but she couldn't shake the lingering effects of her imprisonment. It had scared her down to a place she hadn't been since her father died. At the time, she'd had Daniel to lean on, and now she needed him again. He arrived at the appointed time, Liberty trotting happily at his side. She ran up to Anna and nuzzled into her lap.

She wished that was the way humans could be—happy and easy to please. But men and women alike had egos, and those needed to be fed. They either accepted the world as it was, or they tried to change it to be under their control. But not a dog. A dog was happy to eat, sleep, snuggle, and do it all again.

Daniel sat down next to her without a word. She wanted him to speak. Wanted him to talk first. He tried to talk about what had happened, what she had said, but there was something between them now. Maybe not so much a wall, but a fence, perhaps. It was something one could see through, even to the other side, but there was no breaching it entirely.

"It's a beautiful day," Anna said finally, once Liberty had curled up at her feet.

"It is," Daniel said.

They both spoke at the same time, and Daniel motioned for her to go first.

"How long does it take to get past this... fear?"

She'd said little about her imprisonment. She was both embarrassed and depressively reflective.

"There is no one way, Anna," Daniel said. "Some people get over it fast and others take years."

"Tell me what to do," she said. "Tell me how to get over it fast."

He shook his head. "I can't. There's no magic recipe. You know what I went through, the pain I felt, the utter devastation that I'd taken my life into. And you know what I had to do to get through it. But you're not me. You need to find your own way."

Those words felt like a life sentence without him.

"I need some time," Anna said. "The Fund needs to shore up its defenses. I'm sure Yegorovich won't stop now. If anything, he's probably hungrier than ever to get his hands on me and the others. Not to mention our money."

"Where will you go?" he asked.

"I'm not sure yet."

She wanted him to say that he'd come with her, that she

didn't need to be alone. She wanted him to tell her that they needed to be together and that he would help. But he said none of these things. How her anger wanted to rise.

She wanted to scream at him. She wanted *him* to scream. She wanted him to look like he felt something, because right here and now, the Buddhist monk routine was the last thing she wanted.

"I'll always love you, Daniel Briggs," she said.

He nodded again. And for the briefest instant, he couldn't lock her gaze.

"I know," he said. "And I'm sorry I can't give you what you want. I can't explain it. There's something else I need to do and I'm afraid that if you stay with me, you'll be disappointed in me."

She grabbed his hand and held it close. "I could never be disappointed in you."

He smiled. "You are right now."

Anna did her best to smile. "Maybe a little. But I know you, Daniel Briggs. You're a good man. It's why you've taken my heart."

"I'm sorry," he said.

And that's how they left it, with an "I'm sorry" and a place marked for another time.

She would leave without him, and he would go and find whatever it was that he was looking for. And when he looked into her eyes that last time, Anna realized something that she hadn't seen before. It was that fire she'd seen when she first met him—that simmering anger at the world. It was there again, though she wished it wasn't. But if it was, this was probably for the best. Daniel Briggs had work to do, and the best thing he could do was to do it on his own.

She knew that for sure, staring into those blue eyes that barely quelled the raging fire behind them.

CHAPTER SEVENTY-SEVEN

VIRGINIA WALTON - PARIS

The debriefings were done. Days spent in a dreary room answering every question from the CIA interrogators. There was no longer a reason to lie. She told them everything. Where she'd come from and how she'd ended up where she was. That she lived a somewhat peaceful life for so many years until one day when she received a call from someone who knew everything about her. No matter how many ways they asked her, she didn't know who that person was. They were always cloaked in secrecy, but they knew intimate details. It's just so. And the promise had been, if she hadn't done what he asked, that certain actions would be taken. She was glad that Adam was there when she answered that particular question because he was the one she was trying to save. And even though she'd done such awful things, killed old friends, practically unraveled the network, here she was, standing next to her old flame in the very same spot where he thought he'd killed her.

"Do you ever think about the day we met?" she asked.

"All the time," Adam said.

"What do you remember?"

"I remember how confident you were, how beautiful you were. I'm pretty sure you could have kicked the crap out of those Legionnaires. What about you? What do you remember?"

"I remember your smile. So innocent. I thought you looked uniquely American. Like you'd just put away your baseball glove and finished some apple pie. If you weren't the poster boy for the American dream, I don't know who was. You were my challenge. I figured if I could turn you to my will, I could turn anyone."

Adam chuckled at that. "That's funny, because in my memory, it didn't take much at all to convince me. I was naive back then. Show me some pretty legs and a flashy smile and I was all yours."

"You don't give yourself enough credit," Virginia said, and then she took his hand. "I haven't said this yet because I wanted to tell you when it was just the two of us."

He raised his eyebrows. It wasn't really just the two of them. Others were watching, like the first time they'd stood here. If she did anything wrong, a dozen operatives were ready to swoop in and save the day.

"I wanted to say I'm sorry for everything. All that I put you through, you never deserved it. And you definitely deserved better than me. But I love you, Adam Stokes. I have from the very first moment you smiled at me. I just didn't know how to process it."

He squeezed her hand. "I always knew and that's what pissed me off, that you couldn't say it. I think we both could have done some things differently."

She felt better after telling him. For a time they gazed all around them, taking in the city where they first met, where they'd fallen in love, where they'd learned so much about each other and yet kept each other at a distance. Then, with a touch of sadness, he realized it was time. She'd done her final duty, mended the old bonds.

After a leaden moment, she let go of Adam's hand and cut deep lines into her wrists. She then pocketed the tiny blade. Blood gushed forth at once and she was glad for the darkness because the blood was coating her dress as it dripped like warm rain down her fingers, down her legs.

"I'll miss you," she said to him.

"We'll see each other again," he said. "I promise."

He would know soon enough.

She leaned over and stood on her toes, kissing him on the cheek. "I love you," she said.

And before he could react, before he could grab her, she dived straight down into the river. She felt the current pulling her as her blood mingled hotly with it. She said a silent goodbye, swam deeper, deeper, and deeper still, confident that they wouldn't find her alive.

The Duchess bid adieu to the city she so loved and the man who had captured her heart.

Je t'aime...

EPILOGUE

YEGOROVICH - LOCATION UNKNOWN

Yegorovich toweled off the sweat and stretched his quads. They weren't quite as limber as they used to be. A seven-mile run wasn't bad for his age, and he didn't feel too winded. Still, he would have loved to have those younger lungs back. He was well aware that he yearned for youth like a starving man yearned for food, but he was getting better about that now. Younger women helped, a better diet, plenty of exercise, and of course, his favorite of all things—fresh air.

This house he loved more than any of the others. It was small, unpretentious, but all alone and more than a thousand acres that was all his. He could walk, run, hunt, and all that completely naked if he preferred. Nobody would see him except for security and the servants that did their best to stay invisible.

There was a platter of fresh melon waiting for him in the kitchen. He loved fresh fruit because he'd never had any as a child. He'd gotten by on rations divvied up by Communists in Moscow. He'd done much better for his people. They could eat anything from anywhere in the world. That was the enticement of capitalism. He embraced it, though he'd been careful to build his own brand of the economic model. Something to suit his tastes, something to be controlled by his urges. But here in his own home he could have whatever he wanted, including fruit. The chef had done a good job. The melon was fresh and cool and cut into perfectly even sections.

He has soothed the ruffled feathers of the security people in Moscow. They had dead men to account for. And while they hadn't completely bought the story of Chechnyan terrorists, they'd been somewhat appeased by the money he'd transferred to their accounts, and by the direct missions he'd allowed deep into Chechnya.

The military had been another matter. He had generals itching to move on Belarus. There was discord there. Elections had gone their way, but apparently democracy was once again on the upswing in the former vassal state. He would deal with that later. The military had to make sure he was safe. They tried to insist on soldiers following him around everywhere, but that was not to be. He personally selected each man and woman who accompanied him. It was one of the things he insisted on and one of the many things people grumbled about. They knew that when Konstantin Yegorovich picked the man or the woman, then he controlled that man or woman, and control was the name of the game.

He went to the steam room that he'd had installed the year before. It was one of his favorite rooms. It smelled of lemongrass and lime today. It was quiet, the perfect place to think.

He'd gotten minor assurances from Cal Stokes. Really, they were payoffs, bribes to make sure that he wouldn't go to the press. Furthermore, the money ensured he would not try to retaliate for his two kidnappings. He knew that his longstanding debt to the elder Calvin Stokes, even though it had been repaid, was still lingering. He had a certain yearning to know more of the younger Stokes. And now there was an uncle!

How interesting. Konstantin Yegorovich loved interesting tidbits. He loved to search for signs intertwined.

When he emerged from the steam room, a plan had begun to form.

A harder line was needed. He'd start with his own people and move on from there. He'd give Brandon Zimmer a piece of his mind, maybe threaten him a little. He would throw some money around. He wanted the Americans on their heels. He already had one conversation with Zimmer, and during that little chat he'd been nothing but amiable, treating the kidnapping as if it had been an unlucky mistake. But they both knew differently. Since those days had passed, Yegorovich had kept in almost constant contact with Edmond Flap. It turned out the American president was a little too curious about the goings-on in Russia. Flap didn't ask for specifics. He knew that Yegorovich would provide them when needed.

The updates kept coming, including a handful about Anna Varushkin. She'd left the States and was somewhere in Northern Europe. Flap didn't know where, but he would find out. They would craft a scheme together. The CIA director knew better than to get in Yegorovich's way.

The one thing Yegorovich wanted right now was the money sitting in the Fund. Imagine, pulling up the bank records and seeing *trillions*. He smirked to himself. Those trillions would buy him a mercenary army that would help him wreak havoc on the world. Those smug Germans who'd forgotten what their once allies had done in World War II.

The British who were always poking their nose where it didn't belong. Even the Japanese with their haughty business leaders and rigid standards. And finally, the Americans. Yegorovich figured it wouldn't take much. For a country that looked so stable, it was amazing how easy it was to jar it from its perch.

Exposed energy grids, accessible politicians, citizens who liked to congregate in huge numbers. There were so many targets. It was a matter of choosing a dozen and watching what happened next.

But that was a plan for another day.

Now, he would take a cold shower, replenish his energy reserves, maybe have dinner out on the patio. Then he could go back to those scheming politicians and those crooked billionaires. He would show them all. He would soon be untouchable.

He was undressing in his bedroom when there was a knock at the door.

"I don't want to be disturbed," he said.

"Mr. President, I thought you would like your evening pre-dinner drink when you got out of the shower."

It was this private chef. While Yegorovich was annoyed, a drink sounded good. He'd taken to drinking gin recently—Hendrick's with a squeeze of lime and a dash of syrup, stirred with ice and poured into a crystal coupe.

He unlocked the door and looked down to see his private chef on the floor, a neat, red hole in the middle of his forehead.

The weapon appeared next, followed by a hand and an arm and a face he did not recognize. The weapon gestured for Yegorovich to go back in the room. He did, moving backward slowly.

"What do you want?" he said, trying to sound bored, but annoyed that there was a hint of jitteriness in his tone.

"Just you," the man said.

And then he pulled the trigger twice.

Yegorovich barely felt it, because the bullets tore through his brain, obliterating all fear and cognition.

Matthew Wilcox looked down at the body of the Russian president. It was amazing what a little homework could do.

"Problem solved," he said.

He began whistling Tchaikovsky's *1812 Overture*, looking around satisfactorily. And then he left the room, a trail of complicated consequences in his wake.

Come join my private network at TeamCGCooper.com.

A portion of all profits from the sale of my novels goes to fund OPERATION C4, our nonprofit initiative serving young military officers. For more information visit OperationC4.com. Help us build Camp Spartan.

A LETTER TO READERS

Dear Reader,

I hope you enjoyed *Matters of State*. This novel allowed me to continue the forward progress of my writing career by exploring new ways to present my characters and their backstories. It also allowed the Cooper Clan to explore Paris, Rosemary Beach, and dream of one day building Camp Spartan for the recipients of Operation C4 scholarships.

It's been a busy year. That crazy virus hit the world. I ramped up Cooper Academy to homeschool all three of our kids. I've written some great novels. We're back on the travel wagon again, finally.

All in all I've been very lucky. Much of that luck comes from your support. From my family to you, thanks for buying my books, becoming part of Team Cooper, and just being a friend. I could not do this without you.

Feel free to send me an email to say hello. It's cgc@cgcooper.com. Yes, I answer every email myself. I'd love to get to know you. I can't wait until that can happen in person. Fingers crossed.

Keep livin'.

Semper Fidelis,

C. G. Cooper

October 2020

The Cooper Clan living on a houseboat in Paris, France during November of 2019.

ALSO BY C. G. COOPER

The Corps Justice Series In Order:

Back To War

Council Of Patriots

Prime Asset

Presidential Shift

National Burden

Lethal Misconduct

Moral Imperative

Disavowed

Chain Of Command

Papal Justice

The Zimmer Doctrine

Sabotage

Liberty Down

Sins Of The Father

A Darker Path

The Man From Belarus

Matters of State

Corps Justice Short Stories:

Chosen

God-Speed

Running

The Daniel Briggs Novels:

Adrift

Fallen

Broken

Tested

The Tom Greer Novels

A Life Worth Taking

Blood of My Kin

Stand Alone Novels

To Live

The Warden's Son

The Interrogators

Higgins

The Spy In Residence Novels

What Lies Hidden

The Alex Knight Novels

Breakout

The Stars & Spies Series:

Backdrop

The Patriot Protocol Series:

The Patriot Protocol

The Chronicles of Benjamin Dragon:

Benjamin Dragon – Awakening

Benjamin Dragon – Legacy

Benjamin Dragon - Genesis

ACKNOWLEDGMENTS

A BIG thanks to my beta readers: Nidza, Larry, Earl, Don H., Carl, Glenda, Gale, Marry, Paul, Connie, Bob, Nancy, Julie and Don G.

ABOUT THE AUTHOR

C. G. Cooper is the USA TODAY and AMAZON BESTSELLING author of the CORPS JUSTICE novels, several spinoffs and a growing number of stand-alone novels.

One of his novels, CHAIN OF COMMAND, won the 2020 James Webb Award presented by the Marine Heritage Foundation for its portrayal of the United States Marine Corps in fiction. Cooper doesn't chase awards, but this one was special.

Cooper grew up in a Navy family and traveled from one Naval base to another as he fed his love of books and a fledgling desire to write.

Upon graduating from the University of Virginia with a

degree in Foreign Affairs, Cooper was commissioned in the United States Marine Corps and went on to serve six years as an infantry officer. C. G. Cooper's final Marine duty station was in Nashville, Tennessee, where he fell in love with the laid-back lifestyle of Music City.

His first published novel, BACK TO WAR, came out of a need to link back to his time in the Marine Corps. That novel, written as a side project, spawned many follow-on novels, several exciting spinoffs, and catapulted Cooper's career.

Cooper lives just south of Nashville with his wife, three children, and their German shorthaired pointer, Liberty, who's become a popular character in the Corps Justice novels.

When he's not writing or hosting his podcast, Books In 30, Cooper spends time with his family, does his best to improve his golf handicap, and loves to shed light on the ongoing fight of everyday heroes.

Cooper loves hearing from readers and responds to every email personally.

To connect with C. G. Cooper visit

www.cg-cooper.com